THE STORYTELLERS

CARON MCKINLAY

BLOODHOUND
— BOOKS —

www.bloodhoundbooks.com

Print ISBN 978-1-914614-91-0

To Gillian, Amanda, Francesca, and Paola –
For their unconditional love.

CHAPTER 1

Ronnie – Liverpool

*S*ingles Night. When conjoined, there can't be two more desperate words. Unless they're speed and dating.

It's busy. Plenty of people dressed up in their peacock finery searching for connections. Hip-hop tunes blare through mists of discomfort. How will the lonely voices converse tonight? I'll need a few drinks to get through this. At least they only have ten minutes each.

I sip my pina colada and glance over at Mr Nobody Number One. The bar is sophisticated, dark and just the right side of expensive. His Primark sweater in bright purple is not. I promised myself an end to this. I never learn.

Another sip of my drink and Mr Nobody edges his chair that little bit closer. His breath reeks of beer. He better watch out. I bite.

He tells me how frustrated he is. He's always horny but can't get it up. His girlfriend left him. She cheated. It affected his confidence. I call him on his bullshit. He's not practising a hard-on with me. At forty, I've heard every line.

As he bumbles an apology, I'm already thinking of chicken fried rice and getting home in time for *Casualty*.

Slouching back in my seat, I take a deep breath in preparation for Mr Nobody Number Two. He has thick lime braces that hold up plaid pantaloons. You can't call them trousers. These are billowing breeches all tied up with an eighties lilac belt. His long-knotted beard is speckled with dregs of the salted nuts he's piling into his mouth. And as he talks, specks of brittle and half-eaten shells spurt out. They scatter around us. I try to be polite. Sincerely I do.

I pluck a pink umbrella from my drink and drain the glass. As he drones on about his model train collection, in intricate detail, I crack and crunch ice with my teeth. Then he produces a small gold case and retrieves a toothpick from it.

It's sad. But I'm out.

You'd think as you get older it would be easier to find "the one", but it's not. Only the dregs are left. The dumped. The unwanted. Men who have been deemed unworthy by the rest of womankind. They should wear warnings slapped across their head. Cheater. Liar. Married. Peter Pan.

A buzzer rings behind me and a woman sheathed in pink shrills, "Time's up. Move on." But that's the problem. I've been moving on for so very long.

Drinks are lifted. Chairs pushed back. A man to the left of me dawdles, drains the last from a whisky tumbler and looks to his left and right. Weighing up his chances. In shoes too high for her, Miss Pink strides forward and ushers him on.

Escaping towards the light of a neon exit my heel catches in sticky carpet. And as if in slow motion, I begin to topple until a stranger engulfs me into his arms and breaks my fall. I gasp and shrug him off, but he pulls me into a dark quiet corner and pushes me firmly against a wall. He's wearing tight black jeans and a cream polo. Taller than me, broad shouldered, his eyes emerald green. How have I not seen him before? He's gorgeous.

He sweeps my hair over my back and traces a finger down my neckline. Tendrils of vanilla scent drift towards me. Potent. Compelling. I want to taste him. "Beautiful pearls," he whispers. My breathing grows faster and a flush warms my skin. He smiles, leans in and brushes his lips against mine. I've no idea why I'm allowing this to happen. Perhaps it's the drink and the model train engines.

His grip on my hair tightens and his breath grazes my skin. "Tell me you want it," he says. I do. I really do. But not like this. I'm nobody's bitch. Who does he think he is? I push him away.

He falters, throws his arms wide, then does a mock bow. It's like he's playing the part of the gallant hero in some costume drama from the BBC. A hand is held out in greeting and his eyes flicker with challenge. "I'm Graham. Pleased to meet you."

"Yeah. I bet you are. The question is. Am I pleased to meet you?"

"Perhaps not yet, but you will be." He winks.

I shove past his audacity, strut into the night and walk towards the taxi queue. My hands find their way to my teeth and red varnish chips from my fingernails to colour the night.

The arrogance. The confidence. Those emerald eyes.

Should I be pleased to meet him?

CHAPTER 2

Nikki – Blackpool

*S*tumbling past a greasy café, an empty table screams *leave the diet one more day.* I'm easily persuaded. I mean, who actually likes starving themselves. Plus, a raging hangover is such a good excuse to eat. So why not.

Plastering on a smile, I approach the counter. The smell of bacon crisps the air and my mouth waters at the thought of a sandwich with lashings of butter and brown sauce. Maybe even some grated cheese sprinkled on top. But probably plain toast or a fruit salad would be the best choice. So boring though.

The woman behind the counter rubs the back of her neck. Then she picks up a pen and small notepad and stares. Under pressure, I order my usual breakfast of a fried egg roll and a Coke then flee for the corner booth. You can hide there.

Maybe that's why last night's dirty pig never said goodbye. Maybe Mike was too embarrassed to be seen with me in daylight, someone bigger than a skinny size ten. Or maybe he had a girl-friend waiting at home. Screw him. Oh, wait, already done that.

A fit of giggles swamps me but then a sudden tear makes me feel so alone. Blackpool's great for meeting people. Everyone's on holiday and looking for fun. But I want something more than a one-night stand. Maybe it's time to go home.

A deep cough interrupts my thoughts. Someone's standing at my table. There are plenty of empty places, why choose mine? I gaze up through my lashes to tell them just that, but my stare meets the most gorgeous brown eyes and my voice kind of goes. He's about thirty, twelve years older than me. But who cares. He's dead handsome.

A small white plate is balanced in front of me. "Ciao, miss. I bring you the egg roll." With a flourish, he sets it down and waits expectantly. What's he waiting for? It's an egg roll and he's acting like we're in a five-star restaurant instead of a cheap greasy café. My manners return and I mutter *thanks* and lower my head, hoping he'll go away. But he still stands there waiting, watching. The bloody weirdo.

What's supposed to happen now? I'm not going to pick it up and start in front of him. You can never eat a fried egg roll without the yolk dripping down your chin and onto your clothes, no matter which way you bite into it. It's worse if you've put ketchup on. You never know what end is gonna squirt out then.

"You will enjoy the egg, yes?" Oh, my good God. What is it with him and eggs? Suddenly, he picks up my plate and holds it up near my face. I jump back in my chair.

"Why not you eat the roll I make?"

It's like getting a telling off from my dad. What's wrong with this guy? Does he have some kind of egg fetish? I should have ordered the fruit.

And then he opens the roll and lifts out the egg. It's fresh, straight out of the box, like you'd buy them from the shop. He holds it up between his finger and thumb. "See? I don't cook. The egg it raw. It funny, no?"

I turn towards the woman at the counter. She's fanning herself with a screwed-up newspaper and blowing kisses towards us. They're all mad in here.

He looks down at me and a smile lifts his tone. "Maybe it no funny. I see beautiful girl but she sad. I think how can I do the chitty chat. How they say, cut the ice." He shakes his head. "But it no work."

My head fizzles with a burst of excitement and I giggle, finally getting the point of being egg stalked. He howls with laughter, slamming his hands against his thighs like it's the funniest thing in the world. It isn't. But it's cute, I guess.

"I am the Giovanni," he says and I kind of melt.

Well, you would too at his accent and swoony good looks.

CHAPTER 3

Ronnie – Liverpool

I throw off my black satin duvet, hurl myself from the bed and race shivering into the shower. The scent of vanilla musk froths and drifts into the air. Its aroma reminds me of Graham and my thoughts float back on a soapy bubble to two nights before. There had been something about him. Something heady. Intoxicating. My defences hadn't been down for such a long time, but he'd entranced me that night and as I lather my arms, his touch is still there. There were a lot of losers there that night including myself, but he was different.

What would have happened if I'd shaken his hand? Where might we have ended? A shiver tingles through me. There's only one way to find out. I'll drag myself back to the singles club. He might be there, and we'll see what happens. But this time I'll be the one taking the lead. In the meantime, I must get to school.

Thick clusters of girls, with skirts hiked high above their knees, shriek in the school playground. The usual group of boys gather close by. Thank goodness they're all in uniform.

"Girls! Skirts please."

"Yes, miss," comes the automatic reply.

They'll have hitched them back up their legs by the time I reach my office. It's our little game of "Groundhog Day". The film, not the myth.

Brian, my deputy, struts towards me in a brand-new suit that's just a tad too bright. What new shadow will he cast my way? He compounds his usual insincerity by flashing a cold smile.

"Morning, miss, going to be a tough one today."

"We'll be fine, Brian. We'll show them we're brilliant."

He snorts loudly and hammers in his last nail. "Yeah true, true. But if the inspection fails, you'll lose your job and we'll need a new headteacher. That'd be such a shame after all your hard work." He'd love nothing more. His creeping to the governors has already shown how much he'd love to replace me.

"Won't come to that, Brian. They'll see how great we are."

I really pray I'm correct and turn to inspect the hall. The literacy noticeboard outside the English department has three mistakes. Fuck. Ripping it down, I turn back to Brian and say, "There are spelling mistakes on here. You were meant to check all the noticeboards. Get it changed right away, please. I'm off to the Year Ten assembly."

I've no more time for his shit today.

The hall in sunshine yellow has inspirational quotes papering its high walls. No one ever pays them the slightest attention, but I live in hope. Exams are fast approaching. They need to take them seriously, ignore the idle gossip that rules their lives and focus on what really matters.

After fifteen minutes of statistics and the importance of being kind, the children fidget in their seats. It's time to let them go.

"So, good luck. Let's show these inspectors today how proud we are of our school. Enjoy your lessons and let's leave quietly by the first row." They file out, trying to hide a buzz of conversation. Hannah, the receptionist, in her fake Chanel suit, totters on high heels as she weaves her way through them. By the urgency of her tight lips, this is it. I stand still and inhale deeply.

"The school inspectors have arrived and apologised for being late. They seem nice. I've put them in your office with a cup of tea."

Yeah, they always seem nice.

Outside my office door, I pause and smooth my hands down the creases in my suit. I fuss with the buttons on my cream blouse and run fingers through my hair. Fuck this fear. I've worked years for this moment. Finally, I'll be proven right. I'm more than ready for this. Pushing the door open, I greet the men who will decide my fate. "Good morning, I'm Ronnie Stevens, the headteacher. Welcome to our school."

"Good morning. Sorry about missing assembly. The traffic was awful even though we stayed nearby last night. I'm Andrew, Chief Inspector, and this is my colleague…"

I blink once, twice. My hands tense by my side. Nothing I do can change who he is.

"I'm Graham. Pleased to meet you," he says.

What the fuck is going on? Brian the weasel bumbles in and his desperation to be seen knocks me forward into Graham's upturned grin. I spring back. My fingers clutch the black pearls of my necklace. My mother's, my usual comfort. But Graham stares and the ghost of his voice uttering *beautiful pearls* whispers through the air. I tear my hand back to my side. He winks. Get your fucking act together, Ronnie. He's just a man. So what if he's had his hand up your thighs? Above the waist, I'm all head-teacher, but below I'm a quivering mess.

The stairway doors bang open and Mr Young, a science teacher, bounds through. As usual, he's flustered and his big face is rosy red from climbing the stairs. I hush him with a glare and reluctantly ask Brian to take the inspectors to their first observations. I hate letting go of the reins, but it will give me time to clear my head and give myself a shake. When Graham cheekily pokes his tongue out as he leaves, I'm appalled.

Turning to Mr Young, I ask him, "What's wrong?"

"Miss, come quick, two boys have jumped out the classroom window and I've no idea where they've gone."

"Tell reception to phone and inform their parents. I'm on my way. And, sir, don't ever leave your classroom, especially not when the inspectors are in."

I storm off towards the playground, furious with the boys but even angrier at myself. How can I let this affect me so much? And the way Graham is revelling in my anxiety is infuriating. But it's my fault. I know better than to shit on my own doorstep.

The boys are hiding behind a dirty yellow skip, snatching sneaky cigarettes before lessons. Another three have joined them and when I shout "Boys!" they jump in unison. They need to get a better lookout. I confiscate the cigarettes. They're my brand and might come in handy later. I give the boys a stern warning, the usual detentions and send them on their way. Then I stride off to the staffroom hunting for chocolate.

At the end of the school day, the inspectors sit down with their official folders and regulation façade. Brian edges his chair away from me and smiles towards them. The rat. Hannah has just served tea and KitKats. I'm too nervous to even think about taking a break. What have they found? Have we done well? And will Graham stop with his deep meaningful stares? The chief inspector tugs at the cuffs of his tweed jacket and begins.

"Thank you for allowing us to see the school." *For fuck's sake get on with it.* "I'll start by stating that we agreed if we had children, we'd be happy for them to attend here." The relief flows over me and I deflate into the orange plastic chair. Brian's smile slips from his face and patches of damp spread under his arms. So much for his Lynx effect.

"I'm committed to giving children a second chance and your school does this," the chief inspector says.

Under the table, Graham's foot rubs against mine. The shock makes me kick him. I sit up straight and throw him a furious glare. How dare he? This is a professional meeting. If people find out, we'll be fired. Yet my pulse is racing. His daring lights something inside me. I glance sideways to check Brian the rat hasn't seen. He'd bloody orgasm at such a find.

Graham begins his feedback as though nothing has happened. "I'll be taking your behaviour model to the local authority as an example of excellence." He believes in the same things I do and he thinks my way is the best. I grip my pen to hide my pleasure. He gives another smile, but I suppress mine. I'll not show this fucker a single flicker of emotion.

After a while, the chief inspector leaves to observe the after-school drama club and I tell Brian to accompany him. As I stand, Graham loiters at the door, his dark eyes searching the length of my body, exploring my face. I try to quench my climbing excitement and reach for a bottle of water. When I bring it to my lips and swallow, he licks his lips. I really shouldn't. It's high risk. But my feet edge over to the corner of the room.

"Come closer," I command. His eyes smoulder and his mouth breaks into a lazy grin. It's time for me to take control. Regain some balance of the situation.

Fastening my hand around the curls of his hair I pull his lips to mine and grab the firm flesh of his arse. In response, his hand rises under my skirt, but I slap it away. "No." Gripping his hair tighter, I draw his head down. I can also do deep stares.

Tilting my mouth to his lips for one more taste, my body

leans in for more. But I remember where we are, smack his arse and push him through the door. "Later, Graham."

He laughs and almost dances. His eyes sparking with the game. "You're stunning, Ronnie. Let me take you out for dinner."

I hesitate. I would love nothing more, but the school comes first. "Not until after the final report."

Before he turns the corner, he winks. "'Til we meet again, gorgeous." And with a quick wiggle of his bum, he strolls away.

Laughing, I close the door, collapse onto the carpet and throw my head back in laughter. What a day. I thrust a fist into the air. We've passed. We've done it.

And after years of searching, maybe Graham is the one.

A mist gathers at my feet. Pungent. Salty like the scent of the ocean. And it's rising, snaking under the door, searching for me.

A scream echoes within the room and I realise it's me.

"It's time," someone says. And I splash into the sea. The waves call me anew. I stand and face them. How many times have I done this now? The singles night. The school. Graham. But the waves, with their same old recollection, draw me in, welcoming me home.

I'd forgotten this part. I always do.

CHAPTER 4

Nikki – Blackpool

*I*n the shop, with its sexy sheer sleeves, the new black dress was so classy. The sort of dress Giovanni would love. I wriggle and squeeze myself into it and turn, expecting the reflection of Marilyn Monroe. But the mirror shouts: *you look six months pregnant.* The memory of last night's cheeseburger fills me with disgust. The dress is so clingy even my moles are mountains. I rip it off.

Little drops of sweat drip from my nose. And my last hope, the pink glitter sheath, peeks from my bag.

Now, pink is my colour, everyone says so, including my mum. A princess colour, all girly and full of sugary flirts. Just like me.

I pull it on and throw a wink at the mirror. This is me and all my sexy glances. And this is me, hand on hip, standing seductively at the bar. The dress gives my boobs such a nice round shape, all perky and full, and my arse is fabulous. He'll love it.

Swigging a last slug of lager, I grab my handbag. I'm so excited for our first real date. Blowing a goodbye pout to the mirror, I open the front door and pause. Will he introduce me as his girl-friend? How grown up would that be?

He isn't here yet. It's eight p.m. and the restaurant is buzzing. People are chatting, sharing pizza and the waiters are walking around with drinks and orders. The place is dark, with red walls and candles burning on checked tables. The rich odour of garlic blasts the air and the heat of baked bread wraps around me.

Where the hell is he? Inside the entrance, I wait, biting my nails. This is our first public date and it's so fancy. A swig of vodka would help, but I'd better not. Don't want to look like an alcoholic. I'll wait until I go to the loo later, then fish it out of my handbag.

I smooth down my dress and suck in my tummy. I hope when he sees me, he'll think I'm beautiful.

The room explodes into a blast of noise. Startled, I edge back into the wall. A bunch of Italians trying to out-stage each other is so loud. "*Ciao, come stai*, Giovanni?" the waiters all call.

He swaggers through the restaurant, like a movie star attending a red-carpet premiere. All lights are on him. Staff clamber to greet him, to pat him on the back. Even the customers turn to bask in his presence.

He's beautiful. That's not a word you'd use for a guy, but it fits him perfectly. It isn't just his hair, his eyes, his golden skin, or the tiny little dimples that crinkle near his mouth when he smiles. It's his dazzle.

A tiny blonde smothered in foundation and squeezed into a pink miniskirt totters towards him, a glass of red wine in her hand. Who's *she*? Pink is my colour, not hers. He grabs her around the waist and kisses both cheeks of her perfect little face. She giggles and offers him the wine. I hope she topples over on her stupid bloody heels and falls face down into a plate of bolognese.

Giovanni ambles through the restaurant and stops at a table to ask the diners how their food is. My eyes widen when he grabs a spare spoon and helps himself to the man's dinner. But the man laughs. "It's not as good as yours, Gio." Giovanni helps himself to some more.

The man looks up, a wide smile on his face and Giovanni confirms, "The food it is good here, yes? The choice you make very good, but it needs more of the salt." The man stands and they hug, patting each other's backs. Giovanni turns his gaze to the other diner, probably the man's wife. She quickly covers her plate with her hands. And a burst of laughter escapes from my lips. I would do the same.

Music blasts the room and from the kitchen a couple of waiters carry a fancy birthday cake to one of the tables. The room becomes silent and everyone turns round. I take the opportunity to edge away from the wall.

"Bella. Bella Nikki. What you doing? Why you be hiding?" Giovanni strides towards me and gathers me up like a feather in his arms. Kissing me softly on the lips he escorts me to a table in the back. It's so sweet when he pulls a chair out for me. No other boyfriend has done that before. Well, I guess they couldn't. The seats are glued down at fast food places.

"You beautiful, my Bella Nikki." He lifts my hand to his lips and my head swirls with what must be romance. His mouth sends hot sparks against my skin. And when he strokes my fingers, I want to rip his bloody clothes off. But he stands.

"I go now. You stay here and me be back soon." He kisses the top of my head and ruffles my hair, and I sigh in annoyance. We've just sat down. The smile drops from my face. Why isn't he calling a waiter over? Some romantic dinner date this is turning out to be.

In a sulk and grabbing my vodka, I jump up and strut to the

loo. My friend, Suzie, thinks he's too old for me, but all the guys before him are like little boys. Giovanni is a real man, tall, broad and confident. His size makes me feel all protected and safe like my father used to do, once upon a time. But not if he's going to leave me all alone. Like my father did too.

Practising a pout in the mirror, a thought crosses my mind. Maybe he's talking to that blonde bitch. Maybe she's batting her fake eyelashes at him. Men can't be trusted when it's thrown on a plate for them. Taking a quick gulp of vodka, I stomp back. I'll rip her pretty dyed hair out.

He's in the galley kitchen and calls me over. A waiter offers me a stool to watch him cook. I sit down with my head propped up on my fist and glare at him. My feet kick against the stool. This isn't how it's meant to be.

Over a hot stove, Giovanni tosses herbs, spaghetti and butter together. His eyes are intent on his creation, his lips humming a soft tune. The scents of basil and melted butter waft along the heated air and my hunger rumbles. As he grates parmesan over the dish, he looks up with eyes that glisten. "For me, Nikki, the food, it is the love. My mama, always she give us lots of food. The more food she give, the more she love you too much. The food you eat tonight. It has to come from my hands."

My pulse races and a giggle of bliss runs through me. Smiling, I sit up straight. Maybe this is the right way after all. I was so wrong to doubt him.

Has Giovanni burnt something? Because there's a mist wrapping around me and its damp breath makes me cough and splutter. I try to disperse it with my hands, but it's growing thicker. It trails up my nose, invades my mouth and I sneeze and sneeze.

I've no idea where it's come from or why it's after me. I stumble down from the bar stool, but my feet lift off the floor and I float into the air with my dress spread out all around me. I cling to a ceiling light and shout, "Help," but no one answers. Why can't they see me? Am I dead? An angel fluttering above them? I'm glad I wore pink. The mist has no answers, and it drags me higher and higher.

At first, I've no idea where I am, but the sea appears and yes, I've been here before. I plunge into the water. Then as always, I rise to a custard yellow sun, my feet stuck in wet sand.

Waves crash towards me. Hypnotic. Seductive. Pulling me back. But before their memory grasps me, before I enter the greasy café, a woman further down the sand appears. She too stares out over the water as if in a trance.

A man watches us both.

CHAPTER 5

Mrs Hawthorne – The Beach

Ocean waves lap against my ankles and the chill startles me into a sharp breath. Where am I? Sands stretch into the distance adding a sense of bleakness to the place.

Gulping salt-tinged air, I close my eyes tightly. Try to focus. But there's nothing solid to hold on to. Everything keeps shifting. My feet sink deeper into soggy sand.

Waves unfurl on the shore, their hypnotic rhythm filling the air. To the left of me, they lap at the ankle of a young woman standing just like me. On the other side, the silhouette of another woman cuts against the blinding sun. But as each wave hisses its retreat, something is changing.

My most precious memories are fading. Smiling faces flicker in and out, young and old. Children playing hopscotch, a woman brushing a young girl's hair, a baby crying. In desperation I clutch at the air, fingertips tracing the past. But the memories slip from my grasp and continue to fade. Tears roll down my cheeks with the effort of holding on. A child with a red kite, his smile wide. My hands reach out to touch the string but it's too late. It's gone.

Seasoned with the salt of sea spray, my loss sharpens. There's no fight left in me. Wringing my papery hands, I step out of the surf towards the lure of a distant shack.

As though my movements have broken their reveries, the other two women follow behind. The younger is barefoot and wearing a pink party frock. Her blonde hair tumbles down onto her shoulders. The older one is about forty, brunette and is dressed in a smart trouser suit. The heels of her shoes sink into the sand as she walks. As they get closer, their wide eyes tell me they're as lost as me. I don't speak for fear I won't know my own voice.

We meet before the shack, a café with driftwood walls that could have grown out of the sea itself. A rough uneven counter runs along its length. There are three bright yellow bar stools, but none of us sit. I suspect they're as frightened as me. But then the lady in the trouser suit barges towards me. "I'm Ronnie. Who the fuck are you? And how did I get here?"

Her sharp words startle me and I stumble backwards in the sand, but my fall is broken by the young girl's arms. As she helps me regain my footing, she asks me if I'm okay then she turns to Ronnie and says, "What did you do that for? She's an old woman."

Ronnie scowls. "And who are you? Are you both in this together?"

I stare blankly at Ronnie. What does she mean? The young girl strokes my arm as if it will calm me and responds, "I'm Nikki."

"What's going on?" Ronnie asks her. "How did I get here?"

Nikki shakes her head. "I don't know. I don't know how I got here either."

They both turn to me and glare, but I've no explanation to offer. I simply don't care.

Ronnie lifts a hand to her head, rubs her face. "The last thing I remember was our school inspection."

"I was on a date," Nikki says. "It was lovely and romantic, but it's fading and I can't remember who it was with anymore." She looks around the beach, at the bar stools and then out towards the sea. "But... the waves. I remember the waves." She twists a strand of hair in her fingers, tugging at it, distracted. "And I've seen you before, Ronnie. You stand on the shore staring out at the sea. But I don't know how I know that." A tear slips from her eye. It glistens and shimmers down her face. "Do you think it's a dream?"

Ronnie tears off her jacket and throws it to the sand. The grains flutter up and sparkle in the sunlight. "If this is a dream you couldn't both be here. I wouldn't be dreaming and talking to people I don't know." She pinches her skin and slaps her arms. "See? That hurts. It wouldn't happen in a dream." Her voice becomes a whisper. "But I think I've seen you before, Nikki, too."

How can they know and not know each other? It doesn't make sense. Someone is lying. Probably the someone who brought us all here. If I cared what happens to me, I'd figure out who.

From the back of the shack, an aged man shuffles and stands behind the counter. He's dressed formally in a bartender's crisp shirt, black suit and polished brogues. His long tangled hair is tied back casually from his face and appears at odds with his attire. He smiles, although the smile never catches his eyes. It seems painted on.

"Greetings. I'm the Gatekeeper. I guide those who seek to move beyond this place."

Nikki's face echoes my own bewilderment and dread. Who is this man? But Ronnie's hands clench into a fist. "Oh, I might have known. Stand back, ladies, here comes the cavalry to mansplain," she says. Nikki giggles and Ronnie bares her teeth.

The Gatekeeper smiles. "Such impoliteness. Especially

towards one who can answer your queries." His eyes narrow towards Ronnie and Nikki. "Didn't you just ask why you're here? Wouldn't you like to know?"

"Spit it out then, old man," Ronnie says.

He frowns at her. "You should learn to keep a civil tongue in your head. Until then, you deserve only the unvarnished truth. You're both dead."

Ronnie kicks the sand. "Dead? You're mad, look at me, I'm right fucking here."

Nikki reaches out to Ronnie, as though she wants to hold her hand. "This isn't right. We can't be dead in all this light."

"And how did you both get here?" he says, tone calm, eyes burning stronger than the sun.

Ronnie's head twists left to right as if searching for an answer. "Well if it's not a dream, we must have been passengers on a cruise. It sank and we're its only survivors." The Gatekeeper shakes his head and takes a step towards her. She backs away. "Or you kidnapped us all, you dirty bastard."

The Gatekeeper's eyes cloak in scarlet, his pupils dilate, the sky darkens. I flinch in confusion and a dark dread slashes, slices and cuts through the air.

Ronnie stands still, her limbs trembling. Nikki grabs her hand and drags her towards me. We crouch down and huddle together in the sand that circles around us. But I'm not afraid. I've just let them shape me.

When Nikki talks, it's in the softest of whispers. "Is it a dream then?"

"Does it feel like a dream?" he says. "Is this heat a dream? Is the sand beneath you a dream?"

I pick some of it up and as I let it drop between my fingers, its coarse texture grazes my skin. This is no dream.

He points a long finger at Ronnie and Nikki. "You both died a long time ago. But you're stuck here, on this beach, in limbo, replaying the same scene from your life over and over. Why do

21

you think you are drawn back to the waves time after time after time?"

Ronnie's head shoots up and she unfurls her legs but Nikki hushes her and pulls her back down.

"Beyond here is the Afterlife, a place of beauty and peace. All you need to do, to move on from this beach, is show me what love means. For only those whose hearts are filled with love may enter." He smiles again, but his eyes are still pools of dark scarlet. We three are reflected there as if we belong to him.

"As for those who don't know love?" He nods back towards the waves. "You may return to limbo where eventually, over time, you'll simply fade away."

A flash of bile burns the back of my throat. I swallow it down and concentrate. Perhaps his words will fill or release me. I'm slipping away.

He wraps a large block of ice in a tea towel and slams it hard against the counter. I jolt and he waves his arm, the gesture taking in the three of us. "All each of you has to do is tell me and the others your story and to help you I'll grant you snatches of memories as we go along." He grabs thick chunks of ice and drops them into three tall glasses.

Ronnie turns and jabs a finger in my chest. "I was happy before the old woman turned up. I'd passed my school inspection. Everything seemed so real. But even that's fading now."

He pours white rum into the iced glasses and throws in some diced pineapple. "Then if you were happy, Ronnie, genuinely happy, go back to your spot and stare at the waves. Your memory of the school inspection will come back, but you won't move on from that."

Nikki grabs Ronnie's hand. "Don't go, Ronnie. Stay here," she pleads.

I lower my gaze to the sand. I don't care what any of them do. They can say what they want. I'll stay until the rest of me fades away.

Once more the sun sharpens the sky and the Gatekeeper places three cocktails onto the bar. "Storytelling is such thirsty work, ladies. Please take a seat and help yourselves. Ronnie, since you've so many questions, why don't you start? Think of love and I'll take you back there."

Nikki whispers, "It's okay, Ronnie, I'm here."

CHAPTER 6

Ronnie – The Beach

*H*is knock-off Armani is shit. Who does he think he is? But more importantly, who am I? Where have I been and how the fuck did I die? I've been trying so hard to remember since this arsehole turned up, but I can't.

All that's present is the waves. Even the memories I had before are gone. And of course, this idiot standing here like some crazy Old Testament Moses guarding the gates of Heaven. I've to fight to get in. And not just fight. No, I've to prove that my heart is full of love. What does he want a love story for?

Nineteen Fifty: Hello and fuck off. We women aren't swallowing Valium for the nauseous boredom of daytime TV or being chained to a man's kitchen sink anymore. We're perfectly fine on our own. Some of us have careers. Christ, I hope I've got a decent career. I need to work out how to get out of here.

"Ronnie, you may go back to the waves and limbo anytime you wish. Let them take you. Carry you away."

"Are you fucking mad?"

This man is a psycho. How the hell do I make sense of this? Can't trust him. What if moving on is worse. Much worse than this. And anyway, I like watching the waves and drifting. Don't I? It wasn't so bad.

The Gatekeeper smiles again but his dark eyes remain fixed on mine. I want to punch him. Smash his head against the driftwood wall and laugh at his predicament. "If not the waves, Ronnie, then perhaps you should focus and listen."

He's off his bloody head. I'm not taking any more of this shit. And he stinks of rotten fish. Like a decaying Captain BirdsEye dug up from the seabed.

"Listen, Ronnie."

Standing there like he's our saviour when he's really a prick.

"Calm down and listen."

How dare he talk to me in that tone? And then it surrounds me. Our song.

Falling from the stars

Love dust sprinkled skies

The images assault my mind so forcefully that I collapse to the sand. Our first dance. His hand in mine. The taste of his lips. The love in his eyes. "Graham." And I want to curl up in his arms.

I want more, not just the same old daily pattern. Not the same old scene. The singles night. The school inspection. There must be more than that. And I let myself remember another time. Another place.

Tit for Tat.

And his eyes are exactly where I want them. Focused on me. Adjusting my pencil skirt so that a glint of flesh flashes his way, I comb a hand through my hair and smile up at the stage. He drops the mic for a second time, bungles his words and presses the wrong slide. I laugh and when the crowd joins in, his face burns crimson. It's so unlike him. Of course, the delegates at the conference haven't witnessed my game plan. It's taken a while to action.

For the last few weeks, I'd ignored his calls, played hard to get, too busy, unreachable. Not that there were many to ignore. He wasn't chasing too hard. There'd been no frantic memos stacked high on my desk urging me to contact him and the calls had tapered off a few days ago. I'd guessed he'd other fish on the hook and didn't have much time to pursue me. The minnow that didn't fall for his charisma. The one that swam free.

I'd needed to change that, so I'd scoured brochures searching for his name and found an education conference where he was giving a keynote speech. Luckily for me, the front row still had vacant seats. No one liked the first row. They all preferred to sit near the back. They could snooze there, nap off the boozy lunches. But not me. I wanted to be seen. Full on and centre stage. I booked a seat and then went into Liverpool for a killer outfit and heels. As you do when you're fixed on winning the prize.

The applause snaps me back to the present and I dip down to retrieve my handbag from the floor, allowing my breasts to spill from my sweetheart top. Time to head to the bar. I'll wait there with a few cocktails and a good-looking man. To up the ante until Graham seeks me out, which he will of course. I throw him a wink as I strut past and he grins back. Snared. Like an irritant inside a saltwater oyster.

The bar is quiet except for a few scattered men who obviously saw this as a jolly and couldn't be arsed with the learning part. Although they'll make good use of the old boys' club to promote their careers. A lot of whisky will be served tonight and drunken promises held to ransom in the morning light. I jostle onto a bar stool and order a long vodka. Near the entrance to the hotel, a piano plays. It doesn't take long for someone to slither beside me.

"Hey, darling, you here for the conference too?"

Not an original line and the *darling* makes my hands clench. But with his smart suit and good looks he'll do. Graham won't know he's a caricature that every woman has met before. I slide my smile his way.

David, or DavieD as his friends call him – he capitalises the D out loud as if it's a badge of honour – is here to network. What a surprise. Over the next forty minutes, I learn he's the youngest deputy head in England and is on fast-track to being a head. Of course, he couldn't have achieved any of it without his young, devoted wife who supports his every move. He loves her dearly and is so lucky that she's a traditionalist and enjoys being the shadow to his light. He never asks me one question. I don't care. He's only a pawn in the game.

"But what happens at conference stays in conference, right?" he leers.

An ostentatious bottle of wine appears on the counter. Its intention is to impress me and open my legs while his wife sits at home with a nice cup of tea. I chew on my lip to stop from blurting out *pig*. Instead of spewing out words, he should oink. With his face getting redder from the alcohol, he even looks like one now. A room key swivels in front of my nose. He turns it around to make sure the P for penthouse stands out. Oh, how thrilling. A trip to paradise for little old me.

"You fancy taking this wine upstairs, darling? We'll be back down in time for the networking event."

I'll need to tell him to fuck off. I reapply my lipstick for dramatic pause. His tongue flicks across his lips. And a hand clasps my shoulder.

"Ah. There you are, Ronnie. I see you got the drinks in." Graham grabs the bottle of wine and ushers me over to a green velvet sofa near the piano where jazz notes soften the atmosphere.

Davie shouts, "Hey!" and steps towards us.

Graham smiles. "Oh hi, Davie. Tell the wife I'm asking after her. Tabitha, isn't it? And congrats on the new baby." Davie stares, mouth open and fifty quid poorer, and trudges back to his seat, big D shrivelled between his legs.

We sink into the sofa, but once Graham pours the wine we shake with laughter. "Poor bastard," Graham says.

"Poor Tabitha," I reply.

The bar becomes louder. People are enjoying pre-dinner drinks and the strengthening of old alliances. Lots of new posts will be made here tonight. None will be advertised until the new term but they are already done deals. The arse kissers move higher with the right accents and public school connections. When you come from nothing it's hard to smash through. The word *child* won't have been mentioned but budgets and bigger class sizes will bring praise and handshakes.

Graham brushes a strand of hair from my face and his touch reminds me of how close we're sitting. His arm draped along the sofa behind my head feels like it belongs there. How did that happen? When he whispers into my ear, the touch of his breath makes me feel faint. "You hate all this as much as me, Ronnie. So why are you here? Is it for me?"

The pianist plays the first notes of "Falling from the Skies" and I hold out my hand, the wine masking the vulnerability that's always with me. "Dance with me, Graham."

And we do, just us two on a small starlit square, my head on his shoulder, his arms tight around my waist. When the next song begins, we continue. And it's so calm. So peaceful. The music and us.

He closes the door while I sit on the bed. Gorgeous. Great arse. Funny too. We've laughed so much at me turning up and trying to put him off his speech and the day in the office when he did the same to me. He's charming. But that charm would win others too. Laugh them into bed. Make them feel safe. He walks over and pulls me in for a kiss and I push him to the floor.

He needs to remember me. I need to be different from all the rest. As he laughs and moves to rise, I push him back down. "Stay," I command. His eyes narrow, but he obeys and remains fixed in place. I unzip my pencil skirt, pull it down, step out of it and fold it onto the chair. My fingers linger on each button of my blouse before it's placed on top. Turning towards him in only my heels and underwear, a rush of power pulses within me.

I strut towards him and slowly circle his body. He moans and his hand reaches out. I bat it away and stretch over to the bedside cabinet, take a sip of my drink and smile. I have him now.

"Ronnie," he pleads.

Placing a finger under his chin, I tilt his head towards me and say, "I prefer my men naked and kneeling."

He winks. I slap him. Stare. Then he undresses. How excited he is.

Under crisp Egyptian cotton, we're cuddled together in bed, spooning. We've only slept a few hours. I trace his fingertips and kiss them softly one by one. He gathers me tighter into his arms and whispers, "Ronnie, you're amazing." I snuggle in deeper. He is too. Everything about him. "I mean you're so beautiful and smart," he says.

He kisses the back of my neck and I smile, pulling his hands tighter around my waist. I imagine us taking long walks by the sea, laughing in the breeze, a dog running by our sides. Chatting in the kitchen while he pours some red wine and the table is set with candlelight. Sharing popcorn and beer while we watch an old movie. Lying in bed side by side reading our favourite books. He'd sleep on the left and we'd always kiss goodnight.

"But I've just come out of a ten-year marriage. And I'm not

ready for a relationship." A shiver chills me. But I hold still, force myself to continue to trace the lines of his palm. Gently. Not digging my nails in.

"Ronnie, I don't want to hurt you, that's why I'm telling you now." But he'll hurt me. All of them do. I hold on tight and don't show a flicker of emotion. "Ronnie, what I'm trying to say is…" Yeah, yeah. It's him, not me. And can he stop using my name in his effort to make it personal? We both know what this is.

I turn round to face him. My tone is light and free. As free as he wants himself to be. "Graham, don't be daft. It's only a fling, isn't it?"

As he caresses my breasts and teases my nipples he continues, "I'm glad we're on the same page because I won't ever fall in love with you, Ronnie."

Oh, won't he? We'll see about that. I never run from a challenge.

CHAPTER 7

Nikki – The Beach

I couldn't follow all of Ronnie's story. Everyone says I'm too scatterbrained, maybe they're right. All I know is I want to go home. I'm only eighteen and I shouldn't be left here all alone, not with these strangers. I want my mum. My feet are sinking in this stupid sand. If only there was somewhere to run to but there's nothing, nothing but water. And it's so bloody hot it's burning the soles of my feet. Can somebody help me? It might have been better watching the waves. What was I watching again?

"You used to love the heat, Nikki. You loved the warm sand. Feel the heat and remember," the Gatekeeper says.

"I can't. Let me go. I won't tell anyone about you or this place. I promise. Honest, I won't."

"Wiggle your toes in the sand, Nikki. Let the soft grains fall through your footsteps and take you elsewhere."

Why won't he help me get away from here? What have I done to him to make him so mean? But then on the heatwave floats a memory of a different kind of sand. It hovers there with the rattling noise of fairground rides and children's distant screams. There was sand that you made into castles and water you carried from the sea to build moats.

"And where were you, Nikki?"

Ribbons of memory float back. There was a tower and donkeys and kiss me quick hats. Pink sugar candyfloss. Blackpool. I'd been working in Blackpool. How exhausting it'd all been. Too many late nights after work. Too many one-night stands who fled out the door as soon as they thought up an excuse like their dog had hurt its paw.

Guys who promised the moon and stars before a fumble in bed. Who'd swear they weren't like other men and were full of respect. They'd disappear without so much as a kiss goodbye in the morning. So depressing.

Tears tumble as the memories return. I've never loved anyone. No one ever gave me the chance. No matter how hard I tried.

"Can you smell something, Nikki? Is there something cooking?"

The only smell is the salt in the air, nothing else. I slump to the sand in despair. But then a hint of garlic wafts in on a breeze and the scent of fresh warm pizza dough warms my senses. Thick sauces bubble in pots as he stirs, smiling through the steam. His joy embraces me. "Gio. His name is Gio and it was the first time we made love."

He sits on the tattered sofa with a glass of red wine in his hand. His long legs stretch out in front of him and his feet rest on my wee pine table. I'm sprawled alongside him, gazing up, entranced. But should I trust this guy not to break my heart?

"Nikki, why we no play the cards. Be exciting, no?"

I sigh. We've been playing all week. There isn't much else to do because Gio doesn't like pubs. He can't be bothered with drunks and their stupid arguments. I guess he sees too much of it at work.

It's annoying because it's great to get dressed up for a night out on the town, all the glitter and sparkle and the buzz of getting ready, wondering what's going to happen. But I've given up asking. I'll knock back sambuca with my mates instead. It's more fun anyway.

That leaves us with the cinema and TV, but the film he's watching is rubbish. Well okay, there are other things like nice brisk walks or jogging or other goody-two-shoes stuff. What kind of idiots do those for fun? But cards? Cards are bloody boring.

I jump onto his lap, wriggle and give him come-to-bed eyes until he spoils the moment by asking if I have something in my eye. I slump back onto the sofa, fold my arms and sulk as he watches his crap film. This is my best satin nightie too.

I'm only eighteen and it's like going out with a pensioner. I'm not playing more cards tonight, no chance, no way. I mean he's only thirty and could go to a club if he wanted. No one would say he was too old if he dressed more casually. I grab a tin of lager from the coffee table, pop the ring off and take a deflated swig.

And why hasn't he ever tried to shag me? Is he too old to do that too? Maybe he's being respectful. Yeah, that'll be it. But I want a shag and I'm gonna get it. How else will I know if he likes me or not?

I inch back closer to him, flicking my long hair so that it falls forward onto my face. I hope he'll notice it and romantically sweep it away. Dead clever, eh?

Gio grabs me and pulls me onto his lap. He says in a soft whisper, "Bella Nikki, your eyes, they the blue Siciliano sea." He brushes my hair away and stares at me, his big brown eyes darker than before. I giggle from the nervous tension building inside me.

He hushes me softly and says, "You like we make the love? You sure?" Oh, my. It worked.

He traces the outline of my jaw and I close my eyes, unable to watch him. He plays with my hair then kisses my ears, my neck and my shoulders before finally reaching my lips. I kiss him back shyly and nuzzle against him. This is more like it.

Fingers glide slowly up my calves, past my knees and onto my thighs. He lingers there, stroking, teasing and dispersed in my moans is a sparkle of giggles.

He removes my nightie and lowers his lips to my breasts and my body trembles as he kisses and nibbles. I want to touch him but I'm not sure how. I've had one-night stands before but always when drunk. I've never been there. Like, right in the moment. I never remember details the next morning. It pains me to even think of how my flabby thighs and stomach might look to him.

A soft push and he places me down onto my back and peels off my thong. He groans and a flick of his tongue brushes his lips, but my legs close tight to hide from his stare. Why doesn't he turn me over and shag me like the others? I twist away from him and bury my face in a cushion. He'll think me a fool, but no one has really looked at me before. Never seen me as a person. Just a thing to have some fun with and move on. He might see the pain hidden under my skin and I can't have that.

A whisper in my ear. "My beautiful Bella Nikki." And he lifts my face to his and kisses the tip of my nose. So gentle. A touch that tells me *good girl* and that I'm special. I cuddle into him and he kisses the top of my head.

Gio is showering. I swig down more lager and try to stop grinning like a love-struck teenager. It's so uncool and anyway, my cheeks are hurting. When he calls me *Bella Nikki* it melts my soul.

In fact, his accent is as hot as hell. I'll ask him to talk in Italian more when we shag next. Or as Gio puts it, make love.

I yawn. Three a.m. and I really need to get some sleep. I've work tomorrow and the bar will be busy. It should have been my day off, but I agreed to do it because they're short staffed. I really wish I hadn't now. Why the fizz did I open my big mouth?

Slamming the door, I stomp through the hallway and hurl myself onto the bed. I need to phone Suzie. She'll have finished her shift and still be awake. I'm bloody raging. I can always tell.

"You're fucking kidding me. He shagged you then got all dolled up with aftershave and went out for the night? And left you there?" She's furious for me.

"Yeah, I can't believe it either. I told him he's a blooming idiot like."

"Where was he going?"

"I dunno, Suzie. He wouldn't say, not even after I kicked him," I sob.

"You kicked him? Oh well, he deserves it. Who the fuck would do that? I hope you told him to never come back."

"He's got a key, remember? And my shitty lock doesn't work. Do you think he's married?"

"What? How the hell could he be married? He's with you all the time. Nah, he's probably off seeing his mates. Don't worry about that, like."

"Seeing his mates at three in the morning? Prossie mates, you mean."

"No. His mates from the restaurants and that. God sakes, calm down."

"I doubt it. We just shagged. He told me he was falling for me. I bloody believed him. But he can get lost after this. I should have known. They're all the same."

"Wait and see. You never know."

"And why would he have half a bottle of bloody aftershave on if he was only seeing his mates? Nah. He's away shagging some other lassie, or maybe even his wife."

"Hey, Nikki, I've gotta get to sleep. You do too. Try not to worry. Sorry, but I'm dying on my feet here. Give's a phone tomorrow though, eh?"

"Yeah. Sorry. I needed to talk to someone. Thanks. Night night."

Well, some pal her. She couldn't get off the phone quick enough, selfish bitch. I've listened to her disasters and emergencies a thousand times. I've always been there for her, always had the time. But obviously she can't be bothered with mine.

I gaze around my bedroom. It's all so grotty. Mismatched floral curtains hanging at the windows, so thin that the sun glares through in the mornings. Pink woodchip paper peeling from the walls and a huge damp stain above the ceiling light that gets darker each night. The chintz carpet is so bare that the floorboards show and I've cut my feet a few times on the old nails that poke through. The only other piece of furniture, a cheap white chest, stands in the corner. Two of its drawers are broken and pieces of clothing hang out.

No wonder he doesn't want to stay here, what a dump. I pull up the duvet and cocoon myself in its warmth. I'm an idiot for trusting another stupid guy. Tears fall as I try to sleep.

My nightmares are so vivid. So real. You're dreaming, only dreaming. I tell myself no man is lurking at the bottom of the bed. But still, it feels real and I can't wake myself up. Move your body. Lift an arm. But my body won't respond, even when I think it has. The man gets closer to the bed and I'm shaking inside. His cold hands slither around me and prod me. *Move*, I shout to myself. Move now.

Hands shake my shoulders, my eyes burst open and squint

against the light. A huge mass looms over me. He really is here. It wasn't a dream after all. A scream tears from my throat.

Gio jumps back. "You are crazy woman. Crazy. Why you shout like this?"

Sighing with relief that some nutter isn't gonna kill me, I untangle myself from the duvet and sit up, staring. He laughs and says, "Watch out, my Bella Nikki. Watch out for the rain." Then, like a magician, he throws bundles and bundles of banknotes onto the bed. They flutter down. I'm covered in them. They blanket the whole bed, piles and piles of them. He throws another handful into the air and grins down at my huge eyes and open mouth.

I'm filled with horror at first. Has he robbed a bank and the police are chasing him down? Am I an accessory? Will the door be rammed open in an early morning raid? But then a smile spreads over my face and I clamber to my knees. The notes are crisp in my hands and I fling them up in the air to tumble down around me. I could get those new shoes. Maybe a new matching handbag. He's not gonna miss a few tenners, is he?

CHAPTER 8

Mrs Hawthorne – The Beach

*N*othing connects. These young women's passion so remote and distant. My hands, wrinkled and lined with age, rise to my throat. All those years of life, slipping away. Times of laughter and love. Maybe tears. It should be worrying to be dead, yet it's freeing.

"Mrs Hawthorne?"

There it is again, that voice. Where's it coming from? Should I respond? It's so very peaceful here and the waves are beguiling.

A persistent tapping on my left shoulder. "Mrs Hawthorne, you must respond. If you want to move on you must show me what love means." It doesn't matter what these strangers think of me or how I died. Why not drift, fade out and dissolve? But then a sudden surge of loneliness makes me shudder and a strand of my hair tumbles to the sand.

"Unclench your fist, Mrs Hawthorne." A small piece of sea glass nestles in my palm. It's so beautiful, cornflower blue, so very rare. It's formed from early Milk of Magnesia bottles. How did I know that?

And then like the waves to the shore, he crashes into me. His blue intelligent eyes, cornflower blue like the sea glass in my hand. His loving awkwardness. His soft smile. His silk voice. I clutch onto the memories, begging and grasping for more, afraid they too will evaporate like the ones before. They're all I've left. I open my arms wide as if to gather them in and soon every void in my mind is full of him.

"My Charles."

~

"Do you mind if I sit here?"

I do mind. I want to be left alone with a moment or two free from the angst, but nod politely. "Of course not." He sits rigidly at the other end of the bench. He's in his late sixties, probably the same age as me. I fan my face. Even in a short-sleeved top I'm sweating, but he's dressed impeccably in collar and tie.

A grassy hill stretches before us, past our little bench, down to the river. Clusters of families sit with picnic baskets and bright coloured blankets. The smell of burgers and sausages hangs in the air and a small group gathers around a smoky barbeque. A few boys kick around a football. Behind us, children shriek with delight in a small playpark.

On benches like ours, couples whisper their secrets to each other. And the world softens for a moment.

His little white dog circles around his feet then slumps wearily onto the grass. Unexpectedly, a wash of emotion passes over me and I bend over, sobbing. As if someone has punched me in the stomach rather than crushed my heart.

He doesn't speak for a moment or two, but he's looking my way. "Sorry for the intrusion. I wondered if you were quite all right. May I be of some help?"

I mutter, "I'm fine, thank you," then avoid his gaze. My handbag is lying on the grass. It has attracted the attention of some of the park's bees. Hopefully, a gentle kick with my foot will make them settle elsewhere. But instead, this angers them and they buzz closer to me. Much more of them than I first thought. I scream and draw back.

His body jerks at my sudden alarm. "I'll get it. I'll do it. You stay back!" He leaps to his feet but forgets about the little dog lying curled up in front of him. He trips, the dog yelps and anxiously circles him. "Jack! You silly dog," he shouts, as though the dog itself has caused the accident.

The dog's leash winds itself ever tighter around his ankles. He flails at the bees buzzing around his head and topples forward like an oak tree being felled in slow motion until he hits the grass with a soft thud. The dog barks excitedly and jumps around him. Then the bees fly off, as though their job is done. And despite myself, I burst out laughing. The noise is alien. Sadness has been a part of me for so very long.

He blushes. "Hello, I'm Charles. I'm so sorry about this quite ungentlemanly display." I laugh even more at his formal language and he disentangles himself and sits back on the bench. His salt and pepper hair is full, swept back and in need of a good barber. His voice is soft, the tone educated. Repeatedly he puffs on an electronic vape, inhaling as if it were oxygen. It barely leaves his mouth.

Pulling out a packet of cigarettes from my rescued bag, I turn towards him. "Would you like a real one?"

"Why not, I think that would be a splendid idea." He leaps from the bench with childish joy but trips again and knocks my cigarettes out of my hand.

"You're so clumsy." I grin, as he bends to retrieve them. He smiles and we light up. A little girl with hair in red-ribboned bunches giggles as she skips past our bench. Her mother lifts her and twirls her high in the air. Their laughter cleanses our silence. "How long have you been on the vapes?" I ask.

"Let me see. It must be about five years now. But you always miss the real thing."

Blushing, I shift position on the bench. "Oh, I shouldn't have given you that."

He smiles. His blue eyes are intelligent but spilling with sadness. Something has hurt him. I'm sure of that. He turns and says, "Isn't the park lovely. Who'd have thought that this was in the heart of Edinburgh? I often used to walk Jack here, but I haven't for a while. This is the first time in months. One does forget how beautiful nature is."

"One does, doesn't one," I tease. "It's my first time here. I found it by accident, but yes it's peaceful." I won't tell him my real reason for being here. Why would he even care? What would it matter to a stranger?

"In August, they've a festival, with second-hand bookstalls, craft beers, llamas for the children to pet, burger vans. Not that I eat burgers. I've been vegetarian for years. Never eat something that once had a face, I say."

"Oh, you're a vegetarian? I bet you're a hippy as well! Two of the things I can't stand." It's a joke, but maybe with a hint of truth. "The festival sounds great though. I bet it's really busy then."

"I'm sure it is but, in truth, I've never been. I don't like crowds much. I prefer the walkways along the canal, although I do have to keep an eye on Jack. It isn't the first time he's tripped me over and I wouldn't like to test the depths of the water. Once we took Jack…" His head lowers to the grass and his voice breaks. "My wife died."

The words are so bleak, so void of any intonation. His pain is so intense that I could reach out and touch it. He's broken, perhaps even more than I am. He continues, "Jack is my only reason to live on. Once he's gone… well…"

Charles stands. "Apologies. I need to go." And he grabs Jack from under his feet, cradles him into his arms like a newborn baby and walks away. From the way his body shakes, he's crying. Jack's fluffy face peeks over his shoulder as he stumbles across the grass. Even he is forlorn. Charles is drowning in sorrow and needs someone to help him breathe.

But that person isn't me. I've nothing left to give, for my pain is as deadly as his. I have to get back to the room soon. My sisters will be scared. Yet something draws me to him. Perhaps it's his kindness, or that he's made me laugh. And then it comes to me. Maybe Charles is the one I can save. I shout after him.

"Charles, I'll be here tomorrow. Same time. Same bench."

The park is almost deserted, perhaps because it's a Monday afternoon and everyone else is back at work or school. Or it could be because rain is forecast. The sky is heavy, dark thick clouds getting closer. But I'd promised Charles that I'd be here. A dog barks, making me look up and smile expectantly as I walk, but it's some silly stranger with a pet poodle.

In my Waitrose bag, the titbits jostle against each other and their rustling delights me. I'm rather pleased with myself because I remembered Charles is a vegetarian and bought lots of cheesy things and salads. None of them look that appetising, but maybe he'll be enticed by the strawberry tarts. Carefully avoiding a patch of hard sticky gum, I settle down onto the bench, take a deep breath of fresh air and grab a cigarette from my cardigan pocket. I've put some doggy treats in there for Jack.

I blow out smoke. I placed my tartan rug in my bag this morning. Charles's eyes will sparkle with delight at my thoughtful little gesture. He'll lay it down gently on the grass and we'll sit there drinking and eating, dunking our crisps into dips. We'll have our own little picnic. We'll be part of the fun.

My hand grazes against the ragged edges of carvings that have been cut into the wood of the bench. My fingers trace along the ridges. I wonder who MK and LG were and if they're still in love. Perhaps they too once sat on this bench waiting for someone. Longing for something delightful to happen. Scraping some stray hairs back from my face, I shiver and pull my cardigan tighter. The wind has a bite now.

A quick check of my mobile. No messages. At least nothing bad has happened since I left. It will be fine for a few minutes more at least. It isn't something to think about now. My next cigarette refuses to light, the flame of my lighter blowing out again and again. My hand cups around it to shield it from the breeze and I sigh with relief at the first exhale. Maybe Charles isn't coming after all. The picnic bag leans against my feet and I kick it away.

Another check for news from my family on the mobile. All is quiet. Googling *poodles* for something to do leaves me lost in a trail of clickbait. A Labrador in a pink tutu laps ice cream while a toddler sobs beside him. I chuckle but feel sorry for the poor child. According to the number of likes and comments, it's only me that sees the cruelty.

Charles appears fidgeting in front of me. He doesn't know what to do with himself and he stares down at the grass.

"Where's Jack?" I ask.

"Oh." Charles spins around and searches the park. Steps one way and then the other. Has Jack scampered off somewhere? I jump up to help but we move forward and awkwardly crash into each other. Charles jumps back as if burnt by the contact. "Actually, I forgot. I left him in the house. It's a bit cold for him today."

I burst out laughing.

"What? Did I say something funny?"

"My God, he's a dog. They're meant to be outside. It's hardly bloody Antarctica."

"Well, I have to look after Jack. He's all I have left." Charles's shoulders slump and his eyes redden as if stung by the bees from yesterday.

"Why don't you sit down?"

And he does, as far from me as he possibly can, his body pressed in tight to the arm rest. He lifts his vape to his mouth.

I'm so damn sorry for him. But what should I say? Ask about his wife? Would that make matters worse? Or do I look like a selfish bitch if I don't? It's almost like he's built a shield around him, armour to keep everyone out. But he's come today. He's come out to the park. He's come to meet me.

He's dressed so faultlessly. Perhaps a little old fashioned, but he has style. Beige cords, cream linen blazer, blue shirt and, peeking out from his top pocket, a matching polka dot handkerchief. That handkerchief is so quaint. The picnic. That will cheer him up. "I've got us something to eat. And I remembered you're a vegetarian." I smile. "We've got cheese and fruits I've never heard of before. Let's have a picnic just the two of us. You know, like all those people did yesterday."

Charles stares down at his empty hands. "I'm not hungry, but you go ahead."

I swallow hard to keep the disappointment at bay. So much for the picnic and my excitement sharing it. Ages spent in Waitrose choosing just the right thing. What a silly waste of time. I don't even want to think about the tartan rug sitting lonely in my bag. I grab a cigarette and without offering him one, light up. Neither of us speaks.

Magpies shriek hungrily at a clump of leftovers that lie discarded at the river edge. A small boy, about three, dressed up as Batman, is perched high on his father's shoulders. He giggles and babbles as they both make their way to the exit. A low drone cuts through the park and the smell of freshly cut grass drifts along to our bench. Why would someone mow when rain is imminent? I wrinkle my nose and reach into my bag for a tissue. Another check of my phone.

"I'm so very sorry to have distressed you," Charles says.

"I'm fine. It's the freshly cut grass. I get hay fever."

He tilts his chin down and leans forward. "No, I was rude. It was unforgivable of me. I'm so sorry to have upset you. It's… I'm not at my best at the moment. We've been alone, Jack and me, for quite some time. I might have forgotten how to be around people. Especially when they show me kindness. Do forgive me."

"It's fine, Charles, really. It's hay fever. Don't be daft. You've not done anything wrong. I was disappointed, yes, but it's not an issue. It was a silly idea. I have them all the time."

"It wasn't silly. It was kind. And me? I've been a big buffoon about it. Perhaps we could have a little something to eat now?"

My mobile buzzes. I grab it and as I listen, my world disintegrates. The picnic, the bench, the park, none of that matters anymore. Somehow, I make it to my feet. "I need to go, Charles."

He moves towards me and gently pats my shoulders. "Are you quite all right? May I help? Do you need anything?"

I snatch my bag, throw it over my shoulder, then scream in frustration when its contents tumble out. Cigarettes scatter all around my feet, my phone and purse lie upended on the bench and the silly tartan rug settles across Charles's brown brogues. As I gather everything up, he offers it back to me.

I push it away, shake my head and tell him to keep the useless thing. "Just let me go. My father is dying."

As I turn and stride away my vision blurs, my legs tremble and an intense pain grips my body. It's as though I'm gliding along the pathway, that my feet aren't touching reality. I can't endure going to see Dad and yet, how can I not?

Charles's words sail towards me. "Same bench. Same time. Tomorrow."

CHAPTER 9

Ronnie – Liverpool

*I*t's time for plan *snare him* to spring into action and what better timing than today. Valentine's Day. *Carpe Diem.* I've a change of sexy clothes in my bag for the scene. Graham won't see me coming.

It's been about two months. Very casually, we're dating. I say that, but it's rather rigidly set. I'm his Wednesday girl and I never sleep over. I guess someone else has Thursdays and Fridays. As for Saturdays, he likes to go out by himself.

"A Saturday night is great for pickups because there's no work the next day. Everyone's out for fun," he said, while I smiled and pretended his words didn't pulverise my self-esteem.

But it won't matter in the long run. None of it will. For I'll win. And that's all that matters. Right?

I'd chosen the presents carefully. Nothing expensive that would make him think that I was being too serious. That would scare him off. And they have to remind him of me. I'd bought three.

Exhibit A: Black Fred Perry polo shirt in skinny fit. He loves to wear his clothes tight, to show off his muscles. So, he'll love this and realise I know his style.

Exhibit B: Small stuffed red devil in satin shorts. It holds a little red heart but, because it's disguised as a saucy devil, I'll get away with it. Subtle, but not full-on hearts in your face.

Exhibit C: Red velvet flogger. We haven't used one of these and he'll fantasise about its touch and me brandishing it. Job done.

Of course, he won't buy me anything. Graham doesn't believe in Valentine's, for all the usual excuses men give.

In the pub at the end of his street, I sip white wine and wrap my weapons. I keep my eye on the window in case he drives past. This has to be planned perfectly. I have to make sure he's in. Now, do I write *Love Ronnie* or just *Ronnie* on the card? Will the word *love* scare the shit out of him, or will he see it as a throw-away phrase? I could overthink this for hours, so before I change my mind, I scribble *Love Ya*. There, laid-back, but still getting the word invading his personal space.

Telling the driver to wait, I jump out of the cab, ring the bell and arrange the presents at his front door. I will myself to walk away slowly back down the path. It's Thursday and if my timing is right, he's still at home. As I lift the cab handle, he appears.

"Ronnie?"

With a casual Farrah Fawcett flick of the hair, I turn and smile. "Oh hey, Graham. Didn't expect to see you."

He stands with the presents awkwardly held in his hands. "You shouldn't have done this. But thanks."

"Aww, it's some little things I picked up at the shops. Thought you'd like them." I'd taken hours choosing, but he couldn't know that.

"Why don't you come in, Ronnie? You didn't need to leave them and go."

The temptation to comply is overwhelming. He's stunning. But I've got plans for tonight and, as gorgeous as he is, they don't include him. "Sorry, babe, gotta run. It's Thursday and I've got a hot date."

With that, I enter the cab and wave bye. As we drive off, my head is giddy with the thrill of it all.

I place the champagne flute on the mirrored table and kick off my red heels. Soft music serenades candlelight that flickers shadows across the bedroom walls. I unzip my leather skirt and undress. As I wrap myself in a silk kimono and let my hair down, a shiver of anticipation runs through me. I adore these first few moments.

Graham knew I went on other dates. He went on them too. But I've never made it so obvious before. Fuck, I've never turned him down before either. He'll not be happy. What with him thinking he's God's gift and all that. His face dropped like a prune when the cab drove off. It was hilarious. And a taste of his own blunt medicine.

As I slip under the velvet throw of my king-size bed, I test that everything is within hand's reach. I hate when I've to get out of the warmth again.

Graham never showed jealousy. In fact, he encouraged me to go on dates, although he didn't like to hear about them in any kind of detail. It just made him feel better about doing it himself.

It normalised his behaviour. But he'll be seething tonight, being turned down for someone else. Especially when he has my presents to remind him of my sweetness. The sugar someone else will get. Ah well, enough of him, it's time for my hot date.

I reach over to the bedside cabinet and take a sip of champagne. Delicious. Then I grab the family tub of chocolate ice cream and the TV remote. As the soaps play, I swirl the chocolate around my mouth and let the stress of the day melt away.

"There's something for you on your desk, miss. It arrived by courier at seven this morning." I thank the school janitor and walk up the staircase to my office. What new hell will this be? It will be a miracle if it's the new textbooks I've ordered.

I open the door. The room is fragrant with the heady scent of lilies. And on my desk sits a beautiful bouquet wrapped up in pastel cellophane.

My breath falters. How gorgeous. I never receive flowers, not even on my birthday. Who could have sent them? But, then a thought hits me. They'd better not be from Big DavieD.

I grab the card. *Thanks for the presents, Ron. Hope you had a good date yesterday. How about dinner tonight? Graham x*

And just like that, I've been promoted from Wednesday girl to Friday. I'm going up in the world and am so much closer to the prize. As I walk to the playground, I hum the tune to Blondie's "One Way or Another".

I might not sing like Debbie Harry but fuck, I have her sass.

CHAPTER 10

Nikki – Blackpool

"*T*wo double vodkas and Coke, lots of ice."

Bloody cheek. I haven't even asked them for their order. So rude. Not even a *please*. I pretend I haven't heard and make myself look busy arranging wine glasses on the shelf below. They're in their thirties, boobs spilling up over low-cut tops, tight miniskirts up to their arses. They're a bit too old to be dressed that way. Heavy red gloss is slathered across the blonde's pout and she keeps batting away a fly that hovers near her mouth. I'd pay that fly in sugar if it got stuck to one of those lips.

"Excuse me," she says.

"Oh, I didn't see you there. What can I get you?"

"Two double vodkas and Coke."

"Ice with those?"

"Yeah, thanks."

I prepare their drinks as they chat and giggle with each other. I've been in the job a few weeks and I bloody hate it. The constant noise, the yelling, the dollybirds. Most of all I hate the red aprons and hair-in-ponytail rules. It makes me feel so ugly when everyone else is all dressed up for a night on the town. The two women whisper together, so I grab the ice bucket and edge closer to hear.

"He's here." The brunette giggles. Giggling like a teenager when you're thirty-odd is really pathetic.

"So he is. He's gorgeous, eh?" The blonde slathers on more sticky gloss then throws the tube into her tiny glitter purse. The fly still hovers. Go on Mr Fly. You can do it.

The brunette turns towards me, looks at the drinks in my hand and taps her red talons on the counter. I slow down to annoy her and select each piece of ice with the silver-plated tongs as instructed by Mr Health and Safety on my first day. Let them wait. The blonde bursts into action, poking her friend. "Don't look. I said don't look. He's coming."

Caught up in all the excitement, I crook my neck. These women are as high as kites. Although I must admit, I'm dying to see this god for myself. The brunette adjusts her boobs and the blonde flicks back her hair.

"Ciao," he says and kisses both their cheeks. Their arms wrap around his body and they do a little threesome jig. I slam their drinks on the bar.

I can't actually believe it. The god is Gio. And as they totter off on their five-inch heels he throws a wink at me. I bat it back with a scowl.

Gio had asked me to come work here so that we could spend more time together. Both of us worked nights and he said it made perfect sense for us to do it together. It kind of did, but I hate the garlic that stinks through my clothes while every other woman wafts strawberries and flowers. Are his air kisses really just for tips? He'd better not be playing me for a fool. But then why would he want me to work with him if he's lying all along?

"Two cappuccinos, Nikki."

Great. I wrap my blistered hands in a wet dishcloth, hold the jug of milk under the steam tube and stand back from the violent hissing. The milk froths and gurgles and as usual splutters all over my hands. I hate the bloody machine. I slosh the boiling milk into the coffee cups and the waiter rushes them away. I really hope every other customer tonight hates coffee like me.

I wash the milk jug, run my hands under cold water, then rub them down my apron to dry. The air is smothered with the scent of cheese and freshly baked dough. A tang of hunger ripples in my stomach and I sneak two mint chocolates, the ones meant for customers, into my mouth. The chocolate melts deliciously but I hate mint.

The restaurant is closing and drink orders have been stacked high all night. I've hardly had a moment to stalk Gio's whereabouts. He could be snogging someone behind the fake marble pillars for all I know. But surely not. All the flirting for tips is to help us save, or so he says. A bushy moustache with its stout manager attached twitches and calls my name. "Nikki, we're running out of beer. Go run down to the cellar and bring up a few crates. I'll man the bar."

I nearly freak out on the spot but manage to keep myself still. "Um. Lorenzo? Can't you get the beer? I'll stay here."

He shakes his head and his moustache bristles as if it might flee for freedom. "No can do, Nikki. It's your job. Come on, I'll open it up for you."

I'd rather face the evils of the coffee machine. He pulls up the wooden lid of the cellar and switches on the dim light. There's a flight of rickety steps going down and crates of bottles in various sizes spread across the floor. I can't do it. But if I don't, I'll look like a fool or, worse, get fired. And we've been saving up so hard.

I move tentatively, downwards, one step, two steps, then

freeze. Something scuttles along the cellar floor and I scramble back up. I imagine little beasties running up and down my arms. Shuddering, I scrub them away. "I can't do it. I can't."

He scrunches up his nose and narrows his eyes, the moustache twitching to the right. He leans over me and says, "It's your job and I'm not going down there in this new suit."

What a big pig. I back up against the wall and burst into tears. I hate the dark and all those creepy crawlies. I can't stand them. I'm not going down there amongst them all. He huffs a huge, exaggerated sigh and is about to say something else when, to my horror, Gio walks in. Fabulous, now he's going to see me snivelling. Will the night get any worse?

"Nikki. Why you cry?" Gio booms as he strides towards the bar. He turns towards Lorenzo. "What you do to Nikki?"

"I told her she'd to go get the beer, Giovanni. It's her job."

"You touch her?" His face is thunderous with rage.

"No. No. I only tell her go down the cellar and get the beer." Mr Moustache moves towards me and I can't breathe, so I push him away. He staggers, teetering over the cellar opening until his hand grabs the counter to steady himself.

Bloody hell. I run off to the ladies' toilet, bolt the door and sink to the floor. What a fool I've made of myself. There's no way I'm coming out of this toilet tonight.

"Nikki?" Gio can call all he wants. I'm not going to answer. Reaching over for more toilet roll, I blow my nose. "Nikki. Why you be hiding? Come out now."

"Get lost!"

He's taken ages to find me. He doesn't even care. "Nikki, you don't need go the cellar." Oh, has Mr Big Moustache gone down himself after all? Good for him. But I'm still not moving. "Nikki, come out. It's how you call silly billy." Who cares? It was bad enough that I felt like shit before but now it's even worse. Panda eyes isn't a good look. "Nikki, I go. I be back."

Great. Now he's left me and I really wanted him to coax me

back out. Flushing the toilet, I wet some tissue and rub under my eyes. Maybe I'll run out now, go through the back door before anyone sees me leave. But I don't have my purse or keys for the flat.

Gio slumps down to the floor, his back thumping against the door. "Nikki, I have the cheese pizza and the Coca-Cola and the ice. You eat, yes?" Hell, I'm starving. I imagine the taste of the gooey melted cheese in my mouth and the sharp fizz of a cold Coke. But I'm not going to give in. I'm not a dog performing tricks at the promise of food. A paper plate with a slice of pizza slides under the door and before I know it, I've taken a huge bite.

"You were chatting up those women all night and giving them kisses. I saw you." Gio laughs. It makes me angrier and I throw the half-eaten pizza at the toilet door. "It's not funny."

"But it is, Bella Nikki. I tell you many time. I nice, we make more money. The money we need for the restaurant of ours. This pizza it cold." He's told me that before. Lots of times. We've been saving up for a few months, ever since the big win that he'd scattered all over my bed, and I can't wait until we have our own place. It's our dream. I've already planned the colour of the table-cloths and designed the menus.

"What happened with the cellar?"

"No need worry. I tell manager I go for beer. There is lots there now. I got it and next time you tell me. I go again."

"But I feel like an idiot, Gio."

"No, the man he the idiot, not you. Me I do not like the shark, so I no go deep in the sea. Same thing."

"What did you tell him?"

"I told him my Nikki she no like the daddy with the long legs. So, she no go again." Laughing, I open the door. He stands, kisses my forehead and twirls me up in his arms. He always makes me feel so protected. He isn't going to be like every other man. I need to trust him more. "After we eat, we go casino. We make lots of money tonight for our restaurant then you no need do the drinkies again."

I've always wanted to see the casino, but he normally doesn't let me go. He always says I'll ruin his focus. I bet it's all swanky and buzzing with excitement. How much will we win?

CHAPTER 11

Mrs Hawthorne – Edinburgh

*T*here's an urgency trying to push me forward, a compulsion to race along the sterile corridors, sprint through the haze of lemon bleach. Everything is telling me to run. Run. Dump that silly bag, throw that stupid coat off, remove those shoes. Run. Run. And save him.

But I can't move. I'm too afraid. I slump into a hospital chair.

I remember the dad of my childhood, the one who chased me and my sisters through golden dunes. "Catch me, Daddy! Catch me!" we'd scream in excitement, hoping we'd be caught up into his tanned arms. He'd throw us into the air, twirl us around then laughingly toss us into the sea. The coldness of the water would shock us, yet our shrieks of delight would bounce off the waves. And he'd stand there watching, so happy with himself that he'd made us laugh.

So strong is my memory that I can smell the salt of the sea

and if I look hard enough, I might catch a glimpse of us, all those many innocent years ago, still playing in the waves.

You never quite knew what was true about my dad. Had he really been to Africa or walked three hundred miles home because he'd spent all his holiday money at the races? Had he swum the Channel not once, but twice? Lived in Hollywood?

Long ago lazy Sunday mornings. Me and my sisters listened for Mum to go downstairs to prepare his usual Sunday stew. As soon as she did, we'd throw back our blankets, run through and excitedly climb into his bed, clambering all over each other to get the best spot. Cuddled, cossetted and safe, waiting for a tale from our very own storyteller.

"Once upon a time, there was a man walking home drunk from the pub when he suddenly tripped over a ten-pound note and fell down an open manhole into a jungle with ferocious snakes and venomous lions…"

My sister, Judy, always replied, "But, Dad, it's snakes that are venomous and lions that are ferocious."

"Not in this jungle," he'd warn, blue eyes sparkling. "It's the snakes that are ferocious here!"

Then he'd jump and tickle us and we'd all giggle and wriggle and shout, "What happened next, Dad?"

I have to face those ferocious snakes alone now, so I stand, put on my armour of a brave face and brace for the moment.

Turning the corner, I enter the ward and walk through the green cubicle curtains. My younger sisters, Judy and Mary, sit huddled around his bed in frigid silence. Ashen and drained like ghosts. We're all so old. We hug, then I cautiously turn towards Dad. His head hangs limply to the side, his eyes vacant, skin ash grey. The shock makes me step back, disbelief pressing a fist to my mouth. I'd seen him only twelve hours before. He'd been sitting in the care home garden overlooking the park. Joking, a cup of tea by his side.

I turn away from the horror, shield my face and flee from the ward. Mary runs after me and puts her arms around me, but I shrug her away. I need space, somewhere to breathe. She sighs and goes back to the vigil, but it's a while before I compose myself enough to return.

A nurse walks by. I stroke Dad's head and want to fall to my knees and beg. Please bring him back, please save him. I want her to know he isn't this old man choking for breath. He isn't this stranger with sunken bones, gasping and rattling. He's young and handsome, funny and cheeky. Bold, yet shy when he is in posh company. He has the twinkle of the night stars in his eyes and he likes to sing all the wrong words to all the old musicals and dance badly at parties all night. He loves books, movies and stodgy cakes. He's a gadget man, although he can't fix anything, and he loves the soaps on TV. How will he know what happens in *Emmerdale* now? He doesn't deserve this.

I want to scream to her, "That's my daddy."

But I don't. I just sit there instead, like the coward I am. Silent like the rest. All three of us dazed and numb. Accepting.

I edge closer and hold his frail hands in mine, paper-thin skin, so cold. The same hands that once shovelled heavy coal in cramped dark mineshafts, that hoisted bricks up onto strong shoulders, that sat me on his knee.

Moistening his cracked open lips with sticks of pink sponge, I tell him, "It's okay, Dad, I'm here. You waited and I'm here. Everyone is here. We love you. We love you so very much."

My voice breaks and I swallow back the emotion, my throat burning with the tension. For now, I need to be strong, he won't hear my tears.

And I release him.

"It's all right. We'll be okay. You can go. You can go now, Dad. Go and see Gran. We love you."

As the last callous breath leaves the man he once was, my childhood truly dies.

I kiss his lips for the last time and tell him, "It's been a wondrous fairy tale. A glorious fantasy of jungles and hump-backed whales. Princesses fighting with green, silvery dragons and Batman rescuing them all." I grip his hand tighter. "On days when things get too hard, I'll remember you and us. Goodnight, Daddy, sleep well."

The next day dawns like nothing momentous has happened. From my window, the birds still shriek and the dustbins on the street still clatter. How can that be? We should have all stopped with him, ceased to exist. It's wrong, disrespectful. Who will fill his space? An image from the care home tears at my mind and I shake my head and banish it. I can't remember his face that way. Where are all my tears? Don't I care enough?

My hands tremble and the cigarette lighter slips from my hand to the wooden floor with a crash and clang. I flinch from yet another intrusion and struggle to find my breath. The lighter is Dad's. A gold tarnished Zippo we'd bought a few birthdays ago. John Wayne etched on the front and his name, *Cash*, on the back. Like a little boy, he'd bounced in his chair when he first saw it. Rubbing a finger along the worn grooves, I can almost feel his touch. I flick the lighter on and off and stare at the dwindling flame until the gas runs out.

My sisters phone and invite me round, but I can't bear to go. All their children, all their friends, all the small talk and nibbles. I slump back in bed, wrap the duvet around me and close out the world. But then I remember Charles. He'll be waiting at the bench, in the park, just outside the care home.

I press my lips together and chew on the thought. It will be impossible to move from this safe haven. My body is too heavy to face the task. Nothing left of me to give, not even a tear. But Charles will be there, waiting. Somehow, I know if he has to, he'll wait the whole day. My hand finds its way to my mouth and my teeth tear at the ragged skin near my nails. When the sharp sting of blood arrives, I welcome it. There's no choice but to go. Even if it's for a minute or two. Guilt has shadowed me since last night. If I add any more, I'll suffocate.

I shuffle from the trees. The bench is empty. Charles must have either left or changed his mind. I haven't the energy to care which, but I rest here for a while. I light a cigarette and the smoke curls into the air. A thought flashes through my mind. How would the burning tip feel against my skin?

"Jack! Jack, come back here at once. Don't jump up. Get down." As Charles comes bounding, arms flailing, Jack drags his long leash and barks at my feet. "I'm so sorry about Jack. Jack, get down. I must have missed you when you arrived. I was sitting by the river, but I did keep an eye on the bench."

"It's fine, I've only just arrived."

"Oh good, good." He looks around and pulls Jack tight on his leash. "Well, I wondered if you would care to perhaps come sit there with me. It's behind us. A rather lovely little spot. The breeze from the river is delightful."

"Okay," I reply with a shrug and pick up my bag and follow Charles down.

It's a longer walk than I expected. We leave the main path and instead follow a shallow dirt track. The trees are thicker down here and the riverbank less kempt. I can't see our bench. But Charles is right, it's peaceful.

"I hope you like it," he says as he leads me round a corner. And there, spread carefully along the grass, lies my tartan rug I'd left last time. On top, a wicker basket lined in red gingham is full of sandwiches and slices of cake. China plates with delicate roses lie next to white napkins and crystal wine glasses. A bottle of wine sits inside a steel bucket that brims with melted ice. "I thought we could have that picnic," Charles says.

My eyes brim with tears and a sting of emotion steals my breath. I crumple, dizzy, to the grass, drenched in sweat. A hard lump somewhere in my throat threatens to choke me.

"I'm dreadfully sorry about your father. How is he?"

"He died."

Charles opens his arms and, sobbing, I collapse into them and weep for the longest time. And Charles, releasing his own grief, cries too. Under a canvas of careless clouds that scatter the sky, he holds me, until soft shadows lengthen and mask our pain. Afterward, I wonder if that's why he chose such a secluded spot.

We're sipping wine and gazing at the river. "Charles, why don't you get a mobile phone so we can text or call or send photos to each other?"

He jumps up excitedly from the rug. "What a truly great idea. Now, where would one buy one of these mobile objects? One of the sorts that does all that?"

And I astound myself with a laugh.

CHAPTER 12

Ronnie – The Beach

*H*e stands on the other side of the counter smiling down at us crouched in the sand. His stupid cocktails are sitting on the bar and if he's not careful, I'll throw one in his face.

He grins. "Well, Ronnie, at least you made it to Friday girl."

Cheeky bastard. I rush to my feet. He's getting it now. The old woman stays on her knees, but Nikki leaps up and tugs my arm.

"Please, Ronnie. Don't do anything mad. I need to find out what happened after the casino and I want to see Gio again."

"My father died. It was Charles who saved me," the old woman says. "We shared our grief. But what happened next?"

They're both looking at me with tears in their eyes as if I'm the bad guy. As if all of this is normal and I'm spoiling their fun. The slap of the waves on the sand is like the tapping of a branch on your window late at night, when the wind is high. It makes me grit my teeth. Will it never end? I shrug Nikki off, walk over to the bar and let my fingertips trail along the rough driftwood surface. He leans forward and I smell the cheap pomade in his black curls. I pick up a glass.

"What the fuck is going on. And you'd better have an answer, or I'm going to do some serious damage." I smash the glass against the wooden edge of the bar.

Mrs Hawthorne jumps up and grabs my wrist. "Don't you dare," she hisses. I'm not sure whether it's the shock of her sudden appearance or the strength of her grip, but I step back and drop the glass.

"What kind of person are you?" she says. "I've just remembered my father died, lived through all the grief again and you haven't even asked me how I am. And as for Operation Snare Him. He told you he'd never love you and all you can think of is how to change his mind. You and your hot date with cold ice cream. It's pathetic. You're lying to yourself. But Nikki and I had real lives. She had Giovanni. And I had my Charles. And you're not going to stop us from finding out what happened."

I want to retort, but she's right. Nikki has found someone who loves her, who showers her in money, and their life ahead together looks sunny. And Mrs Hawthorne has found solace in her darkest hour. When all seemed lost, there was Charles, with his silly picnic. Do I have the right to deny them?

The Gatekeeper steps around the counter. "Fear not, ladies. Our stories will unfold. Indeed, in this place," he spins around, his open arms taking in the sea and the beach and his ramshackle shack and the three of us, "it's memory that binds humans together."

We back away from him and our hands find each other.

"I'll tell you a little story," he says. "Once upon a time there was a woman, April, locked up in a medical institute. She'd been in a terrible car crash and had suffered horrific head injuries. All her memories were erased. She couldn't even recognise her own face." He stops and takes a slug of rum and coconut from one of the two remaining glasses.

"Each morning, when April got out of her bed, she'd no idea where she was, or who she was. When she walked to the toilet, she had to navigate her way by following the hospital signs. But one morning, having done that once, the next time she remembered how to get there in the afternoon."

He twirls the ice around in his drink. "Imagine April's relief. Her memories were coming back. At the doctors' urging, she'd begun a diary and on that day, she triumphantly entered *At last, I have begun to live again.*"

Mrs Hawthorne's fingers curl tightly around my palm and Nikki shakes.

"And so she approached the doctors, demanding release. And her physician merely smiled sadly at her. 'Turn the pages,' he said. And so April flicked through the pages of her diary, to the previous day, the day before that, and the day before that. It went on for hundreds of pages. And on each page, in her own handwriting, was the phrase, *At last, I have begun to live again.*"

The Gatekeeper tilts his head back and swallows the last of his drink through tight lips. His eyes are crinkled at the side as if it's all a big joke and he's keeping his laughter hostage.

"It's my decision that you'll be like April. You'll remember precisely what I give you to remember. We'll focus on those memories that you call love and the feelings you experience in that moment of time. What better way to get to know our little group of ladies without the distractions of others?"

"What the fuck do you want from us?" My hands shake as much as Nikki's and my legs are weak. What if I don't like what I find? What if Graham is a liar, a user? Just like all the others. What if everything is a waste of time? What if there is no love? What will happen to me then? Will I stay here forever, trapped by the waves?

He smiles again like a snake slithering its tongue out, testing the air.

"Why, Ronnie. What else? We need to know what happens to our Friday girl."

And, with that, the memories crash over me.

CHAPTER 13

Ronnie – Liverpool

A toothbrush. So innocuous. Yet symbolic when next to his on the bathroom shelf.

I'd "forgotten" to take it home so I could check the next time I visited that it was still on display. And now after a few weeks it's claimed permanent residence. Does he have a hidden cupboard somewhere with a huge box of them, all branded different girls' names? I slosh my mouth clean and make a note to check the house next time he's out.

He steps out of the shower drenched in the scent of vanilla rose. "Ronnie, I love the new body buff."

"Told you. I'll get some more next time I'm in Boots."

He flutters small kisses on the back of my neck and I grab my dressing gown from the hot towel rail we'd installed last week.

A few months have passed and we've slipped into a semblance of normality. Clubbing. Shopping. Cuddling in bed, kissing and watching old films. We often discuss school strategies over a

Chardonnay, his intelligence spellbinding and his astuteness making me hot.

And day by day, piece by piece I'm moving in. Cementing my rank, creating bonds and securing my place in his life.

Exhibit D: New mattress from John Lewis. We shopped for it last Saturday amongst all the other happy couples starting a new life. We'd laughed and laid down, testing them out like they do in those TV romcoms. Normally, of course, I'd be strutting through, sulking at anyone who dared come near. But this was fun me. Happy me. Perfect girlfriend.

Exhibit E: Hairspray, hairbrush and a box of tampons in the bathroom cabinet. If any other woman sees them, they'll understand this is someone else's territory.

Exhibit F: A range of silk chemises and knickers that lie folded in a bag under a bedroom chair. The pile is growing and soon he'll have to offer a small drawer.

He said he'd never live with a woman again but, here I am, becoming more visible every day.

He preens and primps in front of a free-standing mirror. Black tight polo, black jeans. His pulling outfit. He's off out on the hunt with his shady little bastard best pal.

"How do I look?"

"Gorgeous as always," I reply. It isn't a lie.

It's Saturday night. I've moved up rank again. But there's a test I'm not sure I'll pass. And he's so happy, so excited and oblivious to my pain. But why would he notice? It's me who designed it. To prove my worth. To prove I'm different. All part of the *snare him* plan.

I sink back into satin pillows with my new book and hot chocolate by my side. He leans down and I kiss him goodbye. I keep my voice light and as he bounces down the stairs, I shout, "Have fun, babe. Go do your thing."

"Thanks, honey. I'll try not to wake you when I get home."

The door slams. I must be mad. Throwing the book across the

room and stomping downstairs, I grab a bottle of vodka from the freezer. Graham can go fuck his hot chocolate. It will probably be the only thing he doesn't fuck tonight.

How will I get through the next few hours? The pain burns my stomach. How can he leave me like this? In his own home, under the blankets with a book, while he goes out on the hunt. Dirty rat.

But it had been my idea. Earlier, over breakfast, Graham had gone on and on about how much he liked me. And to be fair he showed it in every way he could: flowers, cooking us dinner, asking me to stay over more and more. Except for one thing. He didn't want a relationship and wanted to still play the field. Bastard.

So, I'd said, "Graham, I'm not a jealous person. I don't care if you have sex with someone else. I know that's all it is. Just sex. It's not what we have." He'd jumped on that, nodding. Yes, yes. "But I hate lies. I hate deceit. You must be honest about it. No cheating behind my back."

Another nod. And to prove my point and to become his one and only Saturday girl, I'd scaled up the game. "In fact, Graham, there's no need for me to go home today. I'll stay over. But you go out. Do your thing as usual. I'll relax and see you when you get home." His mouth shot open but after further discussion, we agreed. This is why at one in the morning I'm on the kitchen floor, drinking ice vodka and obsessing.

I can't get my head free from him. Is he dancing or is he already fucking someone? Is she better than me? Younger and firmer? Maybe kinkier? Oh, she'll have a better arse. He's an arse man after all. I rub my hand along my own arse cheeks, disgusted at how flabby they are. Maybe I'll disguise myself and go to the club and spy on him.

Why am I doing it? Am I challenging myself? Seeing how far I can go? Because I can't have meant those words. The pain is too fierce. I could walk out. But then we'd be over. It would all have been for nothing. But how can he hurt me like this? I'd told him it was okay. I'd given the green light. And men? They hear what they want to.

I return the vodka and grab a can of soda. Being drunk isn't going to help. I have to make sure I play the role when he gets back. I have to do that sober.

Six a.m. He gently slides into bed, carefully lifting the blankets so as not to wake me. But I sense every move. I've been looking out from behind the curtains to see who drops him off. I do that yawn thing to show I'm not fully asleep and curl towards his treacherous body. He smells of lemons, the vanilla rose sullied then showered away. Like a child, he'll need to be forgiven. I lay my hand on his chest. "Hey," I say. He wraps me in his arms and his tears feed the drought of my emotion. I have to stand fast.

"It's okay." I laugh. "You haven't done anything wrong."

"I fucked someone tonight. She gave me a blow job in the taxi then I stayed up all night screwing her. I didn't think of you once, Ronnie. Until now."

I want to punch his fucking face in or take a knife and cut off his dick. I want to hunt down the girl, feed her it and watch her choke on her greed.

"That's what you went out to do, babe. Good for you. And you're home now. None of it matters."

He shrugs off my embrace and lies flat on his back. His eyes stray to the window and the flickering street lamp. "My wife and I, we got divorced and it was all my fault."

Just nod, Ronnie. Don't speak. Don't say what you really feel.

"I'd an affair." No surprise there. "We met when we were fourteen, still at school, really naïve. Neither of us had even been kissed before."

Well, you sure as fuck are making up for it now.

"We got married, both of us virgins at eighteen. I wanted to be the perfect husband. She deserved that."

But you couldn't keep your dick in your pants, right?

"But then I made new friends at university and started clubbing. At first, it was just for the dancing. But suddenly I saw this new world and I let temptation in."

Shut up, Ronnie. Don't talk. This is important. This is ammunition.

"My wife saw sex as a means of procreation. It was never for pleasure and had to be done efficiently. Masturbation was a sin. They said it could lead to homosexuality. And I'd been caught a few times. She reported me to the elders and my parents."

What the fuck. I clasp a hand over my mouth to keep my words in.

"It was embarrassing to be chastised in front of everyone. My whole community was disgusted but then I made matters worse by having a few flings. A one-off might have been forgiven, but I couldn't stop."

He swallows hard. I place a hand gently on his thigh and wait.

"I was shunned. Excommunicated. My wife divorced me and the whole church turned their back. It's not a religion like yours, Ronnie. It's nothing like being a Catholic. It's a cult. Even now no one speaks to me, except my mother, and that's in secret. I no longer exist."

His voice breaks.

"The shame of that never leaves me. So, you see, Ronnie? If I couldn't do it for my wife and my parents, I'll never do it for you. And I care so much about you that I don't want to hurt you."

I pull him into my arms. What a horrific weight to carry. And I get it. The years we all spend fucking around, experimenting, trying things out. He'd never had that. And he wants it now, but he can't take any more blame. No matter what he feels for me.

"I'm going to say something, Graham. And I don't want you to reply. Don't talk. Okay?"

His body tenses.

"I love you." I silence him with a kiss. He crumples into my arms.

But do I really? Or do I just want to win? Any normal woman would just walk away. But I'm not just any woman. I can do this. Just not this way. I can't be oblivious to all the facts. I must find a way to take control.

CHAPTER 14

Nikki – Blackpool

Sweat drips from Gio's brow and he wipes it along his shirt sleeve. It's disgusting. I can't be arsed with it anymore. I sit down on the carpet and burst into tears. After a minute or so I look up through my lashes to see his reaction, but he hasn't even noticed. So I cry even more.

Four hours of hell and I'm exhausted with it all and, minute by minute, our savings are slipping away. I hate the place. And I hate Gio. His stupid dreams and big ideas mean nothing at all.

The casino isn't glamorous and fancy. Well, the free drinks are. When I found out you didn't have to pay, I regretted not ordering something expensive. And, guess what? You get fancy meals too. Proper meals made by chefs. But the rest of it. Nope. Not fancy or glamorous at all. It's all dingy and stinks of damp desperation. The freebies are to keep you there and disguise all the squalor. If you leave for a drink or something to eat you might not come back. And they can't have that.

I get up from the floor and slump into a red velvet chair. There's no point putting on a show when he doesn't care. A woman glances over with sympathetic eyes. "Are you okay?" she asks in a hoity-toity voice.

Obviously not, but it isn't her fault and she probably feels as bad as me. Like Gio, her guy is probably slouched over blackjack too. "Yeah, I'm just a bit fed up. It's boring."

She laughs and sips a glass of wine. I change my opinion of her immediately. "I don't see what's funny, actually."

"Oh, doll, you've got a lot to learn. I guess it's your first time?"

I should tell her no, that she's got a bloody cheek. But then she might ask me questions to see if I'm lying. And I really don't have a clue, so I tell her the truth. "Yeah, it's my first and last time. I'll never come back."

She nods like I've said something really good and I'm glad I've not lied. "What happened then? The guy you're with seems to be losing a lot at the tables."

A huge sob lodges in the back of my throat. I gulp it down. "Yeah, he's an idiot. He's been playing for hours and losing all night. I don't think he has anything left."

The woman clicks her fingers towards a nearby server and grabs two champagnes. She offers me one. I don't fancy it and screw up my face. "It's just cheap fizz, but it's nice. Go on, it'll cheer you up a bit," she coaxes.

I smile. "Okay."

"You're young. Eighteen or nineteen?"

I nod and drink some more. I'm not guessing her age because under all the make-up I haven't a clue, she could be anything between forty or fifty. I glance over at Gio, but he's oblivious to anything around him, his focus solely on the cards.

"So, do you live with your parents still?"

"No, my mum and dad split up. She's in Scotland and I moved down here about a year ago. Don't know where my dad is and I don't care."

Cheers and applause erupt from the roulette table and a bunch of men pat each other on their backs.

"Someone's been lucky," she says. I wish it was Gio. "More champagne?" She clicks her fingers again.

When I look down, I'm shocked my glass is already empty. "Please."

"So, your guy is good-looking. Much better than mine."

She points over to a guy in his seventies, bald head, huge stomach and very short legs. My eyes widen and she smiles. "As Marilyn Monroe said, don't you know that a man being rich is the same as a woman being pretty?" I'm not sure what she means so I giggle and sip my fizz. "There's no point in you being with that guy if he's skint, you know. You should move on. I could introduce you to a few high rollers."

What is she talking about? So rude. Like I'm going to dump Gio because he's lost. Well okay, I'm pissed off with him. But it isn't her place to say that. I stand angrily and she reaches over and places her hand on my wrist. "I'm just saying, doll. You could make a lot more money tonight if you dump him. All the girls do that. The guys sort of expect it. Are you working alone?"

"Working alone?"

"Yeah. Some girls try it on their own at first, but you're better off in an agency. I run one and with your looks, I'd definitely take you on the books."

On her books? Oh, my good God. Is she? And without thinking I blurt out my granny's old phrase. "Are you, um, a lady of the night?"

She laughs. "I'm a prostitute, doll, the same as you, only a bit savvier. So, if you want, I'll help you. You could earn a fortune. The old buggers like the young ones."

I splutter and cough, nearly choking on my drink. Could this night get any worse? This place can go to hell and so can Gio. I was right about him and his prossie friends. I stand and pull my miniskirt down as far as it will go, in case anyone else gets any fancy ideas. Then I head for the door.

It's dark outside. I could've sworn it was much earlier. But then time doesn't exist inside the casino. Why would they want you to see the hours and minutes fritter by? Gio shouts after me, but there's no way I'm letting on. It has been the most shit night of my life. I mean, do I even look like a prostitute? I'll have to check in the mirror when I get home. Bloody bitch. I should've thrown the fizz all over her.

"Nikki?" He can get lost. I run along the pavement. He'll never be able to keep up. "Nikki, wait. Nikki, why you run? You think I am the Boogie Boogie man?"

I don't want to laugh but I can't help myself. But I don't slow down. And then in the middle of the street, he belts out Shirley Bassey's "Something in the Way you Move". It makes me laugh even more. And since I'm knackered and out of breath, I slow to a stop and cross my arms.

"Nikki, I am the crazy man in casino. I know this." Yeah, he sure was. A big sweaty one. "But we have fun, yes? You like the food. The drinks. The roulette." Yeah, but I know when to stop. He doesn't. "Nikki, why you no talk me?" Because you've lost all our money and ruined our dreams for our restaurant. "Bella? You hungry?" Not going to work, mate. Not this time.

He grabs me and tickles me under the arms and blows raspberries against my neck. "I'm not a baby. I'm eighteen. Stop."

He leans against a shop wall, head down, shoulders hunched and runs his hands through his thick black hair. "I'm wrong tonight. I let the game put spell on me. I not look after you right way. I sorry, my Bella Nikki. I very sorry. This it not happen again."

I glare at him. "You ruined our dreams."

"Why you say this?"

"You spent all our savings, Gio. Everything we worked for."

He shakes his head. He's about to cry. But I'm not going to soften.

"Nikki. Come." He takes my arm and we walk silently towards the bus stop opposite the North Pier promenade. The breeze blasts a chill around us and sweeps old fish and chip wrappers up into the air. The scent of candyfloss mingles with the salt of the sea and sticks like glue to my skin. Fastening our jackets tighter around us, we continue upwards until finally, Gio stops outside a bank. "Here, Nikki. This is savings card. You keep it now. You no trust me. And I no trust me too. This best way. I sorry."

I don't see much point when we're starting from scratch again, but he gives me the pin number, so I check the balance. The six thousand is still there except for fifty pounds. I'd been wrong and it's not all gone. I feel so bad, but I'm keeping the card.

We sit together on a low stone wall and gaze out at the sea. The sun is rising and the first rays of light spin glitter onto the sand. We munch bacon sandwiches and hold hands. He has ketchup and I have brown sauce, but I don't argue about that.

Suddenly he jumps up and twirls me around in the air. "Let's buy the buckets and spades, Nikki. Let's make the big sandcastle." I laugh. It's seven in the morning. He's mad.

He kisses my nose and grins. As he sets me back down, I shout, "Yes let's. One with turrets and a moat." As we run like kids to the nearest shop, I pat my pocket to check the card. I'll need to find a good hiding place once we're home.

Somewhere far from Gio's eyes.

CHAPTER 15

Mrs Hawthorne – Edinburgh

Wild and untamed, the peonies bordering the driveway add a simple grace to the garden. Petals have scattered onto red gravel. I gather some up, cup my hands and inhale their sweet peppery scent. I've always loved roses. The front door opens and Charles walks out and ambles over.

"They're Clarissa's," he says. "She planted them when we first moved in. They're quite beautiful, aren't they?"

"Yes, they're gorgeous." But their velvet touch now feels cloying. I clench my hand, crush them, drop them to the ground.

While I glance over at the house, Charles fusses with the flowers. "I really should get around to putting in some supports for these." Is he also considering his own stooped back?

We've been chatting and texting by mobile for a few weeks. Charles's ineptitude and my impatience for him to get it right make us laugh at ourselves. And late into the night we've cried again and again for our loss. But this, this is a new step. He'd invited me for dinner and this is my first time at his home. We're nervous and uncertain of the meaning.

The house is a grand affair, secluded behind iron gates, its whitewashed stone walls imposing, and I imagine us being served afternoon tea on the lawn. Charles shifts from foot to foot and makes his way to the door.

"Please do come in."

The hallway is floored in rich caramel oak and several rooms branch off from its pale-yellow walls. But it's the view to the back garden that captures my heart.

The grass, freshly mowed, slopes gently down to a hedge of silver beech and wild cherry trees. Smoke bush, broom and rock rose splash hues of purple and pink in the borders.

In a corner a weeping willow romances an old rustic bench with graceful leaves. How I'd love to sit there, a book in my hand, a glass of wine by my side. My father would have loved it too.

"What's in there?" I ask, pointing to a wooden summerhouse.

"That's where I keep the piano. My playing is so dreadfully bad Clarissa asked me to move it out of her hearing range. Philistine." He laughs.

"I bet you're not that bad. Can I see? Maybe you could play me a tune."

"Good grief, no. Even I admit my music is a crime against the arts. Besides, a couple of years ago I found some poor old itinerant had taken up residence and I had to shoo him off, so now I always keep it locked."

Sunshine washes the hall with a golden glow and warm air flows through the open windows. But I shiver, for there's no life in this home.

"Would you like some tea?"

In such a grand house, we're in the humblest of rooms. A brown leather sofa, shabby and torn, is cramped against a wall. And opposite, set to the news, an old box television drones along with Jack's snores. Charles strokes his fur as if he's scared to lose contact, while I perch on the edge of the sofa looking on. A clock on the fireplace strives to tick the minutes away, but they're sparse.

"Oh," Charles says, suddenly remembering he has a guest. "Would you like a tour of the house? That's what one does, doesn't one?"

Ghosts cling to motes of dust as if yearning for lost love. Her photographs in gold and silver are everywhere I turn. In the dining room, napkins lemon with age curl next to white china plates. And I can just imagine Clarissa holding court here, the crystal sparkling, as Charles basks in her light. Each reflection of his past shapes his loneliness sharper.

Does he live in the television room because he can't bear to see all this? Has he built a refuge there for him and little Jack? I'm suffocated by the desperation in the air.

"Charles?" I say softly as if he's made of glass. As if I might break him.

He jumps as if he's never heard someone speak here for a very long time.

"Why don't we go out to the garden and sit? Come on, it's a gorgeous day. We could take some wine out. Let Jack run around while we chat."

Charles almost sprints to the kitchen.

"So, tell me something about psychology, Professor."

Charles laughs at the use of his title. "It's not something I particularly like talking about. No one says to a particle physicist – hey tell me something about physics. Because they already know they're not going to understand the answer."

I nearly choke on my wine. "Very condescending, Prof."

"And it's kind of the same for psychologists. For example, you go to the hairdressers and they ask, *What do you do for a living?* and you say, *I'm a particle physicist* and the conversation ends there."

"So now hairdressers are dumb?"

He shakes his head and continues. "No, no. But if you were to answer, *I'm a psychologist* they might say *Oh you should come to study us, we're all really mad here.* The problem is people think they know what psychology is, but they really don't."

"Uh-huh." I sip more wine.

"And often the results of psychology are really surprising, which will annoy some people. Let me give you an example."

I top up our wine glasses and lean forwards. I love to learn.

"So Harvey Sacks, an influential figure in my field, looked at how we interpret the things people say. One example he was fond of was *The baby cried. The mummy picked it up.*"

I light two cigarettes and offer him one. He pauses to inhale then continues.

"Now most people hearing that would automatically assume that the mother who picked the baby up was the mother of the baby."

"Obviously," I reply.

"But there's nothing in that statement to suggest the mummy was the baby's mummy."

"What! That's rubbish. It's implied in what was said."

He laughs. "No, it isn't."

Shifting in my chair, I turn closer to him, my voice rising.

"But you said the baby cried and the mummy picked it up."

"No, I didn't put the *and* in. You did." He laughs.

"But if he'd said *the baby cried, the woman picked it up* it would have more credence. It's really stupid. Of course, we'd think it's the baby's mother."

Charles slaps his thigh in delight.

"As I said, the results of psychology sometimes annoy. And I think you'll find you're annoyed. And on that note, I'll get us more wine."

"I think we'll need more than one bottle, Charles. This conversation could take a while."

Charles smiles. "I look forward to it."

Two hours later and we're still arguing about the mummy and neither of us will concede defeat. I can't remember the last time I've had such fun. We're on our third bottle of wine and eating pizza when he asks if I like music. I do, as long as it isn't jazz. Which of course turns out to be his favourite. So, we compromise and put on some old Sinatra.

"Do you miss your career?" I ask him.

"Not really, I've done everything I set out to do. And the timing was right to retire. But I may write again for journals."

Being a professor of psychology, every stereotype fits Charles to a tee. But the bumbling old-fashioned exterior hides a sharp wit that charms.

"Do you miss yours?" he asks.

"Yes, every day. I may go back."

He nods, reaches out and holds my hand. And as the music floats around the garden, we lose ourselves in our thoughts.

Crimson streaks smeared with mauve and plum darken the sky. Splashes of colour painted by hidden lights shimmer from shrubs into the night. We could be anywhere in the world.

Charles stands. "I don't dance, normally, but this seems the perfect time to start."

He bows and holds out his hand. I curtsy and fold into him as if it's the most natural thing. And as we waltz on the lawn with uneven steps, the world is a softer place. Less harsh. Less cruel.

"You've saved my life," he whispers, before lifting my hand to his lips. An old familiar feeling awakens inside me. It both terrifies and excites me.

Will he save mine too?

CHAPTER 16

Ronnie – Liverpool

*S*trolling along the corridor, Mrs Wilson from the maths department scuttles towards me. Her brows are furrowed and she fidgets with a pen in her hand.

"Miss. Sorry to bother you but there's a fight in the downstairs loo. I think it's Shannon and Donna up to their usual tricks."

Sighing, I twist my head away from her. Lick chocolate from my lips and slip my Mars bar into my jacket pocket. There's never any time to sit down and eat in school. Even snatched moments of pleasure get ruined.

"Can't you deal with it? I'm about to go into the English department."

She lifts the pen to her lips and chews. "But there's a gang of girls guarding the entrance and I can't get in."

If she can't control a gaggle of Year Nines, she won't last long in her new role. Which means human resources, supply teachers and behaviour problems. I force a smile.

"Okay. Okay. I'm on my way."

She scarpers back down the stairway like a frightened little mouse. Resisting the urge to creep up behind her and shout *Boo*, I follow her down.

As I turn the corner, the girls flee like it's chip day in the canteen.

"Get straight back to lessons," I shout. "We'll deal with this later."

Shannon and Donna are arguing over a boy as usual. I can't bear to go into the details. I give them detentions then stride back to English.

Two more hours until lunch drinks with Tara and I'm counting the seconds.

The pub is one of those chain types with jugs of watered-down cocktails. You'll still get pissed if you drink enough, but you'll spend all night in the loo. It's busy, but then a carvery always attracts fools.

I order orange juice and lemonade, although I'd love a double vodka and lime. But there could be parents here and they'd use it as ammunition if we ever had a confrontation. I spy Tara's blonde bouncy curls, grab my drink and walk over. It's been way too long since I last saw her.

"Hey, Ronnie. How you doing?"

We hug, but only because it's expected. I'm not really into all that kissing and touching stuff.

"How's hubby?" I ask, hating myself for the abbreviation.

"He's as boring as ever. Let's not waste time talking about him."

We clink our glasses together and giggle. I met Tara in a

previous school. She taught art, but she's left teaching now. We hit it off immediately due to our fascination with hangover cures and a shared history of arsehole boyfriends.

"So, what you been up to? How are things with you and Graham?" she asks.

"School's great. I love being the boss."

She throws her head back, curls flying wild, and laughs. It's such a great noise, loud and in your face. Tara doesn't give a fuck about appearances.

"And Graham?"

"Yeah, it's going great. He's gorgeous and so clever. We chat about everything."

"That's fab. About time you had some luck. You've had some right nutters in the past. Remember that drummer guy's wife who turned up at his gig, accusing you of being a homewrecker?"

"Yeah, he'd told me she'd died in childbirth."

We both sigh and say at the same time, "Lying bastard."

"Especially cos I only fucked him cos I felt sorry for him."

"I don't suppose he cared much about why, Ronnie." Our laughter brings tears to my eyes.

A pack of men suited and booted at the bar, drinking trendy bottled beer, tut in our direction. The smallest one, covered in acne, tries to act big.

"Quieten down, ladies, please. We're trying to watch the races."

"Get to fuck!" Tara shouts in her upper-class accent and a couple of women at a nearby table applaud her.

The pack shake their heads, turn their backs and whisper to each other like old mother hens.

"What about that guy you dated who worked on the oil rigs. He was away two weeks at a time? Tommy?"

"Timmy. We never saw that coming, did we?" she says.

"Nope and neither did his pregnant girlfriend when we tracked him down to her house. Another lying bastard."

Tara sips some of her spritzer, then smiles. "Yeah, maybe a boring husband isn't so bad after all."

I nod, although I don't quite believe it.

"I'm going to have to go soon, Tara. I've a meeting at 2.30."

Her mouth transforms into a pout but she quickly recovers it. "That's okay. But since we haven't had much of a catch-up, what about meeting up after school for dinner?"

I really do need to make more of an effort to see her, but there's always something standing in the way.

"Sorry, I need to go shopping after school. It's Graham's birthday tonight and I haven't bought him anything yet."

"Oh, what you getting him?"

"I'm not sure, to be honest. Like most men, he's hard to buy for. I did have one idea but then I thought better of it."

"What was it?"

I lower my voice and lean in closer to her. "Well, don't be shocked, but I wanted to get him a threesome."

"Another man?"

"Nah, a woman but I–"

"I'll do it, Ron," she purrs.

What the absolute fuck. I was about to say I'd changed my mind. That I'd never been with a woman before and wouldn't have a clue.

"Unless you don't want me to, of course." The pout is back.

I've this *don't give a fuck* attitude to keep up. If I back down, I'll look like an idiot. And she's sitting there, so excited. Excited to fuck Graham! Is her life that boring? A queasiness builds within me, a pressure on the nerve of our friendship. If I say no, she might be offended.

But since this is part of plan *snare him* and, since she's offering, fuck it.

"Wow, yeah, course. That'd be great. Come around to the house at seven and I'll tell him his birthday present is waiting at the front door."

She throws her palm up in the air and, like a teenage boy or someone who has lost their mind, says, "High-five." I jump back and nearly fall off my chair. "Come on, Ron. High-five." She giggles. Flushing with embarrassment I lift my hand and gently tap back. She squeals in delight.

What the fuck have I done?

The candles are lit, the bubbles are on ice and I've showered twice. I've never thought about sleeping with a woman before and I'm not sure I can pull it off.

After school, I phoned my old friend, Liz, for advice. She's been married to her wife for seven years. She'd laughed.

"Just do what you like done to yourself, Ronnie, and enjoy."

But this is for Graham, not me. Another experience, a new way to capture his devotion. I only wish I was more confident in the scenario, knew my script and had rehearsed all my lines.

I pop open some fizz. Pacing the room, I drink straight from the bottle as if it's cheap cider from the corner shop and I'm eighteen again.

A flurry of excitement tingles through me. Graham is gonna die when she arrives. But I'll have to control my jealousy, or I'll fuck it up.

The bell rings and the intrusion makes me drop the bottle. I mop up the tension and take a tissue to the champagne.

I open the door. Tara has gone full out and is standing in a raincoat with a red bow tied in her curls.

I call Graham over and she winks. "Happy Birthday. I'm your present."

His eyes widen in shock and I think to myself, *You did this, so make it work.*

Clasping her hand in mine, I lead her upstairs and Graham trails behind.

In the bedroom, to get past the awkwardness of the situation, I pull her to me and kiss her full on the lips. It isn't how they tell you. It isn't softer and sweeter. It feels just the same.

I undo her coat and her body trembles with excitement. Naked, she is stunning. Yet vulnerable. Fragile. An overwhelming sensation to save her consumes me.

Graham approaches her and it's as if I'm looking through a camera lens. The room feels distorted. The walls distant, the figures too near. I crave to stand in front of her, act as a barrier, protect her. But is it her I want to free or the mirror image of me?

"Ronnie?" Tara says, taking my hand and placing it on her breast. She nods, giving permission. She wants this.

"Come on then, get undressed, birthday boy," I say to Graham.

He doesn't need any more encouragement.

Pushing her down onto the bed, I run my hands up her smooth tanned body. With slow flickers of my tongue, I tease her nipples erect. I marvel at how different they are from mine. Short. Dark and thick. She's not me.

Graham kisses her and soon her low moans excite me too. And I whisper, "You're such a dirty girl."

"I am," she says. Voice hoarse with lust.

Graham parts her legs, then with his eyes fixed on mine, he thrusts and enters her.

Opening the back door, I grab one of Tara's cigarettes. If there's ever a time to lapse, it's tonight. I sit down on the stone step, wrap my red kimono tightly around me, light up and inhale. Graham and Tara are upstairs still at it, but I need a break and some air.

Footsteps pad behind me across the kitchen floor and Tara taps me on the shoulder. Her face is weird, all mushy and soft and her lipstick is smudged on her mouth. I guess she gave him a blow job.

"You okay, Ronnie?" she asks, lighting a cig.

"Yeah, I'm good. You?"

"I've had a fucking ball. But why are you down here on your own?"

"Oh, I just thought I'd leave you both to have fun and I needed a drink."

She sits beside me for a minute, exhaling smoke rings into the cold air. We watch them rise and disappear. Then her hand reaches for mine.

"Ronnie, you do know I don't fancy Graham, don't you? He's nice but he's just not my type. It's you I wanted to sleep with. I have since I met you."

What do I do with that information? I lean over, kiss her. Graham walks in, a cheesy grin spread across his face. "Well, ladies."

I fucking hate being called *ladies*. Just call us by our names.

"I've had the best birthday ever. What a night! Tara, thanks so much." He opens the fridge and grabs a beer and a pie that has been there for some days. I don't tell him that it's probably gone off. Then he walks over, bends and plants a kiss on the top of my head.

"And, Ronnie, you're amazing. I've never met anyone like you before."

I've not either, because I've no idea who I am anymore. How far will I go to win this game?

CHAPTER 17

Nikki – Blackpool

Screaming, I jump onto the sofa. Gio runs downstairs in his pants. The baseball bat he keeps hidden under the bed is held high above his head.

"Is it the daddy with the long legs? I kill him, Nikki. I kill the little devil." He swings the bat and searches the air just missing the lampshade that hangs from the ceiling.

"There's something horrible in the fridge. It's freaked me out."

"In the fridge? How it go there?"

"I don't know! Just go get it, Gio."

"Who put it there, Nikki?"

"I don't know. God sakes, can't you just go get it?"

"Calm, Nikki, calm. I go check out the situation."

We'll be dead by then. Gio moves so slow when he's checking out anything.

"Nikki, nothing bad in fridge."

"Then where is it?"

"How I know? I no see it."

Christ. I'm going to have to go back myself and show him. How in the hell can't he see it? It was the same when he couldn't find his socks the other day.

"Stay there. I'm coming through," I shout. I can't understand it. I saw it just a minute ago. A huge slimy thing with bulbous eyes, staring at me when I went in to get butter for my toast. Gio is standing in the corner, the baseball bat hidden behind his back.

"Gio?"

"Yeah?"

"Where did it go?"

He jumps forward and I fall and crash against the wall. In his hand is the ugliest thing I've ever seen. I run back to the living room.

"Nikki? You want some the polpo?"

What the hell, it's disgusting. He laughs and I throw a cushion at him. "Don't ever bring octopus into the house again, Gio. And disinfect that fridge!"

"Aww, try the tiny piece. Maybe a leg?"

I shiver at the thought of that slimy texture anywhere near my mouth. "No! I'm away to get ready for our meeting."

"Watch out for the monsters!" he shouts, and I laugh, despite myself. He's such a big kid.

The space is perfect. Just the right size for eight tables and we could even put a pizza oven at the back. I already imagine Gio swanning about in the kitchen with his chef whites. The walls are dark sage, but we'll brighten them up to Italian red and put little lamps on the tables. And the location is perfect, right opposite the sea and a short walk from the Pleasure Beach. I love it. It's everything we've been looking for over the past few months. Except for one thing. The rent is too high.

"What do you think, Gio?"

"How much?"

I blanch at his abruptness, but the estate agent smiles.

"Just the same as it was last time you asked, Mr Amato. It's a very desirable location and such a good customer base."

"You take the five thousand off. I pay cash now."

I blush at his reply. He's already asked twice and been refused. I want it too, but he's making us look desperate and, of course, she doesn't agree.

"I've other viewers coming next week but I'll hold for forty-eight hours. If you find the five thousand, it's yours. That's the best I can do."

"I find it," he replies.

"Fantastic, I look forward to doing business. You won't regret it. She's a cash cow for sure."

Gio and I walk along the prom, ducking and diving through the tourists with their kiss-me-quick hats and arms full of candyfloss. The smell of fish and chips dusts the air and Gio is as high as the coloured kites flying from the sandy shore.

"Nikki, our dream it come true. I ask my cousin he work for us, he do the dishes. He good man. And my uncle he give me the money. It no problem. We get this, not to worry about. We have our restaurant tomorrow. My Bella Nikki. We do it."

He lifts me and twirls me around.

"That's what we call it. We call it *Bella Nikki*. The best Italian restaurant in Blackpool. You like yes?"

I laugh. "Yes, I love it and, guess what, I love you."

He gasps, lets his knees buckle and pretends to faint.

"You love me? How can it be? Long time now, I be love you. But me I wait to say in case I chasey you away. You take the long time, my Bella Nikki."

Wrapped in each other's arms, both of us so excited for the future, we kiss. I can't wait to tell my mum.

Where the hell is he? He said he was going to see his uncle before work, but that was hours ago and he still isn't home. It's noon and we start work at one. He hasn't even eaten or showered yet. He could've phoned and said what was happening instead of letting me sit here and worry. What if he didn't get the money? What will we do then? I can't bear to lose the restaurant. It means so much to both of us and Gio will be devastated.

I rip the tab from a lager can and check the phone is working. It is. So, no excuse not to ring. Maybe he isn't even seeing his uncle. Maybe he's off with some girl. Well, I'll not be here when he comes home. Stuff him and the job too.

"Hey, Angie, how you doing? Thought I'd give you a phone."

"I'm kinda busy just now, Nikki."

"Oh, okay. Sorry."

"It's fine, it's just I've got the girls around. It's Rachel's birthday, so we're having drinks then heading out for lunch."

The girls laugh and giggle in the background as they sing along to some daft song. Probably drunk already. I swig my lager and can't believe they haven't invited me. Bitches.

"You there, Nikki? Sorry, it's hard to hear over the noise."

"Yeah."

"You coulda come too, Nikki, you know."

"It would've been nice to have been invited, I guess."

"You were, Nikki, you're always invited. But you always say no to everything. Ever since you and Giovanni got together. We never see you anymore."

"Yeah, whatever, Angie. I gotta go. Gio's just made lunch."

I hang up, crush the lager can and throw it in the bin. Bloody bitches, the whole lot of them, and Angie was the biggest bitch of them all. What's wrong with spending time with your boyfriend? They're jealous, that's all. It was different when they had boyfriends and I was sat on my own.

But then I remember it was Becky's birthday last week. I'd said I was going but didn't because I hadn't wanted to leave Gio on his own. And the time before that the girls were going to the new cocktail bar in town and I'd turned that down too. Maybe I'd said "no" a lot lately, after all. But then, that's what you do when you've got a boyfriend, right? There's no point going out partying if you already have your guy. And Gio hates when I'm hung-over and dying in bed.

The door slams and he walks in. Shoulders slumped, head down and body bent, as though shrivelled to half his size. He collapses into the sofa and it sighs with his weight. I jump up in response.

"What's going on? Where've you been?" I demand.

He draws his hands through his hair and shakes his head. "I feel very bad, Nikki."

"Why? What's wrong? Are you ill?"

He mumbles something and I ask him to repeat it, but he walks around pulling at his hair. What's wrong with him? Has his uncle died or something? I've never seen him like this before. "Gio, speak to me. What's wrong?"

"My uncle. He no have money, Nikki. He say he no can give me."

My eyes water but I won't cry. It's just the shock of the disappointment. Gio had been so sure. But it's not the end of the world. Okay, I love the restaurant but there will be other places, other times. He doesn't need to get so upset over it. We'll just work harder and save more. Oh my God, work. We're late. Gio slumps to the floor.

"I no feel well. I feel the faint."

He's pale and his brow looks clammy and hot. I rush to the sink to get him a glass of cold water.

"Gio, what's wrong? Have you got pain?"

"My uncle say there this horse. His friends say it will win."

"Horse?"

"We need money for restaurant, Nikki. I put money on horse to win."

"You bet on a horse? What money, Gio?"

"I think I do this. We get big money. Enough to buy every-thing we need. Make the place nice. Do new sign, buy new tables."

A wave of nausea passes through me and I have to sit down.

"The bastardo, the horse, it lose."

"What an idiot you are. Did you lose all your wages?"

There's nothing at all wrong with him. He's just feeling sorry for himself. I could kill him. How could he be so bloody stupid?

"I no breathe. I no breathe."

"How much, Gio?"

"Phone ambulance. I need go hospital."

I stand up. Surely not. I rush through to the bedroom and grab the stool from the dressing table. Standing on it, I reach under the box that sits atop the wardrobe. I can't find anything. My hands scramble around. Nothing.

"Where's the bank card, Gio?"

"I no can breathe, Nikki. You no understand."

"Where's the bank card?"

"I was try help. I was try get restaurant. Make you happy."

"Gio, how much is left?"

He sobs. "It all gone."

"Hello, Mum, it's me."

"Are you okay, hen?"

"I'm fine, but I'm coming home."

"When?"

"I'm going to catch the train. Be there in about four hours."

"Okay, see you soon. Keep safe. Don't talk to anyone. I'll make Irish stew for dinner, your favourite."

I sit down on the train and burst into tears. What a fool to trust him.

What will I do now?

CHAPTER 18

Mrs Hawthorne – Edinburgh

*E*verywhere I turn, Clarissa is there, judging. I'm suffocating under her glare. And the house has the dark heavy air of a mausoleum. Things have to change. But how? With a resounding thud, he closes the front door and we stroll hand in hand down the driveway. At least she can't follow us there.

"Will they like me?" I ask nervously.

He squeezes my hand. "They'll love you. How could they not?"

I hope he's right. Meeting his friends for the first time is pivotal. Clarissa hasn't been dead for long and there's me. His new... I stumble over a description. New what? *Girlfriend* is too young and makes us sound like teenagers. *Partner* is too formal, like a law firm. I'll let him decide what's right.

"Tell me about them again, Charles."

"Robert worked in finance and his wife, Elizabeth, was a librarian, but they're retired now and spend most of their time travelling in Europe. They're nice people. You'll be fine. Just be yourself."

"Did Clarissa like them?"

He pauses, and in front of a drystone dyke we come to a halt. The wall borders the canal that runs down into Leith. I should walk it one day. Amble into town. Squeals of delight rise towards us as children in bright yellow wellies skim stones across the surface of the water. Their parents look on and a dog braver than Jack paddles beside them.

"Clarissa didn't really like anyone," Charles says.

All that is absent in Charles's house is abundant at his friends' home. The walls of the hallway are scattered with art, small pencil drawings amidst large bright abstracts and grand pieces of tapestry. Three archways branch off the tiled floor. To the right, is a living room with sprawling cream sofas draped with green tartan throws. An open fire sparks embers of warmth and shelves brim over with books. To the left, a large kitchen reveals a fairy-lit garden through its open doors and my heart melts, enchanted.

Chilli and ginger spice the air and Robert welcomes us into the dining room, where across the table scattered glitter dances in low candlelight.

"You have a beautiful home," I say to Robert.

"Thank you," he replies and pours burgundy into wine glasses.

Elizabeth, her dark hair held back with diamante clasps, stacks naan bread next to a bubbling red casserole dish.

"I hope you like chickpea curry." She smiles.

Charles shifts forwards in his chair and I kick his shin under the table.

"Smells delicious," I reply. I detest chickpeas.

As is often the case when old friends meet, they recount old tales, talking over each other and finishing each other's sentences. All the stories centre around Charles and I smile at the appropriate points. An outsider looking in. Yet I hang on to every word, relishing the love they have for him and how Charles blooms in their presence.

Once we've complimented dessert, a gloriously sticky toffee pudding, Elizabeth grabs a bottle of wine and heads towards the patio doors. "Come sit with me outside while the men tidy up," she says. It's time for her to investigate my intentions.

The patio is strung with delicate lights and dotted with plants in terracotta pots. There are four wicker chairs, I choose the one nearest to her, cosying up to any secrets she'll share. I'm desperate to find out who Clarissa was, but don't want to appear obsessive. How to bring up the topic? A gold charm drapes from my wine glass. I run it through my fingers admiring Elizabeth's artistic flair for detail.

"So, you're very different from Clarissa," she says.

I squeeze the charm so hard that its edges cut into my hand. "Oh, am I? I'm not sure, as I didn't know her at all."

I lean forward and nudge her with an inquisitive girls all together type smile. Elizabeth sips her wine and her eyes roam the garden. I don't interrupt the silence.

"Clarissa was a hard woman to get to know."

I check Charles and Robert are still in the kitchen, then pull my chair closer.

"Charles doesn't talk about her," I coax.

"He was devastated when she died. Wouldn't see anyone, just locked himself away in the house with Jack. We were all surprised to hear about you. You've changed him though. He seems back to his old self."

While I'm thankful for this, I'm more interested in Clarissa, so I push the conversation back onto her. "So, what was she like?"

A few dry leaves pepper the table. Elizabeth stands and sweeps them into her palms.

She's stalling and there's an uncomfortable tension between us that wasn't there before. I bring my glass to my mouth to stop blurting something out.

"Clarissa was a ballerina. A magnificent one."

A ballerina? What? How had I never known this? Charles had said she was a dancer. But a ballerina? That's a new level of threat.

My hand clutches my throat. I mustn't compare this new image with my own soft flab or I'll vomit.

"And although that was behind her, she was still strict with her regimens and could be quite the snob. She came from old money and had very fixed ideas. It wasn't always easy trying to be a friend to her. But Charles adored her."

Does that mean he thinks I'm lazy? Elizabeth picks up her glass and puts her arm around me.

"Anyway, enough of all that. You're here now. She's not. Let's join the men for charades."

Dispersed within clouds of laughter, Charles stutters out. "Cycling. Jumping. Roller coaster."

"Time's up," Robert cries.

"Flying in a plane during turbulence. Oh my, you're hopeless, Charles," I groan.

I slump down beside him, curl my feet up onto the sofa. He throws an arm around me and kisses my cheek. The public display of affection makes me glow. "How would one know such a thing?" he says and we all collapse in mirth.

It's wonderful to be part of such a lovely group of friends. I've lost track of mine over the years and it's at times like this that I regret it.

Robert shares another bottle of wine around and Elizabeth suggests a game of bridge. The evening will go on and I'm delighted.

We walk the short distance back home, heady from the wine and exhilarated by the evening. It had been fabulous, such a success, and I'd loved seeing Charles mix with his friends. He's usually quite stuffy and formal, but he'd loosened up tonight. I'm so proud of him and don't want the evening to end.

"Let's play guess that song," I say.

"How do we do that?"

"We take turns humming the intro of a song and the other person has to guess the title."

He bounces in delight as if I've given him the stars from the sky. Snapping and clicking his fingers he sways side to side and hums.

"Dum Dum. Chi Chi Chi. Dum Dum. Chi Chi Chi. Dum Dum."

"I've no idea, Charles."

He repeats it, adding a little twirl as if that will add to my understanding. I've no clue, but he's so funny and carefree, so I join in and we both snap and sway to the front door.

And in that moment, all our age is swept away, every twist and line of our past erased. We're eighteen again and I want the moment to last forever.

"I give in. What's it called?"

"Such a heathen," he replies. "It's the great Miles Davies. A tune called 'Too much'."

"Oh, Charles, how would I know that! It's meant to be old pop songs."

His eyes sparkle and we giggle as he searches for his door keys.

"My turn. My turn," I say, jiggling about on the gravel.

I hum "The Most Beautiful Girl in the World". With Charles by my side, for the first time, the lyrics could be written about me.

He turns back and glares, his eyes hard.

"That was my wife's song. I played it at her funeral."

101

He pushes open the door and a rush of bitter air releases into the warmth of the night. I stagger back from the assault, but I won't cry. Not in front of Clarissa, who watches from the painting at the foot of the stairs.

Something has to change.

CHAPTER 19

Nikki – The Beach

The train dissolves into the salt air. And I stumble trying to secure my feet in wet sand. The Gatekeeper smiles and hands me a strawberry daiquiri.

"Welcome back, ladies."

Mrs Hawthorne is on her knees sifting sand, transfixed on the grains that slip through her fingers. Ronnie strides up, her hands clenched. Always so angry.

"You did the right thing leaving that loser, Nikki. I dunno why you stayed with him so long."

I'm too thirsty to respond and I gulp down my drink. The strawberries taste like summer, but it's chilly on this beach.

"He's old enough to be your father. Why did you go with him anyway?"

She's really getting on my nerves. I honestly dunno who she thinks she is. I've heard her story and she's no Snow White. In fact, she should be ashamed of herself.

"I bet he wasn't even a good fuck." She chuckles, and I can't believe the cheek of her. I slam my drink on the wooden bar.

"Coming from you, Ronnie, that's a laugh."

"What's that supposed to mean?"

I don't answer. The waves are pulling and I want to start again. I move towards their chant, towards Blackpool, egg gate and the greasy cafe, but she tugs on my arm and demands a response.

"I said, what's that supposed to mean, Nikki?"

Can't she see Gio hurt me? What a bitter cow with no thought for anyone else. God only knows what's made her this way. But I'm not afraid of her. I place my hands on her chest and push her out of my space.

"You don't even like sex, Ronnie. You just use it like money to get what you want."

"I like sex all right. But, hey, I'm not the one who was mistaken for a prostitute, hun."

I push her harder and she lands on her arse. "You're prostituting yourself to get Graham to love you. Why would you be so desperate, Ronnie?"

She leaps up and races towards me, her face screwed red in anger. But I shift to the left and she lands flat on her stomach. The sand whooshes up around her and she coughs and splutters. I laugh.

"Ladies, have some decorum," Mrs Hawthorne says.

Ronnie turns towards her, lips drawn, sand falling from her hair. "And you can shut up. Your Charlie boy is in love with a fucking ghost."

Mrs Hawthorne lowers her head and picks up a handful of sand. "Charles does love me."

I throw a snarl at Ronnie. "You're a nasty bitch."

"Oh, fuck off, Nikki. Go play sandcastles with the old bag if you're both such pals."

I stick the middle finger up to her.

The Gatekeeper sighs. "Are you happy with Graham, Ronnie?"

Ronnie nods, and I don't believe her. How could she be happy with someone who fucks around? She just doesn't want to admit it to herself or us.

He turns to Mrs Hawthorne. "And you, are you happy with Charles?"

She looks up, tears in her eyes. "Of course. He's everything I've ever wanted."

Ronnie shouts from the bar. "Yeah, but are you everything he wants? Or are you just his second-best?"

I really hate her. I mean, okay, maybe Mrs Hawthorne is being used. But it's not our place to judge her. And anyway, she's old.

The Gatekeeper looks out to the sea and all three of us watch him. "Love is like these waves lapping the shore. It rises and falls between euphoria and pain. No matter our age, our life is shared with those moments of ebb and flow." He walks over to Mrs Hawthorne and lifts the sand from her hand. "But is love an irresistible emotion sent to taunt, haunt and devour us? Is that what love is?"

He throws the sand into the air and moves towards Ronnie, who's sitting on a bar stool swinging her legs. He brushes the hair from her face and looks into her eyes. "Are the waves set to drown us or wash us free, Ronnie?"

Then he's next to me and as he takes my hand, I remember the same touch from somewhere else in my past. If I could only place it.

"What once delights us soon darkens, Nikki. Is love merely a choice?"

Ronnie runs over and pushes his hand off mine. "Leave her alone. She made her choice. She dumped him. Now let's all go back to where we were, I was happy before all this shit started."

The Gatekeeper smiles. "Happy reliving the same scene over and over, Ronnie? Just stuck here, watching the waves?"

Ronnie doesn't answer and I know why. She wants more. Just like we all do. She wants to move on.

Mrs Hawthorne stands, shakes her dress and takes my hand. "But you *did* dump him. Didn't you, dear?"

And I'm not sure. For just as before, I can't remember anything of my life.

The Gatekeeper throws out his arm, sweeping all three of us in. "Let the stories unfold." He turns to Ronnie. "You're ready to go back?"

"One minute!" I shout and hold out my other hand. Ronnie runs over and her fingers find mine.

"I'm sorry," she whispers. And I nod and grip tight.

The beach fades.

CHAPTER 20

Ronnie – Liverpool

*I*f Graham doesn't stop the car, I'll not be responsible for my actions. I've warned him. He finds it hilarious, but he'll soon change his mind.

"Ronnie, there's nowhere to stop. We're on a motorway."

"Then find a place, Graham. I'm serious. I want out of the fucking car."

"Okay. Okay. Hang on. I'll turn off at the next junction."

On either side of us are bright yellow fields of rapeseed. Their blaze beautifies the monotony, but their pollen assaults my nose. Graham accelerates and the fields blur into the past. I cling to the seat belt, not knowing what the fuck I'm doing here. A few days ago, it had seemed exciting, but I should have known.

The idea came to me as we drank white wine at his kitchen table. I'd mentioned that I wanted to see Paris and he'd surprised me with flight tickets and a box of croissants. Those moments of romance were sparse, but he's falling in love. Why else would he be so invested?

As he cooked a celebratory coq au vin, I thought about the French and their idea of marriage. Their *Cinq à sept* as my old uni friend from France called it. She'd glowed about her husband, his job, his successes. But when she talked about her lover, she'd glittered like a star. Was she worried her husband would find out? She'd laughed at my naivety and told me he'd a lover of his own. No one cared. Marriage was for love and commitment. Lovers were for sex and a bit of fun.

I decided to find some swingers that indulged in wife swapping. Friends were too close to home, but strangers, well, I'd never meet them again. It took careful planning and a few late-night phone calls, but Kirsty and Tom appeared sane and up for it. They were around our ages and not too far away. We chatted about limits and I pretended to be excited, but all the while I was talking my mind into being more French. It was sex. It meant nothing.

When I told Graham about the arrangements he had to sit down from the shock. A minute later he was planning the route.

The traffic slows to a halt and Graham's shiny red Lexus adds a pop of class to the jam in front. Cars edge closer, drivers stressed because they're ten minutes late for their dull destinations. I wish I was one of them.

"I'm getting out!" I scream. Opening the door, I run over to the scruff that borders the road.

There's not much coverage and, glancing over to the traffic, I imagine the passengers squirming with excitement at this sudden bit of action. Fuck them. I don't care. Squatting, I wrench up my skirt, thrust down my knickers and a rush of hot piss splatters to the ground. I sigh in relief. A few horns toot in either applause or indignation. I flick them a finger and wink. It's best to brazen these things out.

～

We're in the Travelodge, sitting in the bar. Apart from an old guy reading a newspaper and nursing a pint, we're the only customers in the pub. Not our usual choice of venue. We much prefer an overpriced cocktail lounge. Graham sits beside me cool, calm and devastatingly gorgeous, a lemonade in his hands. Mine cradle a long vodka, the crushed ice cooling my flushed skin.

We're meeting them here as a safety precaution and then, if all goes well, proceeding to their home. Of course, they really mean they want to score the livestock. Decide if we're good enough looking, or not. Panic springs my fears wide open. What if they don't like me? How would I cope with the shame of ruining Graham's night? I pick up a cardboard coaster and peel the layers apart, an eye on the door.

And in they walk. Kirsty is in her late fifties, with short auburn curled hair. She's dressed in a denim minidress and saggy fishnet tights. A pink rumpled cardigan is wrapped tight across her drooping breasts. It's about two sizes too small and from the fuzzy bobbling of the wool, it's not new. She's desperate, sad and nothing like how she described herself. I'm sorry for her, but I'm fucking relieved. There's no way this will go ahead.

Her partner, Tom, saunters towards me. He's young, about thirty, good looking and dressed in jeans and a crisp white shirt. His cocky grin slaps a smile onto my face. I can't look at Graham or I'll collapse into laughter.

～

The bedroom walls are papered in floral chintz and match the curtains and duvet covers on the single bed. An ornate white dressing table holds a myriad of perfumes and trinkets. Mostly these are coloured bead necklaces and long gold chains with dangling moonstones. On the bedroom door, a nylon dressing gown and feather boa are draped around a silver hook.

A ring of damp surrounds the cheap chandelier hanging from the ceiling. I sit on the bed underneath it. Is there a leak, or has it not been painted? Maybe, if I'm lucky, the ceiling will collapse. Indistinguishable sounds rise from the floor below and I want to tear my hand from Tom's gentle grasp, but I must keep up some semblance of the act.

"Ronnie, you don't want to do this, do you?" Tom whispers.

"Not really. I thought I could, but I just can't. I'm sorry." I blush. There's nothing wrong with him. If we'd met in a club, I'd have exchanged numbers. But lying here side by side is clinical and sordid. I'm repelled by the seediness of it all. He passes me a tumbler of warm vodka. My granny used to have the same glasses in a cupboard in her living room. She kept them safe for special visitors or a wee shot of sherry at Hogmanay.

"It's okay," he says. He moves and sits on the old shabby rug, his hands splayed behind him, helping to hold the weight of his disappointment. I'm almost free, except my thoughts still focus on the sounds below.

"You're beautiful, Ronnie," he says.

But I'm not enough for Graham. What is he doing down there that makes her squeal? Why don't I make those same noises when he touches me? Is nothing special?

Tom stands and combs his fingers through his hair. He's agitated. "You deserve better than this. If you were mine. I'd never share you. I'd keep you all to myself."

"But what about Kirsty? You share her," I retort.

He smiles. "Kirsty's just a mate. I've known her for years. She's a bit kinky and asked me to partner up with her so she could do this swapping thing. We aren't an item. I'm single."

So they had lied about being partners. Does anyone ever tell the truth?

As Kirsty whimpers in ecstasy, I realise my mistake. It's me I feel sorry for, not her.

Tom hands me his business card. He's a lawyer specialising in family law. The idea of that makes me smile.

"Call me, Ronnie," he says. "I'll treat you like a queen."

Waving our goodbyes, I march to the car boot, grab a bottle of wine then settle into the seats. After a deep slug and gargle, I turn to him. "How could you?"

He responds with laughter and I slap his leg. "Aww, come on. It was a bit of fun."

"But she was about sixty. You couldn't have fancied her."

"She was nice. We'd a good time. It was exciting. Didn't you have fun too?"

I didn't. It was as seedy as fuck. And I can't understand why he went through with it. She wasn't his type at all.

"Yeah, it was okay. But mine was better than yours and he told me to dump your arse. Said you didn't appreciate me. Said he'd never share like you."

Graham slows down and glares. "Oh, did he? Bloody fool. You'd be bored with someone like that. I hope you told him to get lost."

And I think, would I? Would I really be bored?

Graham puts his foot down. "Let's go home and get packed. We're off to Paris in the morning. Maybe we'll get one of those caricatures done near the Sacré-Cœur. You've always fancied that."

What might the artist draw when he looks at me? What will he see?

"That would be so romantic, Graham."

"It would, especially in Paris." He smiles and lays his hand on my thigh.

My heart soars up through the sleazy shame of the past few hours. That was just sex. It wasn't romance. It wasn't him and me. It'd all been worth it. Hadn't it?

CHAPTER 21

Nikki – Edinburgh

"*M*um, where's my Coke?" I'd left it on the coffee table, but she'll have lifted it. The three-minute rule.

"I thought you were finished."

"Mum, I'm nearly nineteen, not nine. If I'd finished, I'd have brought it through to the kitchen."

"Aye well, we don't want rats, Nikki." In she marches, duster across her shoulder, hoover in hand. We've just eaten lunch and Mum cleans after every meal or snack. She bangs the hoover against the sofa and I sigh and assume the position. *Sit back. Feet off the carpet. Legs in the air.*

"You can sigh, Nikki, but when I was wee the rats used to jump on us when we were sleeping." She shudders. "Huge as cats they were too."

She'll be telling me next about how Granny tore sheets of newspapers to wipe all their bums in their outside toilet.

113

"Rats wouldn't dare face you now, Mum." She tickles the duster across my face.

I flinch back from the nasty thing. "Ugh. Mum."

"So, what're you gonna do, hen? They're looking for staff down at the new pub. Linda said her daughter got a job there. They pay good wages. You get your dinner free too."

The thought makes me want to vomit. Mum would have a fit if I did. Her special friend Mr Bleach would be out. We'd not be able to breathe through the fumes for days.

"I dunno, Mum." And I really don't. It's hard being home when you're used to your own space. Difficult reverting back to a child. Getting told to make your bed and turn the light out at midnight. Mum's house is beautiful. She works hard for every penny. But it's like a showroom, everything spotlessly clean and in its right place. By just sitting still you are making the place untidy.

"I'm going to get the bairns from school, Nikki. You want to come?"

"Nah, I'm going up to Granny's for a wee while."

"Okay." She puts the hoover away then stands in front of the hall mirror, touching up her hair and refreshing her signature red lipstick. "And, Nikki, that guy you ran away from. You know you're enough on your own, don't you? That you don't need a man?"

I smile. "Yes, Mum, but I really liked him."

"Yeah, I liked your dad too. But that's no reason to put up with men's shit. We've all been fine since he left. Haven't we?"

I nod. But in the beginning, when she thought we were all sleeping, I'd hear her cry every night into her pillow. My mum's too proud to deal with me knowing. She'd hate it. But she's right. We're all much happier on our own. But it doesn't mean I don't miss Dad. And it doesn't mean I don't miss Gio.

"George, will you open the sack up wider? Christ, you canny do nothing right."

"Oh, hush woman. I'm doing it, come on."

Granny and Grandad are in the back garden, digging for potatoes. I've snuck around the back and am giggling at their antics. Grandad is always getting shouted at for something or other. Usually, it's for falling asleep during her favourite TV programme, *Coronation Street*.

"Will you wake up, George, and stop snoring? I canny hear what Ken Barlow's saying."

Grandad would wake with a jolt but always be back snoring five minutes later.

Granny puts her foot on the spade, pushes deep into the ground and digs out a big clod of potatoes. When she throws them into the sack, he's looking the other way and they scatter across his feet. He jumps. And she shouts, "George. Look what you've done now."

I burst out laughing.

"Nikki!" She runs towards me, her smile broad and pale blue eyes twinkling. She wraps me in her love and I cushion in. Grandad ambles over and ruffles my hair.

"It's good to see you," he says. He takes my hand and leads me to the kitchen. At the old Formica table where I'd first learned to bake and where Grandad had fixed the puncture in my first red bicycle, I burst into tears.

Grandad strokes my hand and Granny puts the kettle on.

"Now, now, lass. I hope you're not crying over a man."

"I liked him, Grandad."

"If he's done you wrong, you can't like him now, hen."

"But I can't just switch it off. Emotions aren't like that."

He lifts his thumb to his face and rubs his chin. He doesn't air his opinions much. He leaves all that to Granny. But when he does, it takes him some time to think first. Granny brings over a cold can of Coke and a glass with some ice, just how I love it.

"Granny? How did you know I was coming? You and Grandad don't drink Coke."

She unfurls a tissue from under the cuff of her cardigan and dries my tears. "I always have a can of Coke in the fridge for you. Just in case. I never let anyone touch it. I tell them, you'd better not touch Nikki's Coke, or I'll kick your arse."

We all laugh and she sets down a plate of chocolate digestives. Grandad reaches for two then hands one to Granny.

"As I see it, loving someone is always a choice, Nikki. Do you think I'd still be here loving this old battleaxe if it weren't a choice?"

"What do you mean, Grandad?"

"Every night we go to bed and I choose to kiss her goodnight and tell her that I love her. And then every morning I wake up and choose to love her again. Sure we've had ups and downs, every couple does. Those that don't are liars or hiding the truth. The world can be a harsh place. Lots of things that happen in life can knock you down and take your breath away. You need someone beside you that can bring light. Not just on the days when everything is good, but when that darkness comes too. Your granny, she's my sunlight, always has been. So if I can choose to love, you can choose the opposite. It just depends on whether he brings sunlight that makes you shine in his company or darkness that makes you vanish. If there's more darkness than light, then you must choose not to love and walk away. Never let anyone fade your light."

Granny bats a dishcloth playfully at him.

"You and your poetic words, George. You silly old bat. I choose you to go and pick up those potatoes that are still lying on the ground."

I smile, but there's something in what Grandad is saying. Does Gio bring more darkness than light? At this moment, it's a total eclipse. He's broken my heart and I'll never trust him again.

"There's plenty of fish in the sea, Nikki. But you've got to watch out for the sharks," Granny says.

～

My sister is hiding turnip under her mashed potatoes. I did the same at her age. At least Mum doesn't put it on my plate anymore. Except for peas, and she knows I hate them.

She's standing at the sink doing the dishes before we've even finished eating. I throw a couple of peas at her back and she turns around to scold my sister. I laugh and Mum winks. It's good to be home, but already I'm bored. The doorbell rings. Mum slams her cloth into the sink, then tuts as soapy water splashes out. "Who the hell is that at this time of night?" She hates visitors that arrive unannounced. The house must have a twenty-four-hour deep clean first.

A voice booms through the letter box. "The Nikki, she live here?"

I jump from my seat. Only one person speaks like that. How did he find me?

"I'll go. I'll tell him to get lost," Mum says. My sister, excited by the change in routine, throws mash all over the floor.

The bell rings again. "Hello, anybody alive in house?"

He'll have the neighbours out on the street with popcorn soon and Mum will go mad if she's the centre of gossip. Ever since Dad left she's been a stickler for us walking proud and being a perfect family.

"It's okay, Mum, I'll go. And don't listen at the window."

She scrunches up her nose. "As if I would." I know she would.

Gio smiles up from the bottom of the steps. He holds out his arms for me and I take a step back. A suitcase and a large back-pack sit beside him. Does he think he's moving in? "My Bella Nikki. I come find you."

"Why, Gio? I told you it's over."

"It not over, Nikki. I do very bad thing. I know this. But I not the bad man."

"You ruined everything, Gio. You ruined our dreams."

"But we make new dream, Nikki. You think we have no more the dream?"

I'm not going to be making any kind of plans with him. Twice now he's ruined everything and I'll never trust him. Tears fall from my eyes and I hate him all over again.

I try to close the door, but he runs up the steps and wedges his big foot in it. "Nikki. I love you. Listen to me. My brother, he has the restaurant in Sicily. Beautiful restaurant. It sell fish."

I hate bloody fish. And anyway Gio is a big dark shark. Just the kind Granny warned me about.

"He tell me go Sicily. Go work there with him."

"Go then, Gio. I don't know why you've come here to tell me your good news."

"It is beautiful place, my town. The beach it gold and the sea very hot. I show you best place to swimming. The fish, Nikki, they be beside you. My brother he give me his house. We have own place. You love it. Come with me."

I've never been abroad before. I've walked the sands in Black-pool, but I've never stepped foot in a foreign land. Excitement tingles within me and I find it hard to stand still. But I can't go with a liar.

"Nikki, my family will love you. And this our big chance." We had chances before. He spoiled them.

Gio drops to his knees, places his hands together in prayer and looks up at me with big brown eyes. Rain drizzles around him and a part of me feels sorry for him. The part that loved him. "Say yes, my Bella Nikki. I be the good man. If you give me chance. Come to see the sunlight in Sicily."

The lies. The gambling. The heartache. I should slam the door on his face. But then, the sun and sea. Our own place. A new life far from the dark clouds and the promise of thunder.

And just like Grandad told me to do, I make my choice.

CHAPTER 22

Mrs Hawthorne – Edinburgh

*R*eluctant to say goodbye, we share a bottle of wine over the phone until dawn. Neither of us relishes the silent beds that shun our presence. That's when Charles says it.

At first, it's mumbled, as though he's trying to disguise the significance of his words. But they linger between us, weighty with promise and fear. He says it again, this time surer of himself, but the quiver in his voice can't mask his angst.

"In the quiet hours of your absence, I've been thinking about us and our future. About waking up together, walking Jack in the park, dancing around the garden. We could have a joyous life. Come live with me. Let's not wait any longer to start our 'happy ever after.'"

I've longed for those words. Planted the seeds in his head as we pruned forget-me-nots in his back garden. And each time I went home, I'd nurtured those thoughts by ensuring my distance left a void. A space where he'd miss me. But now that the moment is here, can I do it? Live with a man again? Invest all my well-being in someone else? I've accepted the solitude of being on my own for so very long.

"It's okay. It was a silly idea. I'm just missing you. I quite understand if it's not something you wish to do."

But he isn't all those men that have come before. This is gentle Charles of the cornflower blue eyes. This is my saviour. I can't let "happy ever after" elude me now, not at these late years. And I adore him.

"Charles, I'd love to."

"Oh, how wonderful. How simply delightful." Jack barks in tune to his excitement.

"But."

"Yes?"

"If I give up my apartment, what security would I have? What if it doesn't work out? I'd have nowhere to live. Things do go wrong, Charles."

The line goes silent and my teeth tear at the jagged skin around my fingernails. His answer could change everything. Strip away the façade of his adept Prince Charming.

"Then we'll marry. If something goes wrong, you'll get half of everything. The house. The savings. The pension. You'll be set for life."

A sob tears at my throat. How different from all those men before him. Men who'd raped my emotions and finances. Always hungry, forever needing more to make them bigger, more important, until beside them I'd grown small and insignificant.

"Charles?"

"Yes, yes. It's too soon. A ridiculous idea at our age. Perhaps you'd prefer a little nest egg instead?"

What a kind generous man. But I'm not after his money, just his love. A chance to start something fresh amongst all the death and darkness.

"I'd love to marry you," I say, and he whoops with joy.

"But, Charles..."

"Y-e-s," he drawls out the word, making me giggle.

"The house. Well, it will never feel like mine. Can we decorate?"

"We'll do anything you want."

I stifle a shriek of delight. I can't wait to rid the place of Clarissa.

The next day I meet my sisters for lunch in a local pub, excited to share the news. As usual, they're dolled up to the nines. Gazes straying to younger women, assessing their clothes, their hair-styles. But they only truly compete with each other. It's always been that way.

Obsessed with her weight, Judy prods some dreary salad around her plate. "But you've only known him six months."

Why can't she be happy for me?

"And his wife has only been dead nine months. Isn't it a bit soon?" Mary adds before stuffing a cheeseburger into her big mouth. She'll be on the treadmill for two hours later, working it off. I stab a chip with a fork and reply, "He's everything I've ever wanted in a man."

They glance at each other and pat red serviettes against their tight lips. The waiter brings over drinks and Judy grabs the Diet Coke from his hand just in case it gets muddled in with the two full-fat ones. Heaven forfend.

"You've said that about every other man too, you know. Maybe you should wait a while," she says.

Mary laughs. "True. And anyway, how can you be bothered at your age? Aren't you done with all that fairy tale crap?"

"Just because it didn't work out for you," I retort.

I throw my cutlery down. It clatters to the busy table with a clang and they look up, eyes wide, lips pursed, oblivious to any hurt they've hurled from their caustic tongues. Why is it that, even after all these years, we still play our same roles, still follow the same patterns? The pub is busy. So many people cramped together in such a small space, and the stench of roast beef makes the warm air heavier to breathe. I rise, push back my chair and squeeze through the tight space to escape outside.

The beer garden is packed tight with benches, all of them occupied, but I find a small wall and sit down. Of course, his wife has been dead only a few months, but that doesn't mean he doesn't love me. He's shown it in so many ways. I light a cigarette and inhale until calm has been restored. They haven't even met him yet, so how can they judge him? Charles is awkward in social settings. He'd wanted to wait.

Judy appears and sidles up beside me. I shift over to make room. "What you doing, dafty? Come back in."

She places a few timid pats on my shoulder. She knows I can't stand that sort of thing. But this is her in peacemaker mode and I have to concede. That is how we do things in our sisterly paint-by-numbers way.

"I'm okay. Was just getting a cig." I throw the butt to the ground, stand and stamp it out. She rubs her arms and shivers, although it isn't cold, and her face compresses in concern. A frown magnifies the deep crease between her brows. At sixty the Botox doesn't help anymore and it's hard to see the little girl that once sat on my knee while I brushed her long blonde hair.

"We're just worried about you. That's all. We don't want to see you hurt. You're our big sister."

"I'm okay."

She bends and picks up my cigarette end and throws it into the nearest bin. Everything neat and tidy.

I follow her back to the table. Mary sits with her head to the side, smiling like I'm some unfortunate stray child. I want to slap her face. Instead, I smile back and she says, "Did you watch that new drama on TV last night? It had whatshername that was in that film we watched last year. The redhead. She used to go out with that guy from *EastEnders*."

And just like that, we've moved on. Like so many previous conversations that might have blown us apart, the topic is now buried beneath celebrity news. We often speak about mother and her surface conversations. We'd never been allowed to talk of feelings or emotions. Yet we never admit that with each other, we do exactly the same.

The waiter arrives to collect our plates. He has slicked-back hair and a ruby embedded in his nose. He's young, about thirty. Of course, this doesn't stop Mary from flirting with him, even at twice his age. When he offers us dessert menus, Judy stands in his way.

"No. No. We don't want dessert. We're all full up."

The waiter jumps back, startled, as she shuffles the menus back into his hands. She turns to us and says, "You didn't want anything, did you?"

Mary replies, "Didn't have much choice, Judy, did we?"

I laugh and grab my bag. Lunch is over.

On the walk home I fantasise about what kind of wedding we'll have. What colour dress I'll wear. Not white after the last disaster, but maybe a soft pastel. Should we have a reception? And if we do, where? I suppose Robert will be Charles's best man, but how will I decide between my sisters for best maid? Whomever I choose, the other will be offended. I throw my bag onto the kitchen counter, pop the kettle on and grab my phone. I wait for Charles to answer the call, fidgeting with questions.

"My sisters are delighted. They can't wait to meet you."

"Good."

Something isn't right. His breath is laboured and he sounds like he's been crying. Has he changed his mind?

"What's wrong? Is Jack okay?"

Charles sobs and dread crawls down my spine. I light a cigarette and time stretches between us. Before he composes himself enough to speak, my cigarette has burnt down to the stub.

"I'm quite all right," he says. "Just felt a bit sorry for myself there."

"Why, Charles? What happened?"

"Oh, it's nothing for you to worry about. How was lunch?"

Charles has never been dismissive before. There certainly is something to fret about. I need to discover what.

"Charles, you need to tell me what's happened. We can't marry with secrets between us."

He inhales deeply then sighs as if it's his last breath.

"You caught me at a bad moment, that's all. I'd thought you might like one of Clarissa's rings. She has some gorgeous emeralds and you love those stones. They're no good to her anymore. But, when I went looking, I found a letter in her jewellery box."

"A letter? From whom?"

"From my wife."

His wife? Am I not to bear that title? I detest her, even dead she ruins everything. This was meant to be our day.

"Oh, I'm so sorry, that must have been hard for you. What was in the letter?"

"Nothing. Nothing at all. It was just a shock. She must have written it before she died and then left it there for me to find. But everything is tickety-boo."

We talk for a while about inconsequential things, it doesn't seem appropriate to bring up wedding plans anymore. Then we say our goodbyes, arranging to meet in the morning, but a pain drums in my head much longer. What's in the letter? I need to find it.

CHAPTER 23

Ronnie – Liverpool

*P*aris was wonderful. We took a sunset cruise along the Seine and strolled hand in hand through the twinkling lights of the left bank. Just like a normal couple, and anyone would have said we were in love. I guess one of us is.

We've been home two weeks and there are still hints of that romance, but the edge has returned. The roses he bought me today are gorgeous and in full bloom, but my focus is on the thorns. What price do I need to pay for his love?

Graham saunters into the bedroom, trying to disguise his excitement for the night with a casual stance.

"So, what kind of boundaries and rules do you want, Ronnie?"

I glance over at him, the question catching me off guard. I've not really thought about it. But we've only an hour left. I roll silk stockings up my legs and want to blurt out *it's off*. We aren't doing it anymore. I want monogamy. I want Paris back.

But that would chase him away. And it isn't his fault. He

hasn't had a life like the rest of us. And he'd rather break up than hurt me with a cheater's lie.

"No kissing. No exchanging phone calls. And no emotional connections," I reply.

He nods and splashes on some cologne and through vanilla mist he peels on some tight leather pants. What damn clichés we are.

As we stand outside the sex club, a burly doorman demands identification. He's as intimidating as the secret world hidden within the red door behind him. My tummy spins and I run my tongue along my dry lips. What the fuck am I doing? Graham hands over our passports and after a nod, the door is opened and we enter the main room.

It's dark with black painted walls and low dingy lighting. There's a bar in the corner and a bunch of people are queuing up waiting to be served. Music thumps out from two large speakers on a small empty dance floor. The atmosphere feels sticky, as if it will coat my skin. Couples are huddled together on sofas, while others are eyeing each other up and one woman in her underwear is having a spin on a stripper pole. She's young, slim and tanned.

The air smells of popcorn, a trick the club's implemented to boost sales and conceal the smell of sex that'll soon swamp us. I tug on Graham's arm. I can't do it.

"Shh. You're fine," he whispers.

He guides me over to the bar where we're meant to hand in our drinks. They don't have a licence, but you bring your own. He asks the barman, who's dressed only in a tight lime thong, to pour us doubles. I clutch Graham's hand and cling to the thought that we might escape soon.

As we descend stairs into an even dimmer set of rooms, I spot an empty four-poster bed with vibrators, floggers and whips on display. Graham releases my hand and bounces on the mattress like a child.

"Join me, Ronnie. Come on!" He springs up to grab me, but I step back, evading his grasp.

"No way, Graham. Imagine all the diseases on those sheets?"

"Aww, you're no fun."

I give him the finger, finish my drink and turn away. I'm over-dressed in my miniskirt and strappy vest, yet I'd worried at home it was over the top. I'm going to need more vodka to get through this night.

We walk into a seedy cinema showing hard porn. I'd laugh at the fake moans coming from the screen if it weren't for the number of guys sitting in the chairs with their dicks out, panting along. In the front row, a woman being fucked from behind is giving another guy a blow job. She's having fun. And I clamp down the urge to march up and throw them off.

We move to a red room where a bunch of men stand naked, pressed tight against a wooden wall divider. I'm not sure what's going on, but I can't take my eyes off their bare arses. Some are firm and tight whereas others jiggle like jelly, dimpled and round.

"It's a glory hole," Graham says. "Look at the other side."

That'll be right. I turn to leave, feeling my way out with my palms. A stranger's hand creeps up my skirt. I recoil back in fright.

"No thanks," Graham says politely as if he's in the Savoy.

The guy shrugs and shuffles away and my skin crawls at the ghost of his damp touch.

A clump of bodies are fucking each other in the corridor and we have to squeeze past them to get to the next room.

It's cramped, bodies writhing on a black rubber floor. I fidget and fiddle with the empty glass in my hand, not knowing what to do. Graham edges closer to the action, his eyes almost on stalks. I laugh. He's like the Road Runner hanging suspended in mid-air.

"Meep meep," I say, just for shits.

Graham's brows furrow and he squints at me like I've gone mad. Maybe I have.

"Go on. Join in. You're dying to."

I let go of his hand and push him forward. He doesn't need any more encouragement than that and I sprint from the sleaze and head for the bar.

"Treble vodka, lemonade and ice please."

The bartender has matched his thong with a string vest and his nipple rings poke through the holes in the thread. I should tell him, just in case they catch onto something, but then maybe that's the point.

"Ronnie, is that you?"

My fingers grip the edge of the bar. Who's that? One of the kids' dads from school? Or even worse, a school governor? I can't reply and out myself. Why the hell did I come here? The barman passes over my drink and I gulp some of it down. Look for somewhere to hide.

"Ronnie?"

Oh my God, why doesn't he fuck off? A trio dressed in latex catsuits slides up beside me and leans on the bar. I slip through them and escape. I need to get Graham and get the fuck out of this place. I don't give a shit if he's in the middle of some bitch.

I march back to the rubber room, head down, hair drawn over my face. A hand on my elbow jerks me to a stop.

"Ronnie. It's me, Tom."

Tom? I glance up. I've seen him before, but not at school. It's the guy from the swapping night. The family lawyer. I should have guessed he'd show up here. "Well, well. Where's Kirsty?" I ask, edging myself against a wall, trying to be small, the panic still not fully gone.

He grins. "It's single men's night. She's not here. I told you, she's just a friend anyway."

I nod and slosh the ice around in my glass, contemplating my next move. Should I ignore him or stop and chat?

A woman dressed in leather chaps struts past. Crawling behind her is an overweight bald guy. A furry tail protrudes from his arse and once in a while he stops to wiggle and wag it. She tugs on his leash to hurry him along.

"So, I take it you didn't come here for the ambience," he says with a wink.

I meet Tom's eyes and we erupt into laughter. It cuts the tension and something between us catches and sparks. I've not noticed how his smile lights up his face before.

"No, Tom, it's not quite my idea of elegance."

Our eyes crinkle in mirth and my panic settles. He's an ordinary guy. There's a velvet sofa to the left of us hidden in a corner. It's fairly clean and free of stains, so I smooth down my skirt to cover my thighs and sit. He joins me but ensures there's a respectful distance between our bodies. I like that.

"So, where's Graham then?" he asks.

"Oh, he's in that big room with all the rubber padding. God knows what he's doing." I shudder to signify it's not my kind of thing.

"I don't think God will be that interested, do you?"

He's funny. I like that too. A woman in a maid's outfit jumps onto a guy's lap. The place is so busy that some of the soft action has slipped into the lounge. But here in the corner, it's fine. My hands wrap around my glass. If you ignored the setting, I could be like a mother waiting for her child to run off some energy on a visit to soft play. Graham will be back soon, asking for a drink and a snack, all puffed out.

"So why are you here, Tom, if not for Kirsty?"

He glances over at the moans coming from a corner, then turns his attention back to me.

"I'm so busy at work there's never enough time for anything

else. But, well, a man has needs you know. And this is the easiest way. No strings. No pressures. And then I go back to my desk."

"But don't you want more than just sex?"

"Yeah, of course I do. I'd love to have the white picket fence and all that. But where do you meet someone to devote your life to? At a nightclub where everyone's drunk? It's not like the old days. And with the hours I put in at work, there's never the time."

"Yeah, I get what you mean." I'd tried it too. All those single nights and then running home, full of shame, to eat a meal for one, not two.

He edges closer, brushes his fingers along my arm and looks into my eyes.

"Unless it was someone like you," he whispers. "I'd make sure I had time then."

Giggling like a silly teenager, I pull my arm away and place it by my side where it's safe. I'm not sure how to react. Is he just playing a game? Are these just lines? Or am I really that special to him. He leans in closer and traces a finger gently down my face.

His breath sends a shiver of desire.

"I've thought about doing this since I met you, Ronnie." He lowers his mouth to mine and I lose myself in the tenderness of his kiss.

Hands grab Tom's shoulders and he's torn off me and tossed to the floor. Graham stands in the empty space glaring down at him.

"What the hell you doing, mate?"

I'm frozen to the sofa. I've never seen Graham angry before. He's usually devoid of any type of emotion unless, of course, he wants something. He hunches his shoulder and cocks a fist, glowering at Tom, who lifts his hands in defeat and shrugs. Then he stands and slowly brushes the dust from his clothes. Ignoring Graham, he turns to me.

"Think about it, Ronnie. I'll wait as long as it takes."

And with that, he strides away like prey teasing the hunter to come seize it. I'm not sure if he means the hunter to be Graham or me.

"What's that dick saying? Wait for what, Ronnie?" Graham says, fists still clenched.

"Nothing. He talks rubbish." But I'm secretly pleased. Tom's got balls and he clearly likes me. Maybe I like him too.

Graham grabs my hand. "You've had too much to drink. Let's go home."

Too much to drink? He's never complained before. Then I get it. He's jealous. That's why he's so angry. Aww, have I spoiled his night?

Snare him has a new weapon. It's Tom.

CHAPTER 24

Nikki – Mondello

*B*loody hell. The air blasts me and I stumble at the top of the gangway. I've never known heat like it. I cling to Gio to steady myself. He wraps his arms around me.

"Nikki. Welcome to Sicily. My very beautiful home. You love, yes?"

If I learn to breathe, sure. With sweat sliding down my neck, I take his hand and, on shaky legs, step from the airplane into the shimmering heat and my exciting new world.

After going through customs and collecting our luggage, we step into the car park and some guy yells, "*Si veloce!*" It's Gio's cousin, and I take this to mean *hurry* because Gio grabs our suitcases, throws them into the boot and we jump into his Fiat Panda.

As they mould the air with hand gestures in a language I can't understand, the car tears through the frenzied Palermo roads. The vivid colours that flash by are dazzling and my head swivels around with each new sight and scent. How can all this be just a few hours away on a plane? It's magical.

The car halts and I jolt forwards, crashing into the hot leather chair in front of me. Gio grunts. "It car jammy. We be go soon."

Angry men thrust fists through open sunroofs and a few abandon their vehicles. "*Pazzo. Pazzo!*" they roar, through clouds of exhaust fumes.

Vespas in all sorts of shades weave in and out of lanes and squeeze around us like a swarm of bees. Not even the honk of the car horns frightens them off. Being used to the rules of the road back home, I grip Gio's hand and hold on. But he's oblivious to it all and eggs on his cousin through a red light. We're all gonna die and I haven't even been to the beach. Imagine dying peely-wally in Sicily, with not even a tan.

As we leave the city, the traffic calms, the roads narrow and a mist of fine dust blows against the car windows. Gio offers me a bottle of water. It's grown warm, but I still hold it against my flushed skin. Everything is sticky. My hands. My face. I'd sell my soul for crushed ice.

"*Ti prego, fermare la macchina,*" Gio shouts.

The car jars to a stop. The force throws me back against the seat and the water bottle escapes to the floor. What now?

He jumps out from the car, raises his arms, stretches down to touch his toes and does a little jog on the spot. He grins over to me and rubs his hands.

"Nikki, I no so young, but watch." He ambles over to the opposite side of the road, taking his T-shirt off as he goes, to where trees are growing in rows. My eyes widen in surprise as he stoops, tenses, then pounces and climbs up a rickety fence. At the top, he totters to and fro. He's going to fall. But he balances, reaches out and grabs some of the branches and their hanging fruit. Placing a few in his T-shirt, he rolls it up, jumps down and runs back.

"Nikki, you no taste the orange like this anywhere else."

I can't believe you just pick them off trees here. I'm not even that fond of fruit. I'd rather have a chocolate or a tub of ice cream.

He peels the shiny skin and the tangy scent pierces the air. My mouth waters in response.

"Every time I come home, I stop here. Eat the orange."

He unwraps the last piece of skin and tears the orange in half. The sticky bright juice trickles and dribbles down his fingers. My mouth grows drier and I lick my lips. I want to suck his fingers dry, but I stop myself. It wouldn't be right. Not in front of his cousin.

"But you stole it, Gio."

He shakes his head. "It the orange grove. One or two they don't miss. Open your mouth and taste."

It explodes in my mouth, the juice oozing out and drenching my dry throat, the tart sweetness beyond anything I've ever known. Is this how an orange should taste? It's glorious. Gio smiles, throws one to his cousin, then offers me more.

"*Andiamo*," he says.

Off we continue along the dusty road. The cousin turns on some music. Gio gestures wildly. And me? I sit savouring my new-found passion for fruit.

As we turn a corner, the landscape shifts to rocky shorelines and rugged mountains. In the distance a beach, long and curved, slopes gently into a blue and turquoise sea that glitters in the sun. Its pale golden sand is dotted with pastel-shaded cabins. Lime, lemon and pink. It has been etched from my dreams. I jump up and down excitedly as if I'm five. "The beach, Gio. The beach. Look."

"*Bellissima*. But too hot. First, we see my father. We go later. Not to worry."

My heart sinks and I slump in the seat. In my excitement, I'd forgotten about that part. I hope he likes me.

~

The noise is first. It snakes down the tiled stairway and grows harsher as we approach his father's door. The chittering and chattering, the booming laughter, the clinking and clanking of glass and the giggles of children smashing around. After scrunching my hands through my hair to puff up my curls that sank in the moist air, I grip Gio's hand. He drops it as soon as the door bursts open and I lose him to the crowd.

As I stand on the threshold, they gather him in, draw him into a tight circle and smother him with hugs and kisses. The children dance around his feet, pawing at his clothes, tugging for attention. I'm not sure if I should step in or wait until they finish their greetings. After all, this is his family, his home, and I'm just a stranger to them all. But then Gio opens a bottle of Peroni and joins a couple of men on a balcony. Has he forgotten about me standing here alone?

A little girl about five or six, hair tied up in a cream ribbon and dressed in the sweetest mint dress, bounces towards me. She laughs, points to my hair and says something. But I can't understand her words, so I just smile back. She shouts something across the room to a little boy with thick black hair. He must be two, maybe three, and he scuttles over on his knees to join us. They both babble away and then a third little girl dances over and strokes the silk of my dress.

I'm quite the attraction and they want to show off their new find. Slipping their tiny hands in mine, they gently drag me into the centre of the room. I giggle with nervousness and they all join in.

A volcano of strange phrases erupts around me. They ooze from the luscious lips of the women and spurt forth from the gregarious men. Someone says, "Hello." But I soon realise that's all the English they know and a sheen of sweat glistens on my skin. The strangeness of such a different place makes me feel faint. A woman in a lemon strappy dress offers me a glass of white wine. It's so kind of her and I gulp it down. When I place the empty glass on a table, their stares tell me I've done something wrong.

Gio walks in, holding his Peroni, and if we were somewhere else, I'd grab it and drink that too.

"Where you been, Nikki?"

How dare he. He was the one that left me. "I've been here all the time."

He introduces me to everyone, all his brothers and cousins and I nod and smile. There isn't much more I can do. Everyone seems more friendly now. However, it's weird how the men sit at one table playing cards, drinking lager and the women sit at another, quiet. Maybe it's some kind of tradition.

"And this, this is my father. His name it is Tony."

Gio doesn't look much like his dad. Tony is much shorter, slighter and his hair is white. Even his eyes are lighter than Gio's dark broody brown. But from all the laughter lines etched across his face, he appears kind. Hoping to make a good impression I offer him my hand, but Tony shakes his head, ignoring first my hand, then me. Then he turns back to his friends. My skin burns scarlet and it's not from the heat.

Gio shouts something in Italian to him and then a whole bunch of folk join in, except the women. They just carry on with their sewing, as if it's nothing to do with them.

His brother, Phillipo, edges up to me, his lips torn into a scowl and he whispers, "Go home."

I flinch at his words. I don't tell Gio. What if he bloody agrees?

I wander over to the balcony, hoping that the cool breeze will dampen the burn of Phillipo's words. But the air's too warm and the wound too deep for such a simple cure. I forbid my tears to betray me. But still they run, slowly at first but then faster as if they now have permission. Below, on the ground, a girl in denim shorts jumps onto the back of a lilac scooter. She wraps her arms tightly around another girl with long dark hair and they both laugh as they zip off. They could be going anywhere but I wish I could join them.

"Nikki?" Gio kisses me on the head and with the back of his hand wipes my tears away. "My family, they want me marry Italian woman."

Not someone like me, then.

"They no understand. It take time, Nikki. My dad he no the bad man. He sorry."

But what about his brother and the rest of the family? They're all bloody ignorant. "Why didn't you tell me things would be like this, Gio?"

"I no know, Nikki. I no know. I very sorry. But I love you. That all it matter." And I love him. Maybe he's right and that's all that matters. I let him lead me back into the room. But this time we go together, hand in hand.

Later, from the women's table where I sit silently as the others sew, I glance over at the men with their cards and lager. I want to be a part of their laughter. I can't talk, but at least I could play bloody cards and get drunk. What is this? Nineteen fifty-three?

A wash of loneliness drenches my skin and I long for my mum to say, "Hen, do you want a cup of tea?"

Maybe I've made a huge mistake.

CHAPTER 25

Mrs Hawthorne – Edinburgh

A yellow skip squats on the driveway, an affront to the manicured lawn. We trail back and forth with crates crammed with remnants from the past. We've cleared out cupboards and drawers, stripped curtains from windows and thrown up rugs from the floor. Sometimes we sit on the garden bench to catch our breath, or to argue over a tin of beans from nineteen ninety-four. Yet still, no letter have I found.

"What an utter mess," Charles says.

He steps cautiously over stacks of old books. I reply with the same words I've used many times before, "It'll be worth it in the end."

Then I add some more to his pile.

He's right. Upstairs, which we're redecorating first, is shambolic. But I'm not going to spend another night on a mattress that mourns for their past. I need everything gutted and gone. So out in the skip sprawls the chintz of her middle-class reign and I can't wait for us to sleep in our new virgin bed.

"Let's stop for a cigarette," Charles says as he rubs his eyes and slumps onto the garden bench.

He tends to think of himself as younger than his days, but physical work reminds him of his years. I join him and we both light up and exhale. The smoke curls into the summer air, its sour scent masking the fresh garden bouquet. Charles coughs. He'd been coughing quite a lot lately.

"We really should stop smoking, you know," I say.

"Let's get the bedrooms decorated first."

My heart dips and prickles of disappointment sadden my voice. "Don't forget downstairs, Charles. That needs done too."

He sighs, throws his cigarette to the floor, stamps it dead, tosses it into the skip and slumps back. It must be hard for him to destroy the memories they shared. But he's promised. It isn't like I'm being horrible or changing things for change's sake.

The house is gorgeous, but the décor is decades old and not to my taste. When we make tea, it's Clarissa's kettle we use. When we bake pizza it's her oven gloves that we wrap our hands in. And what kind of woman has patterned china, like my grandmother once had, and floral aprons with gingham bows? The green leather chair in the living room is torn and shredded by dogs they once had. It was her favourite chair. The book she'd been reading last still lies open and waits there. It's crazy to be envious of a dead woman, but I can't help it. I want to deplete it all. The place is saturated with her. There's no space for our own love to flourish.

However, Charles is the kindest man I've ever known. It's cruel to neglect his emotions. He's shown that he loves me in so many ways and here he is showing me again. I walk over to him, unfold his crossed arms, place them around my thickening waist and snuggle him in.

"Thank you for all this," I say, ashamed of myself and my irrational thinking. He doesn't deserve my jealous behaviour.

"You don't need to thank me. I love you and want you to be happy. Excuse me for being a tad grumpy. I'm just tired. It's hard work, all this."

I link my arm into his and pull him up. "Come on, old man. Let's get you something to drink."

He scratches the top of his head, holds a finger to his chin then tilts his head. "Hmm. There's one thing though."

"Uh-huh?"

He lets go of my arm and frowns. My eyes narrow and shift to the red gravel I've been shuffling with the toes of my flat sensible shoes. I'm arranging it carefully into a tall pile. What's wrong now? He points behind us. "We're going to need a bigger skip."

I laugh, bubbling with joy and follow him back into the house. The gravel topples silently to the ground behind us.

Slashes of purple and ruby rose bruise the night sky and I burn candles of jasmine and pomegranate to sweeten the shadows stretching through the living room. Around the low coffee table, I scatter piles of cushions on the floor. The scene set, I slip the box behind me. Charles saunters in with a bottle of red wine, Jack padding along at his feet.

"What are we doing?" he says as he shuffles down awkwardly. Charles is more comfortable in a formal setting.

"Ta-da!"

I hold out the box and he fidgets on the green velvet cushion like a little boy, rubbing his hands together. I bathe in his approval, his excitement warming me.

"I'll have you know I was the Scrabble champion at my old grammar school," he says as he sets out the board and spreads out the letters.

"Game on." I'll be hopeless, but I love breaking through

Charles's stiff shell and showing him it's okay to have fun.

"*Dickhead* isn't in the dictionary." He sighs.

"I think you'll find it is." I add another tile to the end.

He pushes his glasses down his face and peers over them to stare. I laugh at his stern expression made even funnier by his red wine moustache.

"Try *dickheads* then. And that's twenty points to me."

"Hardly the best use of language, but I'll give you it."

Grudgingly he writes the points down on a scrap of paper as I pour us more wine.

Like Charles, my father loved games. Especially ones he could bet on like a round of dominoes at the pub. It's cruel they can't meet each other. He'd have been fascinated by Charles's knowledge, entranced by his tales and rather in awe of his status. I missed out so much in my father's life. All those years wasted, when we didn't talk, didn't see each other. And now, when everything is perfect, his absence is more acute. If only I'd known how much I'd miss him I may have made better choices. He might have too.

Charles is far ahead in points and the distance is lengthening. I stare at tiles that refuse to form sense and hope he can't play his next move.

"*Jezebel*. And my goodness, look. Double and triple points."

"*Jezebel?* That's an old word."

"It still has relevance today," he replies, glancing my way, a smile widening his lips.

Does he mean me? I grab a handful of peanuts and throw them towards him. They scatter around his head and fall to the floor. Jack wakes from his slumber and scrambles to snatch them up.

"Now, now. That's not a very sporting way to declare defeat, madam."

I throw some more. They sprinkle around his head and catch in his thick grey hair. He brushes them off and frowns. Have I gone too far? He leaps around the table, grabs me and pins me to the floor. I squeal in excitement.

"That behaviour is rather uncouth," he says, his face inches from mine.

His hands grip my wrists, holding my arms to the ground and he sits astride me, his breath warm against my skin. My pulse races.

"You're such a sore loser."

"I'm not," I reply, and he grazes my lips with a kiss.

"But I love you," he whispers and brushes the hair away from my eyes.

I sigh and drape my arms around him. The Jezebel that I am.

We lie there for most of the night, Jack curled at our feet. Until the candles burn out and the chill returns.

Charles shoos Jack to the garden before he settles for the night and I make my way up the staircase to get ready for bed. A brown box lies on the second step. Have we missed taking it to the skip?

"Charles? There's a box lying here!" I shout.

I prod it gingerly with my toes. It isn't sealed, so I peel back a corner to see more. Could it be mine? A Hermes scarf appears in yellow and green and I pull it out. Something clatters from it onto the wooden step. Something that's been wrapped up carefully inside. I panic, hoping it isn't broken, and step down to pluck it up.

Charles pushes me aside and grabs it. A look of anger flashes over his face.

"Charles, what is it?"

"You shouldn't have touched that," he says and his eyes flush with tears.

"What is it?" I reply, a sudden weakness in my legs.

"It's just a framed photograph I wanted to keep. It was in the skip by accident, so I retrieved it. It's nothing. Go to bed. I'll be up soon."

Tears drip down his face. Why?

"But you've lots of photographs, they're all over the house. Show me what's so special," I reply with words braver than I feel.

With trembling hands, he turns it around. At first, I'm not sure what it is, then the lines become clear and the shapes make sense. It's Clarissa, draped along the chaise longue that still stands at the top of the stairs. Her dark long hair fanned around her like Medusa and apart from the taunting smile she wears, she's naked. An acid taste floods my mouth.

"Why, Charles?"

His body shakes. It's crushing to witness his pain. I want to run and comfort him, but his next words bludgeon my heart.

"She's my soulmate. I can't. I won't just discard her."

He walks away, cradling the photograph as if it's the most precious thing he owns.

On trembling legs, I walk into the bathroom and hunch over, vomit into the sink. The avocado sink. The one she'd chosen. I stare into the mirror. The silver mirror she once hung on the wall. They must have laughed together and joked about the right height. I see the lines, the wrinkles, the saggy skin. The eyes once bright and turquoise blue that sparkled with devilment, now dull with age. How can I compete? If only he'd seen me younger. I might have had a chance then.

I turn on the taps. Gold ones, of course, because she wouldn't have settled for less. I run my hands under the water, letting it get hotter.

Music drifts in through an open window. He must have retreated to the garden and his summerhouse. I recognise the song. It's the one he played at her funeral. "The Most Beautiful Girl in the World".

"Damn you both!" I scream and slump to a heap on the floor.

The ghost of her laughter echoes around tiled walls.

CHAPTER 26

Ronnie – Liverpool

"kirts."

"Yes, miss."

I flick a glance back. "Girls."

"Aww, miss."

I laugh and enter the lime green corridor of the Humanities block for my appointment with Edward, a business teacher. I'd observed his lesson yesterday and today is feedback. He's not going to take it well. He never does. It's as if he ignores my advice to taunt me.

He greets me with a smile, arms crossed over his chest. I sit down opposite him and take out my folder. "Morning, sir. So how do you think it went?"

He's rigid in his chair and a sneer paints his face. "It went great."

"But some of the children couldn't keep up," I say. He cocks his head to the side, narrows his eyes and slides his chair further back. I brush a crumb from the desk.

Massaging his temples as if I'm a headache he wants to banish, he grunts, "Most of them did okay."

"But that isn't good enough, is it?" I'm sick of his attitude.

He leaps from his chair and bangs a fist on the desk. Sweat soaks through his armpits and spit dribbles from his lips. "This is rubbish. They did all the work." He stamps his feet. "I'm not doing anything else. I'm being persecuted."

"Why don't you take a seat, sir? Let's talk about this calmly."

"Take a seat?" he shouts, and he grabs a chair. It slams against the back wall and crashes to the floor. He's behaving the same way as the children he's meant to help. What a role model.

I want to seize him by the throat, but he'd love that ammunition. "We'll leave this for today, sir. You need to settle down." I stride out, throw a nod to the receptionist, *I'll be five minutes*, and march into the car park. Crouched behind a huge truck, I roar, "Fucking bastard."

I close my office door and slump into the soft leather chair with my chips and cheese. The room will reek of grease for the rest of the day. So annoying that staff will know what I've eaten. Nostrils flaring, they'll enter the room and within seconds, pursed lips will sigh *oh, is that chips I'm smelling?* Fuck off, man. They're not contagious. I delve into the soggy mess but after a few minutes, bin them. Great. Now the room stinks for nothing.

Tom's business card lies on the desk. I've toyed with it throughout the day, coiled and rolled it through my fingers. It isn't as crisp now. I trace the raised lettering with a fingertip. *Tom London. Expert in Family Law.* Impressive, but I'm not a client. Should I trust him? After all, we'd met under unusual circumstances but on both occasions he'd been a gentleman. Mum would have liked him. I can just imagine her saying *Oh a lawyer, that's a good job. Go on. You stick in there, doll.*

A memory of Estée Lauder scents the air and with it a vision of her green smoky eyes, red-stained mouth and platinum curls. Before the cancer stormed and cowed her to her knees, that is. There's a tightness in my chest. I can't go there. But I can dial.

"Well, Ronnie. I didn't expect to hear from you," Tom says.

I shuffle paper around my desk and pick up a pencil. "If it's inconvenient, Tom, we should talk some other time. I hear there's some dogging planned on a lay-by off the M56."

His laughter roars down the line. "You're funny, but I'll pass on that one. Unless you want some company while Graham's off doing his thing. Always happy to come to the aid of a damsel in need."

I smile. Graham would go nuts at him using his name. "So how are things in the land of Tom?"

"Sorry, just a minute…" The call goes quiet. I doodle squiggles on paper. Boxes that get bigger and bigger, and tiny little flowers. I keep an eye on the door. The peace can be shattered in a matter of minutes.

"Sorry, Ronnie. Problem with a client. Are you still there?"

He'd taken his time. "Sure, I'm here but I've not got long."

"Oh, great. I was worried you'd be gone." A clicking snaps down the line. My body tenses. What if someone is listening in? "Can you hear clicking?"

"Oh sorry, sorry. I was clicking my biro off and on."

I smile and flop into the chair. "Why did you want me to call?" My red fingernails tap the desk. If he's just after sex, I'll cut this off now.

Tom splutters down the phone. "Um. Well. Um. I thought it was pretty obvious. I like you, Ronnie. I like you a lot. I'm not sure what the deal is with Graham, but I'd love to take you out. For dinner perhaps, or we could go to the cinema?"

"A normal cinema, I hope."

He laughs. "Of course. Of course. So, next Saturday at eight?" A student knocks gently on the door. Her parents stand behind her. The mother glances at the clock and the father shifts from foot to foot. Obviously antsy.

"Great. I'll meet you outside. I have to go. Bye."

Graham slips into bed, nuzzles my neck and gives me a quick peck on the cheek.

"Hey, Ronnie. Can we talk?" My stomach churns and I put my book down. This doesn't sound good. I stare at my hands then dart a glance in his direction.

"Sure, what's up?"

"It's just. And I don't want you to take this the wrong way. I appreciate everything you do. You know that. No one has ever done the things you've done for me before."

I shift around in the bed. It's so hot. I can't get comfortable. Is he finishing things? "Oh, come on, Graham. Spit it fucking out."

For all his sexual shenanigans, he's prim and proper in his language. He stares at me and raises a brow. Does he believe I give a fuck? I clench my fists and dig my nails into my palms.

"The swinging and sex clubs are great, Ronnie. But well…"

"But what, Graham?" I snap.

He turns his head away and picks up the teddy bear he bought me in Paris. It holds a red velvet heart. There were others on the stall with *Je t'aime* scrawled across them but this one is blank. I still love it. He tosses it back and forth in his palms.

"It's like I'm a dog on a leash, Ronnie. Like that guy you told me about at the sex club, remember him?"

I throw the duvet off and pounce towards him. I'm inches from his face. "A dog on a leash? What the fuck are you talking about? You do anything you want."

He swallows and lowers his head. I want to punch him so

147

badly but force my arms to stay at my side. "Don't you get everything you want?" At least he has the decency to nod. "Then what's the problem?"

Tears trickle down his cheeks. Why the fuck is he crying? Surely, it should be me.

"You're always there. Always watching. Judging. Humouring me like I'm five years old."

I thump the pillow with a fist and glare at his pathetic cabaret. "I let you do anything you want. Anything!" I shout.

He lifts a tissue to his nose and blows. "That's it. You. Let. Me."

I tense from the pain. He leans over and gently takes my hand. I jerk mine away.

My book has fallen to the floor. I bend to retrieve it. I'm going to pack my bags and go home and read it.

"I miss the chase. I miss going out with my mate."

What a selfish bastard. He's had all the sex he could want. I'm sick to death of men. Tired of their wants.

Graham continues, "I'm sorry. I'm not normal. I know you deserve more."

"I do," I scream and throw the book at his scum-ridden back. He doesn't react, just picks it up and hands it back.

"It's not your fault."

I fucking know it's not.

"It's all this religious stuff. I've missed out. I don't want to be like this, honest I don't. I feel like shit. Don't leave me please. If I don't have you, I don't know what I'll do." He crumples into a heap and his body shudders as he weeps. He looks over, eyes stained with tears. "I didn't want to lie to you, Ronnie. But now, look what I've done with my honesty."

I stroke my arms and leave him to weep. I've spent so much time on this piece of shit.

"Ronnie?"

"Yes?"

"I've never felt like this for anyone. Give me a little bit more freedom for a while. It's only sex, it means nothing at all. Then when it's all out of my system. I promise I'll give it all up. It'll be like Paris forever. Just you and me. Just us."

I twirl a strand of hair through my fingers and tap my feet on the floor.

So, he's not rejecting me. He's begging me to stay. He must love me but be afraid to commit. Is there any difference, really, to him chasing women with his mate? At least I'll not have to watch or jeopardise my work. And it's not his fault that he wants to live like a teenager when he was denied it growing up.

He shortens the distance between us. "Please, Ronnie. I need you." He puts the teddy bear in my hands.

But are we back to step one? Is Graham right? Do I deserve much more? Could that person be Tom? I shake my head. That's silly. Tom's merely a weapon and part of the plan.

"Ronnie," Graham cries.

I wrap my arms around him and cradle him in. Stroke his hair gently. There's a part of me that wants to rip it all out, but I don't. "Graham, it's okay, I understand. You go out with your mate. Make it next Saturday. I'll see you Sunday for lunch. But you're buying."

He mutters, "Thanks."

I smile. Tit for Tat. Fucker.

CHAPTER 27

Nikki – Mondello

*S*liding my feet into sandals, I sneak across the room. It isn't easy with flip-flops slapping against tiles, but thankfully Gio stays snoring. When I edge the bedroom door open, sunlight streaks through. I creep into the gap and close it to seal him in the dark. This is my day. My moment.

I unlock the balcony doors of our sixth-floor apartment. We've been here a few weeks. Gio said it's a dangerous place, but it's not any worse than Edinburgh. He's just jealous of all the wolf whistles I get and is being overprotective.

The heat blasts my face. It's unrelenting, even at eight in the morning. As is the noise. Everywhere you look, something is happening.

Women drape clothes over makeshift ropes. Some, on their knees, scrub walls and windows. While others fling buckets of water over bright orange railings to splash onto the road. Voices boom back and forth as hands spin through the air and the mixture of onions and garlic tingles my nose. I look down to the balcony floor.

The wicker basket lies on its side. It must have fallen from the table during the night. I wince when the heat from the handle burns, and I unravel the rope. Now it's time for the fun part. The little green van is below us and young boys are running around with orders. Placing the money inside the basket, I raise it over the side. Sweat is stinging my eyes but I can't let go of the rope to wipe them. Someone laughs and points and others join in. I smile back feeling a part of something. The basket is swinging from side to side, but it's hard to weave the rope through my wet fingers. As long as it gets there, that's fine.

Once it's lowered with all the rest, I watch and wait, hoping for the best. I can't speak the language and I've no idea about Italian money. Gio buys everything but, today, I want to do it myself. When I told my mum about it, she was horrified and wrote back.

That is so lazy. Why don't they just go down to the van and get it? And what if someone steals the money, hen? She doesn't understand the intensity of this heat.

And you'll get fat eating pizza for breakfast. Do they not have Frosties or porridge?

The rope sways and I tug to check the weight. It's heavier. I squeal and roll up the rope. I've done it. Okay, I hadn't needed to talk, but at least it's something. I'm learning my way.

The *sfincione* is still warm. It's like fried pizza from the chippie but wrapped in breadcrumbs. It's become my most favourite thing to eat as it reminds me of home. There are too many fish in Sicily for my grease-loving tongue. Wishing I'd ketchup, I carry it through to the bedroom with a skip in my walk. "Wakey wakey."

Gio grumbles and pulls the thin cotton sheet higher to hide from the light. I sit down on the edge of the crumpled bed, tray in hand and flick off my shoes.

"Wakey wakey, Gio."

He sighs, rolls over and wraps his arm around me. The tray teeters on my knees and I grip it tighter.

"Gio, look. Look what I've got you." He rubs the heels of his hands over his eyes, stretches then sits up and frowns.

"How you do this, Nikki? My brother he is here?"

"Nooooo. I got it myself."

He narrows his eyes. "And you not fall? Nobody shout you?"

I laugh. I'm eighteen, not eight. "Nope. I was fine. Here, try some." I tear off a chunk, pop it into his mouth and place the tray between us.

He looks at me with a gleam in his eyes. "You very clever girl, Nikki."

I punch the air. "They're delicious, Gio. And now I can buy them myself."

He laughs and rolls me onto his lap. "Not as *deliziosa* as you, my Nikki." He licks my nose and it tickles. I giggle. Hands slip under my T-shirt, roam up to my breasts and gently tease my nipples. I tremble and kiss him.

He could have waited. The pizza's growing cold.

I grab the beach bag and sling on my sunglasses. I can't wait to jump in the sea and let the waves wash away the sticky sheen coating my skin. "Let's go, then. I'm ready."

Gio glances over, looks me up and down then shakes his head. "You crazy woman. No."

The excitement slips from my face. What've I done wrong? He said we were going swimming. "What is it?"

"Your clothes, Nikki. You look *puttana*."

"*Puttana*? What does that mean, Gio?" It isn't a good word. He often uses it when losing at cards with his brothers. But there's nothing wrong with me. I don't even have any make-up on. It's too hot for all that.

"We not wear the clothes like this here. You go change."

"But it's a beach, Gio. I've just got a top and shorts on. It's boiling outside."

He stands and claws his hands through his hair. "You change or we no go," he snaps.

I bite my lip and swallow the lump in my throat.

"Siciliano wife she no dress this way. You bring the shame to my family like this."

I throw the beach bag at him and it hits him on the head. Good. Then I run through to the bedroom and burst into tears. I hate this country and I'm sick of all the rules. The shorts aren't even showing any arse, they're down to the top of my knees. And my boobs are covered. Okay, maybe my cleavage is showing, but it's forty degrees and other women walk about in bikini tops and jeans.

Gio has changed. It's all rules, rules, rules. Back in Scotland, he didn't care about any of this crap. I crunch my teeth together. I'm not putting the damn dress on. It has no shape. It's too big for me and reaches my ankles. I'll be like a bloody nun. A drab one at that. And I'll swelter on the beach. Everyone will laugh.

A big black beastie crawls along the floor and I clamp a hand over my mouth to stifle a scream. I'm not giving Gio the satisfaction of being my hero. I jump onto the bed and pull my feet up tight to my chest and stare at it until it disappears.

The buzz of the town drifts through the window and stings the thick silence. People are having fun and I can't even read a book or watch television. Nothing's in English. I stifle a yawn and reach for my box of stationery.

Dear Mum,

I miss you. I miss everyone. Tell Granny and Grandad I love them. It is so hot here. Your clothes stick to you even when you have just had a shower. And you should see the size of the beasties, they are so massive. You'd hate it.

But it is really lovely at the beach. It is like something you would see in a film. Long golden sands and a turquoise sea. When you swim you can see the fishes. Can you imagine that?

I am having a good time, Giovanni is looking after me and his family are all so very nice, so you do not have to worry about me.

I hope you and your pals have a nice time at the pub on Saturday at the talent contest. If Granny goes make sure she does not get too drunk, or Grandad will not be happy. Remember that time at Sunday mass when she was getting communion and was sick all over the priest. Grandad was so embarrassed, but Granny just said she had food poisoning. I do not think anybody believed her because they had all been in the pub with her. So funny!

Anyway, I better go because Giovanni is waiting to take me out for a drive. It is so hot here that it is brilliant to get a breeze through your hair.

I will write soon. Love you always.

Nikki

P.S. Please write back.

P.P.S. Make it soon. There is nothing in English to read here.

A tear drops onto the paper, blotting the blue ink. It spreads when I try to brush it off, but it'll be fine. I can't waste paper and start again. I slide it into a pink envelope and look for a stamp. I've only a few left. Gio hasn't taken me back for more yet.

He shuffles in and stands before me with drooped shoulders. "Nikki. We go beach. You put dress on."

"No."

He walks over, sits beside me and holds my hand. I let him, but after a few seconds of moody silence, I pull it away.

"Nikki, this not Scotland. You have to do things the family way."

I stand and glare at him. "I'm not wearing that minging dress, Gio. If you love it so much, you wear it."

He throws his head back and laughs. "Nikki, you are crazy, Scottish woman."

He slaps his hand against his brow and paces the room. I turn and stare out the window.

"Why you no wear the dress over the shorts. Then at beach you take dress off. Problemo solved."

A bead of sweat drips down my cheek. He walks over and rubs it away. Instantly, another appears. It's hard to breathe in this place.

"Just until we get to the beach, yeah?"

His eyes crinkle, knowing he's won. "*Si*, Bella."

I hope he's telling the truth.

CHAPTER 28

Mrs Hawthorne – Edinburgh

On bended knee, he gazes up, a red velvet box cradled in his open hands. What on earth? The box is far too large for such a small delicacy as an engagement ring. He coughs and clears his throat and I nudge closer to the edge of the sofa. I want to hear every word. I also crave a cigarette in my hand.

"Please forgive me for my poor behaviour. I've realised I'm quite a broken man. Although I was prepared for Clarissa's death, it's obviously affected me far more than I thought."

I shake my head and place my hand on his knee. "Charles, it's fine, honestly. Do get up please."

He brushes me away. "No, please let me finish. I've something to say."

"At least sit up on the sofa, Charles. You'll hurt your knees down there."

The velvet box shakes in his hand. "No, it has to be done this way." He smiles.

Sunlight streaks through the window and brings the teal in the new sofa to life. The silver cabinet that adorns the back wall sparkles with trinkets we've collected on our little trips and walks. The room is so warm now.

"I never thought I'd have to start all over again. I was just waiting for Jack to die then I was going to join him. But that life is the past. You showed me how to feel again. How to laugh and even dance. I owe you my life." A tear slips down his cheek and it's hard not to lean over and brush it dry. The words *please let this be it*, echo like a mantra inside my mind.

"I was in a very dark place with nowhere to turn. But then one day you sat by my side and little by little the light crept back. Marry me and let's make every day as bright as the first."

His words, so beautiful in their simplicity, calm my fears. I am here, alive and not some imaginary ghost of times gone by. My eyes brim with tears. I kneel beside him and cradle his face in my palms.

With one hand on the sofa, he pulls himself up from his knees. "There's one more surprise." He walks over and opens the sitting-room door. Jack bounds in, tail wagging. He's wearing a red bow and around his collar is a garland of paper roses. He's so pleased with himself as he runs round and round in circles.

"Jack. Come here. Settle down." Jack barks excitedly and Charles dawdles after him. I laugh when Jack's floppy ears peek from beneath the coffee table. Charles sneaks under, grabs his collar and makes him sit down. Then he tugs his shirt back into his trousers and straightens Jack's bow tie. Settled, they both look up at me with wide eyes. Gentle cornflower blue and forlorn molten brown. Charles smiles. "Um, so will you marry us?"

How could I not?

If younger, I'd spring towards him and jump into his lap, but creaking bones and sore knees make the journey muted and longer. The decades, thieves of spontaneity.

"Yes. Yes. I'd love to."

Charles's smile spreads to crinkle his eyes and Jack's fluffy tail thumps hard against the floor. My heart echoes the beat. And we cuddle while Jack scrambles between us, licking at our faces as we dissolve into giggles.

Charles says, as he regains his decorum, "This calls for champagne."

Jack pitter-patters beside him through to the newly painted kitchen. He loves the chance of a treat just as much as me.

I stand and search the room for the red velvet box. It's so like Charles to get *just* about everything right. Not under the table, not hidden behind the silver scatter cushions. Where is it? Perhaps he'll serve it with drinks. Not wishing to ruin his theatrical reveal, I sit back on the sofa and tug at the skin around my thumb. Will he remember emeralds are my favourite?

He walks back in carrying crystal flutes and ice-cold Dom Perignon. After throwing a bone to Jack to keep him busy, he raises a toast to us all. "To you, me and Jack." He smiles.

With my fingers clasped around the stem of my glass, I smile back full of delight, not quite believing my good fortune and this wonderful sight. It will be an honour to be his new wife. But then my bare finger glares a warning. I wriggle my fingers in his direction. Surely he'll realise his omission.

"It's rather lovely, isn't it? Not too sharp," he replies.

I flex my fingers out. "There's something missing?"

His eyes snap to Jack, always his first priority which, to be honest, has become a tad annoying. Then they turn slowly to me.

He looks at my hand, at the flute I'm holding, and jerks to attention. "Oh, how very remiss of me, so sorry." He grabs the bottle from the table and refills my glass.

I slump to the sofa and sigh. "Oh, Charles."

His face screws up in confusion, the lines that carve his face deepen and he shrugs. "What? What am I missing?"

In an attempt to brighten my disappointment, I gulp some champagne, but the bubbles slip down the wrong way and I choke on my feelings. Just once in my life, couldn't everything be perfect? He springs over and pats my back. It adds to my annoyance and I snap, "The ring. Isn't there a ring, Charles?"

He flinches at the tone and I wish it'd been kinder. "Oh, of course, I forgot it amongst all the excitement. I'll rectify that right now." His hand scratches through his white hair and he looks around. "Now where did I put that box?" And down he goes on his hands and knees to search the floor.

Jack, alert to the tension and some unexpected fun, scampers over, barking to help with the game. Charles tuts and hushes him away, intent on finding the misplaced treasure. I sip champagne, my fingers tapping against the arm of the sofa.

"Aha, it's here," he says triumphantly and drags it from under the sofa.

Dust clings to the velvet box as if it's been missing for years and not minutes, but it doesn't tarnish its beauty or the promise of what lies within it. Charles's eyes twinkle. This is the moment.

Until Jack barks and the doorbell shrieks along the hall to pierce my heart. The treasure discarded, tucked into his grey cardigan pocket, Charles runs to answer. Voices whisper together, but there's no point straining to hear the words. I'm not interested. Not now.

"It's Robert," Charles says as he ushers him in to stand before me. Neither is embarrassed at this unannounced visit. It's as though his friend has every right to intrude on our biggest moment. I nod, smile and refill my glass with champagne.

Robert fidgets with his tie, tightening it then smoothing it down his shirt to lie flat. "I hope I haven't interrupted anything."

"No. Not at all," declares Charles. With a smile and a nervous hop skip to the sofa, he sits down. "Would you care for some champagne?"

Robert unbuttons his tweed jacket, ruches up his chinos and perches on the edge of a chair. His glasses slip down on his nose and he peers over them. "Are we celebrating?"

"Um, yes. I suspect you could say we are," Charles says.

"Oh. Well if I could just have tea, please? It's a bit early for me."

How dare he dampen my occasion with his humdrum milky concoction? Next, the ginger nuts will be out and the tedious display of intelligence translated in a witty way. Why can't he get out and leave us be? I like him, but he's in the way.

I've waited so long for the perfect moment but, like everything else, it's in danger of being shattered. The first wedding had been a mistake. I'd known all along. Everyone had told me, but I'd never listened to them before, always thought I knew best. Why would I have listened to them then, when there was a beautiful white dress? But I should have paid heed to their concerns. I know that now, of course. Long after it's too late.

"So what are we celebrating?" Robert says, dipping his biscuit in his tea. He probably imagines it's a new journal publication or some sought-after tickets to the theatre. I smile, letting Charles answer. His response will be insightful.

With a gulp of champagne, Charles pauses in the moment, then he lowers his hand to pet Jack. His glance focused on the trail his fingers leave as they weave through Jack's curly white hair.

"I've just proposed."

Robert leaps from his chair and claps like he's giving Charles a standing ovation. "Such wonderful news. Congratulations."

It's all the encouragement Charles needs to lift his head and smile. "Thanks. We're very happy."

"So, may I see the ring? When I get home, Elizabeth will want every detail. Perhaps I could take a picture?"

"Charles was about to present it," I blurt, unable to wait any longer. It doesn't matter that Robert is here. He's his oldest friend, after all, and we at least had enjoyed our proposal in private.

Charles scrapes his hand through his hair and tucks it behind his ear.

A crimson flush bleeds across Robert's face. "Oh, I'm so sorry. I'm in the way."

"Not at all," I say, not wishing further delays.

Charles passes me the box from his cardigan. I smile, stroke the red velvet, and the men stand side by side, waiting for my reaction. I press the delicate silver button and raise the lid.

Not one ring but five. I don't understand. Eyebrows raised, I glance up at Charles. He's wearing a smile that almost makes him shine, but Robert is grim and won't meet my eyes.

"If you would like me to buy you one, I will. But these were Clarissa's. They cost a fortune and she won't wear them anymore. There's an emerald there. It's your favourite stone. But have them all."

Robert groans. "Oh, Charles."

A week before I'd asked Charles to buy me a bar of chocolate at the shop. He had asked what kind, but I'd said to grab anything, forgetting to say not to get me anything with nuts. When he returned, he laid seven different bars in front of me. I'd laughed and asked him why and he'd explained that he wanted to ensure I'd something I really liked. That was precious to me. But this, what is this? Does he not understand the connotations?

"What's wrong? If you want a new one, throw these away or gift them."

Poor Charles. He loves me, of that I'm certain. Of course, it would be silly to spend money when these lay abundant. I can't hurt him this way or be selfish.

I stand and kiss his cheek. "No, I love them. Thank you. The emerald is gorgeous." My throat tightens, from the tears I hold back and the loss of my perfect moment. But my restraint allows the tension in the room to dissipate. And I'm sure that her laughter, which reverberates around us, is simply my imagination.

"I think I'll have that champagne." Robert smiles. But he never does take a photo.

CHAPTER 29

Ronnie – Liverpool

*I*n the en suite Graham's splashing cologne, singing along to a song, getting ready for his night on the town. I don't care, but shape my face into a semblance of sadness. I want him feeling bad at the image of me sitting alone with hot chocolate and a pile of marking. When really, I'll be on my date with Tom. A smile crosses my face, but I quickly hide it when Graham sashays into the bedroom.

For the last couple of weeks, Tom's phoned my office at one o'clock. Students were astounded when I rushed past them and ignored their behaviour to catch his call. They probably thought I'd turned soft. But I loved our quiet chats. Just him and our little oasis. No teenage angst or teacher demands. He shared his love of music, old TV shows like *Kojak* and that he'd always yearned to play guitar. Sometimes we spoke about personal stuff like our upbringing and how our parents had fucked up our views of the world. Mine because they were poor and his because of their riches. Not once did I feel the need to snare him.

Graham edges onto the bed and flashes a shy grin. His usual little boy imitation. He's waiting for permission like I'm his mother instead of his girlfriend. "You sure this is okay, Ron?"

Of course, it isn't. But it won't be me that says *no you're a selfish bastard*. Let him have his freedom and revisit his youth. But I'll be doing the same.

"Of course, go and have fun with your mates. It's fine. I told you before."

He pecks a kiss on my forehead and flees from the room, trying to outrun his guilt. He doesn't want it clinging to his new T-shirt. That would surely dampen his sex appeal. Not that I'll be doing anything like that with Tom. I made that very clear from the beginning. And he's fine with it. He just enjoys my company. I guess he's lonely.

"Ron, I'm off then. You sure you don't want me to come back here tonight?"

"No, it's fine. I'm just gonna get an early night and you'll wake me up. It's been a long week. I'm exhausted."

"So, you'll come over to mine in the morning, then?"

"Yeah, about lunchtime."

"Okay, babe. Have a nice night."

"You too. And wear a condom."

His laugh splinters my civility. It wasn't a fucking joke. The front door slams behind him and I wait. Drum my fingers on the bedside cabinet, flex my ankles until his rat friend's car scuttles along the road towards its dirty destination.

One hour to get ready for Hot Date Tom. I throw the covers off the bed, rip off my nightie and rush to the bathroom.

It's dark and a gentle kiss of rain dampens the air. The streets are quiet, except for a couple of women embracing in a corner. A street light illuminates the drizzle around them and the hazy glow makes them appear angelic. The memory of Tara's smile flashes through me. It makes me sad. I'm always losing friends in some way or another.

The women part and move on, giggling at some private joke. I wrap my coat around me against the rain. We're going to see *Friday the 13th*, an old horror film. Tom chose it. He loves horror and has all the original Hammer House movies collected at home. *Frankenstein* is my favourite. I've always felt sorry for the monster, all alone in the world. But then, if he'd found love, it would have betrayed him eventually. So he was probably better off.

"Hey, Ron!"

I gasp because the voice sounds just like Graham's, but it's Tom and he waves from across the road. I'm glad I've dressed down in jeans and a jacket. He's casual too. Although he's in white trainers and I'm strutting my stuff in red high heels. You can't be too laid-back. Not on a date.

"Sorry I'm late. A spot of rain and Liverpool comes to a stand-still." His blond hair, normally straight, has curled up his collar. It's cute. Perhaps I've been waiting all my life for this. A few extra minutes won't make any difference. He leans forward, brushes his lips to my cheek and unzips his jacket. An urge to flee turns my head away. I'm not sure how to react. For in his hand is a single red rose.

He shuffles his feet, hands in pockets. "Too much?"

"No. Perfect." I smile. "Thank you."

"I was scared you'd snap it in two."

I laugh, he joins in and, somehow, he's holding my hand as we enter the foyer.

~

"Best teacher in the world, huh?" Tom holds up the one surviving mug from the hundreds I'd been gifted over the years. It always sits on my kitchen windowsill wherever I live in the world. Irfan had given it to me just after he turned thirteen. He hadn't seen his fourteenth birthday. He was dead by then. Another statistic of stabbings and gangs. He'd been a great student. A beautiful boy. I remove it from Tom's hands and replace it where it belongs. It needs to feel the sun every morning.

Tom's shoulders drop. "Sorry, Ron. I shouldn't have touched it. I guess it means something special to you. Want to talk about it?"

"No, thanks. Put some music on and I'll grab some wine."

It's weird having Tom in my home. It's like a crossing of lines. But we've had such a good night that neither of us wants it to end. It'd been so funny when the hand rose from the lake at the end of the film and he'd screamed. And it's just a few drinks between friends. Nothing like what Graham will be up to. I grab two glasses and a bottle of red.

Music welcomes me into the living room where Tom is dancing on the sofa. He's weaving my red silk scarf through the air.

I giggle, not quite believing my eyes. "Uh, what are you doing?"

"I'm giving myself up to the moment." He jumps down and saunters over to the window, tilts his head to the side, places his hand by his ear. "Can you hear drums?"

I shake with laughter. His eyes close and he sings along with the lyrics.

I collapse onto the sofa in fits of giggles, my cheeks sore from laughing. He's nuts.

"Tom."

"Yep?"

"Why are you floating my red scarf about?"

He snaps his fingers in the air then places his hand on his hip. "He's from Spain, isn't he?" The scarf twirls above his head then with a flourish he brings it to his feet. "I'm a bullfighter. Olé."

Tears run from my eyes. "Fernando is from Mexico."

"You're wrong. You're thinking of Angelo. He's from Mexico."

"That's the Brotherhood of Man, you idiot. This is Abba. And I'm pretty sure they're both Mexican."

He throws the scarf onto a chair. "I knew that. I knew that." He laughs.

"Super Trooper" plays and he runs over, grabs my hand and pulls me up to my feet. "Come on, let's harmonise. You be the redhead. I'll be the blonde."

"Wait." I grab my wine and down the glass. He does the same.

I narrow my eyes and throw him a glare. He fake flinches, gasps and draws a hand to his mouth.

"I'm Agnetha. You're Frida," I snap.

He smiles and we take our positions, standing back to back. We only stop for wine, the loo and to catch our breath. When "Waterloo" starts, we're too exhausted to even shout the first words. With sweat dripping from our faces we collapse to the floor.

"Ronnie?"

"Yeah?"

"Where's Graham? I've asked you before and you've avoided the question."

I inhale deeply and sigh. "He's out with his mates, clubbing."

Tom shakes his head. "I just don't get it. If you were mine, I'd never leave your side."

"You would, Tom. One day."

He slides along the floor and brushes the damp hair from my face. Placing a finger under my chin he brings my eyes to his. "I wouldn't."

"Yeah, yeah. I've heard it all before." And I had, many times from so many men, all with different faces but spouting the same lines.

"You haven't heard it from me."

"I'm with Graham," I say.

Tom takes my hands into his. "Graham doesn't care about you. Don't you see that?"

Maybe he's right. No one else ever has. But wait, that's the point, isn't it? I have to make Graham love me. Be the perfect match. Everything's going to plan. If it's too easy, it won't be worth it and I won't have proved a thing. But have I got that wrong?

Tom's warm hands reach up and cradle my face. He searches my eyes as if he can read every crack of my soul. All those unsaid hurts that would choke me if I let them out. When he lowers his mouth to mine, I kiss him back. When he lifts my top and touches my breasts, I let him in. We don't make it to bed and it's beautiful to let go. We fall asleep holding each other's hands.

"What's that noise?"

"It's nothing," Tom whispers. "Go back to sleep."

"What if Graham's come over?"

"It's not him, everything's okay."

A rustle in the dark and I spread my arm out searching the floor. I find the top I'd worn earlier and throw it on. "Where are you, Tom?" Crawling over to the lamp, I fumble for the switch to turn it on. Something doesn't feel right.

"Why don't you go back to sleep? Everything's fine."

The glare of the bright light blinds me and I rub at my eyes. Everything is far from fine. Tom is sitting on the edge of a chair, fully clothed and tying his shoelaces.

"What's going on, Tom?"

He smiles. "I've gotta get going. I've a busy day later."

I stare at him open-mouthed, even though I know the rules state I'm meant to smile and nod. Pretend it doesn't bother me. That it's okay for him to fuck and run. Can't show his words, whispered in the night, might mean anything at all. Have to hide the hurt and fake it out.

"But I'd a brilliant night. It's just I'm away for the next six months at the new office in Gibraltar and I've still to pack."

I storm towards him, fists clenched tight at my side. "Are you fucking joking? You're sneaking out at three in the morning?"

A lopsided smile spreads to his eyes and he bends to pick up his jacket. "Aww, come on, what did you expect? It's all part of the game. Look at all the places we met. Hardly take your girl home and 'introduce her to your mother' terrain."

My fists uncurl. Tears spill. The room spins and my head bows. He ambles over, leans down and places a dry kiss on my wet cheek. I'm left there like a used blow-up doll as he strolls down the hall to escape.

I sprint after him, grab the back of his head and wrap his hair around my fingers. He pushes me away, but I tighten the hold. Then I tilt my head and hurl spit in his face. "Get out of my fucking house, you scummy bastard."

He cleans his face with the sleeve of his jacket. "You're a fucking psycho, Ronnie. I pity you."

"Get out. Get out. Get the fuck out," I scream and push him through the door. His foot stops me from slamming it shut and he snarls, "Not a bad fuck. But I've had better. No wonder Graham plays around." He winks and struts down the path like a feral tomcat.

With trembling hands, I turn the key in the lock, slump to the floor, draw my knees to my chest and lean back against the wall. I'm an idiot. Have I not had enough experience to recognise the lure of the bastards? The ones that make you fly with their words then slice your wings with their actions.

My eyes flinch towards the ring of the doorbell. I can't believe he's back. "Get the fuck away from here, or I'll phone the police, you bastard."

The bell rings once more and his hands hammer the door. I pounce to my feet. I'll kill him this time.

"Ronnie? It's me, Graham. Let me in please. I have a confession."

CHAPTER 30

Ronnie – The Beach

Flames rise to smoke the air, sparks crackle, dance and softly fade. Around a firepit, wrapped in blankets, all three of us sit and stare out to the waves. The Gatekeeper in bare feet, with his trousers rolled up past his ankles, paddles there. Occasionally, he stoops to hold a shell to his ear, as if a story will be revealed.

My stomach cramps in spasms. I twist my head to the side, bend over and vomit hits the ground. With the back of my hand, I wipe my mouth clean. Tears drench the sand. How dare he pull me back here? I rip the blanket from my shoulders, stand and yell down, "Get me back to Graham."

The wet sand sinks around my feet as I stride towards him. He scratches his head as he holds a coin to the light.

"I said get me back. I want his confession."

His face contorts into a grin, or maybe it's a grimace. He crouches, dips his hands into the sea and offers me cupped palms.

"These waters are blessed by the Goddess Lethe. They will bring you forgetfulness. Is that not what you wanted, such a short time ago?"

My eyes dart to his hands. I stumble back, slip and fall.

He smiles and lets the water drip slowly through his fingertips. "It would appear you've changed your mind, Ronnie. And you may be right. Is the loss of memory really such a mercy? Lethe had many sisters and brothers. Some were liars, others were storytellers. But she loved them all. We never get to choose our family, do we, Ronnie? But they're the only ones who really know us, don't you think?"

"What the fuck you on about?" I snap.

He waggles a gnarled finger in front of me. "Remember your manners, young lady."

Any closer and I'll take his finger to my mouth and bite.

"Ronnie, you're back!" Nikki squeals, running towards me. And before I get to my feet, she's got her arms around me, squeezing me tight. "Come on. Come sit at the fire and get warm." There's something so sweet about her. It annoys me, but it also brings fresh tears to my eyes. She grabs my hand and I let her lead me back.

She picks up the blanket from the ground, spreads it out between her arms and shakes it. My eyes squint against the sand flying from it.

"Where did the blankets come from?" I ask.

She shrugs and lays the blanket around me. "Dunno. They were sorta here."

I sit down on a boulder. It sends a shiver through me and I lean into the fire to warm my hands.

"And the bar? It's disappeared."

"Yeah, looks that way."

"Great. I could have done with a strong vodka."

Nikki laughs, nods, lifts her knees to her chest and cocoons herself in her blanket. Hawthorne sits next to her with her face scrunched around pursed lips. Miserable old bitch. I need to get out of here and back to Graham. Had he seen Tom leave? Oh God, what if he had. He'd be so angry. And what the fuck was he going to confess?

"He's loathsome," Hawthorne says.

"Who?" I ask. Does she mean the Gatekeeper or Charles?

She rolls her eyes. "Tom, of course. I really dislike him. But how didn't you see it coming?"

"He was a nice guy. He wasn't like that in the beginning."

She laughs. "A nice guy that you met at a perverted sex thing. How unexpected."

A storm of anger engulfs me. I want to grab her blanket and throw it in the sea, but she's old. It wouldn't be right. And what does she know about Tom? Maybe it was my fault. Maybe I reacted too hastily. If I'd let him leave, things might have turned out differently.

"She didn't know he was going to turn out that way. It's not her fault. I think you're being a bit cruel," Nikki says.

"Oh, let her say what she wants, Nikki. She's a bitch anyway."

Hawthorne crosses her legs and brushes specks of sand from her trousers. "I'm only telling the truth. What is it about you that you choose despicable men? Men that use you like a toy. Anyone could've seen what Tom had planned."

Could they have? He'd been different from my normal type. Easy going. Kind. And he'd chased me from the start. Or had that been through our meetings of chance? The praise and declarations he made usually suffocate me but with him, it had been different. Why?

"Are you okay, Ronnie?" Nikki perches beside me. She's rubbing my arm and her face, with an eyebrow raised, tilts too close to mine.

"I'm fine. I want to get back, that's all."

"To Graham?" she whispers.

"Yeah, I need his confession."

"Oh, I wouldn't be in too much of a rush, dear. He probably wants to tell you he has syphilis or that he's got some poor girl pregnant. He's just the type," Hawthorne says.

Nikki gasps and her fingernails bite through my blanket to pinch my arm. Both of us turn and glare over to where Hawthorne sits on her moral throne.

"Not that I would personally be acquainted with such people. I shop at Waitrose."

Nikki giggles and I slap my thigh in amusement. Hawthorne throws us a scowl. We dissolve into laughter. It goes on and on. We clutch our stomachs, stamp our feet and still it comes. Nikki snorts. My cheeks ache. Breathless, we cling to each other, but still the laughter spills from us. It tumbles across the sand and rides the waves where the Gatekeeper stands. He looks over and frowns. A chill floods the air. The fire hisses. Snaps out.

"Look what you've done," Hawthorne says.

I walk over to her. "Oh, be quiet, second-hand Rose."

"I've never worn a hand-me-down in my life, dear."

"Oh? I thought you wore Clarissa's jewellery. I thought you were given a choice of five rings?" Her head bows. But instead of feeling happy, I'm ashamed. What the hell am I doing picking on a woman? An old one at that.

The Gatekeeper thumps an old wooden oar against a rock.

"Five is a special number, Ronnie. You shouldn't be so fast to dismiss such things. There are five waters here: the Lethe, the Acheron, the Cocytus, the Phlegethon and the Styx. Each has its own emotion associated with death."

He turns to Hawthorne. "Sometimes, having five options is a good thing."

I've no idea what he's talking about. He's a raving clown. Five waters and options? Maybe if I pay more attention, rather than obsessing about Graham, I'll figure it out. But I'm more interested in getting back. Nikki is cradling Hawthorne in her arms. Surely it should be her, as the youngest, who's being comforted.

I'm sorry for her, dying so young. She'd be a nice person to know in different circumstances.

"Are you okay, Nikki?" I ask, moving towards her.

She shakes her head. "Not really. I'm scared of what I'll find. What if Gio is just like Tom?"

Oh. It's her turn to go back. What if I get closer to her, cuddle her in. Would I go back too? The Gatekeeper growls. "No, Ronnie. You all take your turns. How could you be judged fairly if you each have unequal time?"

"Judged for what?" Nikki asks. She's trembling and very pale.

"Your love," he replies.

I spit at the ground. As if love might ever be wrong. As if it's ever as simple as one word. And Nikki's eyes glaze over.

CHAPTER 31

Nikki – Mondello

Scraping my hair back into a ponytail, I splash water on my face. It's just gone ten in the morning and this must be the hundredth time. When I catch my image in the mirror I wrinkle my nose and grimace. What a state. The heat has destroyed my beauty routine and left me like a lobster in a frazzled wig. There's no point in wearing make-up. It melts as you slap it on. And believe me, I've tried. Even my mascara dripped into puddles and stung my eyes. I'd never be seen dead like this in Edinburgh, but here I've no choice. How can Gio even fancy me like this?

The worst of it all is the baggy shapeless dresses and the mediaeval rules. Gio lied, and in this heat, well it's just easier to comply. He's become a different person since we arrived in Palermo. Before it was all kiss chase on the beach and shots with my pals but here, he sticks to me like a leech. And when he has to work, I'm grounded alone in this shitty home. With no television,

I sit for hours on the balcony wishing I could join the world. But I'm not allowed.

I drag myself across the hot tiles to the kitchen. Damp foot-prints linger behind me. I'd go back and dance in them, make pretty patterns on the floor. Blast some music and sing like a pop star for a while. But the clammy air has stolen my spirit and I need a drink and ice to revive it.

It's ridiculous to tie rope around a fridge, but Gio says the catch isn't tight enough and we can't buy new. Not yet. My hands grip the frayed ends. Sweat dribbles from my face and my palms sting against the coarse edges. I pull, clutch at a thread but it tears off in my hand and the knot tightens. Sighing, I step back, staring at the stupid thing and flap my tent dress to get air to my skin. What a pig this thing is. There's nothing I can do that will budge it. I stamp my feet and slap its white grimy door.

Running through to the bedroom I kneel and grab the big knife from under the mattress, the one Gio keeps there in case of intruders. Not that anyone would steal from here. Head high, a warrior to the fight, I stride back. I'll carve it, slice it and loot its arctic treasure. One hand clenches around the rope, the other sweeps sweat from my face then lowers to slash. The rope snaps and the door grumbles open.

Cockroaches. Hundreds of them. They scutter out of the cold onto the warm sticky tiles. Soon there's a blanket of gleaming shells. The stench invades the air and seeps into my sunburnt skin. Will it cling there longer because my skin's raw from the sun? A few clamber onto my bare feet. I stand there and let them. Their legs, or feet, or whatever you call them terrorise my toes. My knees shake. Throat stinging from screams.

Someone knocks at the door, shouting. It's a woman. I under-stand some words but can't make sense of what she's saying. She seems scared. Maybe the whole block of flats has a roach inva-sion. And these aren't normal cockroaches. These are the size of a baby rat. Of course, I get it. They were gorging on the food in the fridge. That's why they're fat. I move a foot and then another and back up against the wall. Each step makes me scream louder.

The knocks on the door get fiercer. Someone's kicking it, trying to get in. More than one voice shouting. It could be two, maybe three. But I can't move from the corner. The front door bangs open and footsteps rush towards me. The man carries a hammer, the woman a shoe high above her head. A little girl about three or four totters beside them. In her hand, she trails a pink teddy bear much too close to the floor.

I should run to her, save the teddy before the roaches scuttle aboard and party. She's only a child. Any other adult would put their fears behind them and dive into a rescue mission. If only I could move. But I'm as frozen as I was back at the restaurant at the top of those cellar stairs. And this is worse. Their legs. The smell. We've nothing like it in Scotland.

The man plods across the room and the roaches crunch into inky blots under the thud of his feet. He raises his hammer and shouts, "Bastardo!" Is he gonna kill them one by one? But instead of crushing them, he throws open a door. A broom falls out of a cupboard. He grunts and looks around the small flat. Under the table. Behind the sofa. And in the bedroom. They must think from my screams there's a strange man in here. And they've come to my rescue.

The woman kicks a few cockroaches aside then struts into the kitchen, holding the heel of her shoe like a knife. The man lowers the hammer to his side, shrugs and joins her. The little girl puts her teddy down on the table and picks up the fallen broom. She sweeps the cockroaches out onto the balcony and over the edge. The woman glances down at them as they tumble into space. She pats her daughter's head as if saying *good girl*, then catches my eyes. "*Non ti preoccupare. Sono solo scarafaggi.*"

I lower my head.

Scarafaggi. Cockroach. Another new word.

She smiles, slips on her shoe and walks towards me, arms

wide. She checks my clothes, picks off a roach and throws it to the tiles. "Tutti okay now," she says as she turns me around.

I run my hands down my clothes and shake my feet. The itch on my skin burrows into my mind. I dart out of the apartment and onto the landing, where I stand shaking. Nothing is going to tempt me back in.

The man talks to his wife as they leave. They mention Giovanni's name and something to do with the door. Then they nod and take their daughter's hand. She giggles and turns towards me. I could lose myself in the dark night of her eyes. "Hello. My name it Francesca. What yours?"

I reply, "My name is Nikki."

"Come our house. It safe," she says and hands me her teddy.

Their ivory sofa is too perfect to sit on, my clothes too dark for its sumptuous cushions. On the walls are portraits in thick golden frames and from the ceiling, crystal pendants sparkle from chandeliers. It's like a rich person lives here. A cream cabinet holds gold figurines and many different versions of Mary Magdalene. On each side of the sofa sit ornate jewelled lamps. The scent of leather is fresh and sharp.

I'm thankful when Francesca slips her hand into mine and leads me out to the garden. A scatter of pillows in yellow, pink and green are piled up against an orange tree. A stack of books and dolls lie strewn across them. She sits down on a giant beanbag and tugs my hands to join her. When I do, she smiles and hands me a book. It's in English and she climbs onto my lap and begs me to read.

"We want she speak the English. We buy the books," her mother says. "But come, Francesca. Leave the Nikki alone."

It's strange how the mother is dressed in white shorts and a denim halter-neck. Even her hair is dyed blonde. Is that not forbidden here? I pull the cheap nylon from the heat of my legs. Francesca wriggles up onto my lap, wraps her arms around my neck and says, "Please." I can't resist. She reminds me of my little sister and I nod to her mother *it's okay*. She smiles and ambles away.

When I open the book, tears spring to my eyes. How wonderful to see words I understand once more. How I've missed my own language. Francesca hugs her teddy and cuddles in and I tell her *Once upon a time.*

The fresh scent of garlic and basil wafts around us and her father walks over and hands me a cold beer. Its touch feels delicious against my warm skin. Somewhere a piano plays and a woman sings along to the melody. I place the book down to listen and Francesca leaps up from my lap and grabs an orange from the tree. She offers it like treasure. "You like the *arancia?*"

Arancia. Orange. Another new word. And that's when I remember Gio. I'm not meant to leave the flat. The scuttle of the roaches returns to my skin and I can't help but shudder, but when I look there are none.

Shouts rise from the patio and Francesca tugs on my arm. "*Mangiamo.*" She smiles and I follow her across the garden to a feast of scents, all the colours of the rainbow. Not a beige chip in sight. What if I can't eat it after all their kindness? Her mother pulls out a chair and gestures for me to sit then pushes a plate towards me and motions to help myself. I ignore the salad and the fish with glassy eyes, reach for the thing that appears normal and bite into hot bread. Mozzarella drips around my fingers. I twirl it around and scoop it back into my mouth. Her mother laughs and pulls her chair up closer.

"I am the Paola," she says and pats her hand on my knee. "You okay, Nicoletta? You is happy?"

I crumple into tears. Is it her touch or the way she reminds me of my home? It's so hard here, so far away. Gio's always out working and I've nothing to do. No one to talk to. And the flat is a dump, nothing like he promised. Nothing like this palace.

She takes a napkin to my eyes and hugs me. I hang my head and breathe deep but snot dribbles down onto my legs. I brush it off hoping no one notices. I miss Mum so much.

Footsteps rush towards me and arms scoop me up out of the chair.

"My Nikki. No you cry."

Gio clutches me high in his arms and kisses my tears. He twirls me softly around under the darkening sky. "The Paola she phone me. I come fast I can. I go get the gun tomorrow. I kill all the cock a roach bang bang. You see, Nikki. You see."

The sadness floats away on a giggle and with his hands tight around my waist I lean back and spread out my arms like wings. "Faster," I say.

And Gio spins.

Francesca jumps to her feet and claps in delight. But I don't miss the scowl Paola darts at Gio.

CHAPTER 32

Mrs Hawthorne – Edinburgh

*M*y sisters are coming for lunch. It will be the first time they've been to the house. It's not that I haven't wanted them to before. I just had to make everything perfect. It wouldn't have done for them to witness all Clarissa's things. If her presence was so prominent, they'd not understand she was in the past.

But she's eradicated now, all her finery heaped into skips and rotting in a landfill. Her local artist landscapes are stripped and replaced with more tasteful prints. The chintz of her and Charles's life banished with Farrow and Ball Manor House Gray. Such a more refined palette.

Except for one thing. This urn in my hands, which is adorned with a hand-painted peacock. Apparently, it was her favourite bird. Who would choose a peacock unless they were pretentious and thought themselves something special? Far more tasteful to choose something simple like a robin or even a sparrow. At least they don't parade around in a flashy manner.

With a grunt of annoyance, I finish the dusting and place the urn back onto the shelf. It would only take a smidgeon of a nudge for it to fall onto these wooden floors. It would certainly smash. Contents spilling out like a clump of cement and I'd grab the hoover and that would be that.

My hand clamps to my mouth. I back away and flop down onto the sofa. I must never utter those words out loud. How awful. Anyone else would protect its precious contents and ensure they pushed it back carefully against the wall, not leave it dangling near the edge. They'd have more respect for death. I twist my engagement ring. It's still a little too tight even though the jeweller widened it. My fault of course. I couldn't admit my hands were much fatter than perfect Clarissa Ballerina and had accepted the alteration with a smile.

Charles had lifted my hand with tears clouding his eyes, saying it was fabulous to see it worn again. Our love had never felt so crowded. Ridiculous to have such hatred for a stranger, a woman I've never met, but she needs to vanish so we can breathe. How hard can it be when she's dead?

Jack barks and scampers past me into the hall. I jump up and follow him through. It'll be Charles back from collecting the Waitrose order for lunch. They've such a delightful selection.

"Hi, baby," he says to Jack and crouches to pat him, checking for cuts, scrapes, or missing paws. I roll my eyes behind his back and ask him, "Did you get everything?"

"Yes, absolutely, and a little something to brighten up the dining room too. Just a minute while I get them from the car."

I carry the buffet tray into the kitchen to unwrap and arrange things on a silver platter. It will be such a treat for my sisters to eat something that's not from Asda. It will brighten up their day. When we were children, my mother thought Findus crispy pancakes were the height of luxury. Thank goodness I've moved up in the world since then. I pop the platter into the fridge, grab my cigarettes and lighter and head for the garden.

"Oh, have you got a moment?" Charles says, shuffling behind me. In his hands is a large bouquet and he holds it towards me when I turn. The scent spins around the hall and his eyes on mine sparkle. Like a child waiting for a gold star and a pat on the back. The flowers are magnificent, but peonies are her favourites, not mine. She spoils everything with her intrusions. I gather them into my arms and grant him a kiss. "They're beautiful, thank you so much, darling." I'm rewarded with a lopsided grin and he takes them back to trim and place in a vase.

I cross the garden, sink onto the bench under the willow tree, light a cigarette and breathe in. The branches trail down around me. Swaying gently in the breeze they help to shroud my shame.

I fidget with a twig, pull off a catkin and roll it gently in my hand. Why have all the men I loved not loved me enough? Am I not smart? Are my tales not witty? Do I not measure up to other women's beauty? I've tried so hard to be what they want, but time after time I've failed. I clench my fist and crush the bud until its sticky sap coats my fingers like blood. Even my father abandoned my mother and left me behind. And I try harder than her to be the perfect partner. Yet it's never enough.

Charles shouts from the terrace. "Your sisters are here." He's bouncing from foot to foot, anxious and unsure of himself. I'd better rescue him, he's never great in social situations.

"Yes, one minute." I lift the cigarette to my mouth, inhale until the glow burns my fingers, then throw it to the ground. I fix a smile to my mouth, smooth the wrinkles from my dress and follow him back in.

Mary and Judy were young when Dad left. It was a Sunday afternoon and they were playing in their bedroom with tea sets and dolls. Mum had let them take a jug of squash upstairs and some Jammie Dodgers for a picnic. I was fifteen, in the next bedroom listening to music, when the arguing started downstairs. It happened most weekends, so I didn't pay much attention at first. They'd shout until it ended in Mum crying and Dad leaving the house with a slam of the front door. In the morning at breakfast, everything would be back to normal, as if it never happened.

But this time their voices were low and I couldn't make out some of the words. I crept down the stairs and stood one step from the bottom where their reflections glimmered in the hall mirror.

Mum wrung a dishcloth through her hands, her face red and blotchy as if she'd been crying and Dad stood at the front door with his shoulders slouched. Dad always stood tall. He crouched enough, when working down the coal mine, that when he wasn't working he wanted to be closer to the sky. So I knew something was wrong. A suitcase was at his feet, the same one he packed for our summer trips to Blackpool. Why would he go on holiday without us?

"I'm going now," he said.

Mum replied, "Okay."

And he picked up the case, turned the latch on the door and walked out.

I stood there, blinking back emotion. Something very bad was happening. I wanted to run back upstairs and cuddle my sisters. Protect them from the heartache that would destroy their innocence. But I was wrong. This was our dad. He'd never leave us. I forced my feet forwards, opened the door and shouted. "Dad?"

But he never turned round, so I chased down the path after him. I tugged at the hem of his suit jacket, asking him where he was going, but he pushed me aside, climbed into his car, pressed down the button and locked me out.

"Go home and look after Mum, she'll need you," he said. Then he drove off. Not even a kiss. How could he leave his princess? I stood there for hours believing he'd come back. Change his mind. But he never did.

And that was the last time I saw him. Until fifty years later when my sister, Judy, phoned and said he was dying.

I brush my tears away. What's wrong with me today? I can't let my sisters see me so fractured. Get a grip, you old fool.

Charles has set up the dining table beautifully. The food looks wonderful and the peonies are the perfect touch. No one need know I hate them. My sisters are seated and Judy has brought her granddaughter, Sophie, along. She jumps up and runs over to me and wraps her arms around my waist in a tight hug. I ruffle her hair. "What age are you now, Sophie? Three?"

She sighs and with her hands on her hips says, "No. I'm five of course."

I laugh and my sisters join in. Sophie's the cutest thing. Judy is lucky.

"The house is beautiful," Mary says. "I love the way you've decorated it all. It's really pretty."

Judy smiles. "Mary's right. You'll have to give us a tour later."

I'm light-headed from their praise. Charles carries in tea, the best china, matching sugar bowl, perfectly presented on a silver tray.

Mary grins. "Do you remember when we were wee and played usherettes with Mum's plastic trays? We wanted to be one when we grew up."

I laugh. "Yeah. We thought it was the best job in the world."

Judy adds, "Because we thought we'd get to see all the films for free."

Mary suddenly gasps and leaps from her chair. "My goodness. I forgot about your ring. I've been dying to see it."

Judy pushes back her chair to join her and I hold my hand up as they ooh and ahh. I blush, hoping they don't ask what shop it came from or realise it's second-hand. They'd not understand. I remove my hand and the threat.

Mary turns to Charles. "It's perfect. I'm so happy for you both."

"Thank you. I'm very fortunate indeed," Charles replies.

My sisters smile. It's not a polite gesture. I know them well enough to understand it's genuine warmth. They like him. As I knew they would. Charles is easy to love.

Sophie is fidgeting beside me, kicking her feet against the table, bored with the adult setting and chat. "Let's eat. Charles, serve the tea. And, Sophie, why don't you come with me and I'll get you some orange juice and a chocolate biscuit. You can watch some cartoons in the living room. Does that sound good?"

"Yes, please, thank you." She stands and places her tiny hand in mine. She has such perfect manners, but then I wouldn't expect anything less from Judy. She brought her boys up with the same decorum.

As we walk through to the kitchen, Sophie jumps up and down. "Oh, what a big television. Can I go through and see it, please?"

I tell her, "Yes," and that I'll be there soon with her snack. And she bounces off, with Jack padding softly behind her.

I've missed out on so much. It's no surprise my sisters are so close to each other and I feel left out. Except for the occasional visits, I've been absent from their lives. Too devoted to my prestigious career and the endless search for love. I'd forgotten how happy I could be when it was just us three.

I grab the orange juice and a couple of biscuits and stroll into the living room. Sophie is standing on her tiptoes, her arms stretched out to the bookcase. She's reaching for the urn.

"Pretty bird. I love peacocks. They're my favourite thing in the world."

My mouth opens in shock. I see what's going to happen. She's not tall enough to grasp it and her fingers are spinning it closer to the edge. A few seconds more and it will teeter and fall. She won't catch it because her hands are too small. With a clatter, it will crash to the floor. Smash. The accidental murder of an unwelcome ghost.

My feet are frozen beneath me. Time slows. My hands tremble and shake. The orange juice splashes out over the glass. Jack scrambles towards me and licks the floor.

We're sitting together on the sofa. Sophie giggled when I jumped towards her, thinking I was playing a game. When I moved the urn higher onto a windowsill, her bottom lip jutted out, but now she's fine.

"The thing is, the vase has a special meaning for your Great Uncle Charles. It belonged to a lady that he loved very much but she's gone now."

Sophie settles back into the cushions, curls her legs up and tilts her head to rest on her hand. Her big blue eyes gaze up. "Is the lady in heaven, like my hamster, Flo?"

Strands of hair have escaped from her pigtail. I lean over and brush them back from her face. "Yes, darling, just like your hamster. Exactly like that."

Her lips widen into a smile that displays every tooth in her mouth. "We have to take good care of the vase then, until she comes back. It happens at Easter, my daddy says."

I plant a soft kiss on her cheek. "Yes. You are so right, Sophie."

She beams, proud of herself and says, "Can you switch on the television please?"

And just like that, she's moved on. It's time for me to leave my childish insecurities behind and do the same.

CHAPTER 33

Ronnie – Liverpool

*H*alf term and I'm sterilising the stench of bedroom lies with non-toxic paint fumes.

I plunge a brush into a tin of Dulux, load it thick and slap my rage onto the wall. Scrawling, over and over, *F U Graham* and *F U Tom* until I'm out of space. Teal Façade, which was darker in the shop, splatters my skin and I'm drenched in sweat. I'll need to douse myself in a bath of turpentine. Pity I can't do the same to them. I crumple to the floor, panting for breath. But shit, it's been worth it.

I've demanded the details of Graham's confession, but he thinks he can gaslight me.

Exhibit A: Misunderstanding – He explains that I was upset that night and due to my heightened emotions, I must have misheard him. He uses air quotes to emphasise what he truly said. *If you've someone in there, Ronnie, I hope you're using discretion.*

It's laughable. I'm a headteacher. I'm programmed to distinguish speech. I wouldn't last long in the job if I expelled students for using the word ruck for fuck.

Exhibit B: Subterfuge – He was drunk and desperately needed a pee, but I wouldn't answer the door, so he just said he'd a confession as an excuse to get in. As if.

Exhibit C: Deflection – He changes the subject. Suddenly becomes interested in an issue at school that will reel me in. "Oh, that problem with the English teacher? I've solved it. But if you don't want to hear…" Of course I do.

Exhibit D: Attack – He doesn't understand why I've become obsessed about something he's never said. Perhaps, he suggests, it's me that needs to confess and not him. I give him that. But I still heard what I heard.

It's pathetic and yet I won't drop it. I just can't. He was going to tell me something, but at the last minute changed his mind. Well, fuck that. I'll never let it go. It will twist in my mind and fester.

I pour some paint into a tray and grab a roller. I need to smooth out the words of my anger or the landlord will think I'm a nutter. It's a shame because it's quite artistic. But if anything were to happen to Graham or Tom, I'd be the police's chief suspect.

Not that I'd hear from Tom slimebag again and Graham's keeping his distance. I've had it with men. And you know what? I can't be arsed with this either. I hurl the roller into the tray, strip to my underwear and stamp down the stairs.

There's a pile of student reports on the worktop in the kitchen, waiting for my signature. But I like to read each one and write a personal note. Not in the mood for that. I open the freezer door and grab the vodka.

I sit on the sofa and throw a drink down my throat. The sting of the alcohol makes me cough. But I like it. There was a guy once. Don't know his name. Kenneth or Kenny or maybe it was Ken. It doesn't really matter. Just another bastard. I used to go to the pub after school when I first started teaching. A quick drink always turned into us staying late and dancing. And he was the DJ. Sigh. A DJ. Should've known better. After he wore me down with how special I was, I thought I'd be the one to tame him.

We dated for six months and at first, it was amazing. I even met his mother and loved her. But then the calls dwindled. He stopped coming around as much and when he did he seldom stayed over. He worked nights and his gigs had become busier, plus his mother was diagnosed with breast cancer. She wasn't coping and he'd moved back in to support her. Of course, I understood, but things felt so different. So I tried harder to make his life easier. Bought him small presents to cheer him up and kept things pressure-free. Until I was shopping in Sainsbury and saw them both, him and his mother, at the checkout.

"I hope you're feeling okay now," I said to her.

"Me?" she said. "Nothing wrong with me, dear. Couldn't be better."

I turned to Kenny who shrugged and winked. "No harm done, hun."

I left my shopping in the trolley and walked out. His lies forcing my head low.

The paint's dried on my skin. I scratch the edges and peel it off then flick it across the room. I should paint more. I like the sting. My mum was always decorating. Once one room was finished, she'd start again somewhere else. Maybe she did it for the same reason.

I draw the bottle to my mouth and swallow some down. I need a pee but can't be bothered moving. I cross my legs and hold it in.

The phone rings. It'll be Graham with today's excuse for why he can't come round. But if I don't answer, I'll spend all night overthinking what he might have said.

"Hey."

"Hi, Ronnie. How're you, gorgeous?"

I sit up straight and edge forward on the sofa. "Tom?"

He laughs down the phone. I want to scream but stifle it in. Have to hear what shit he's going to spout.

"I guess you didn't expect to hear from me. What you up to?"

I gulp back some vodka, place the bottle at my feet and force out a laugh. "Course not. I thought you were away with your job?"

"Ah. That fell through. Last-minute thing, you know?"

Fucking liar. "Aww, right. Shame."

"Anyway, what about you? What you up to?"

That's twice he's asked that now. It's obvious what the fucker is after. "Nothing really. Having a drink and chilling out."

"Sorry about before, Ronnie. I shouldn't have said the things I said or acted like such a prick. That's not who I am. I guess it was the drink and the stress of leaving the next day. I meant it when I said how much I like you. I've missed you these last few weeks."

I missed him too. I'd looked forward to his daily phone calls in school. The rushing to my office, like a teenager again. He'd made me laugh. Softened the edges of the day.

"So what about it, Ron? I'll come round. Make it up to you?"

Hands stray to my arms, scrape the scabs of paint from my skin and my lips transform into a smile.

"You were a bastard, Tom."

His sigh is loud. Dramatic. "I know. I know. Let me show you I'm not that guy. Please, Ronnie. You know me better than that. I was a dick to lose you."

Another gulp of vodka. I swirl it around my mouth, savouring the acidic burn. "Okay."

"Great. I'm outside in the car."

"Outside? Outside my house?" I'm in underwear and stink of sweat. Splattered with streaks of paint. I stand, stumble and lean onto the chair. I've also had too much to drink.

"Give me five minutes, Tom. I need to get changed and run to the loo." I cut him off, run into the kitchen and grab the washing-up bowl. Then scramble upstairs, pausing to cross my legs once or twice as I go.

At the top, I pull my knickers down, hobble through the bath-room door and squat. The gush of piss makes me sigh. But no time to loiter in the minute. I jump up, brush a comb through my hair and throw on some oversized sunnies.

There's a knock on the front door. I run to the bedroom window. Open it wide. Shout "Just a minute," then bend, lift the bowl and haul it over the side to drench the dirty rat.

I laugh and hold my hand to my mouth. I'm scared to look but dying to see at the same time. It's batshit crazy, but he deserves it. I stick my head out the window and look down. "Piss off!" I shout.

"Are you fucking crazy?" Graham shouts. "What the fuck was that?"

My mouth falls open. I pull the window shut and close the curtains. Slouch down to the floor. What the fuck have I done?

Showered and subdued with a glass of red wine, Graham sits on a stool behind me as I stir-fry some chicken and rice.

"So, I take it the piss was meant for Tom?" he says.

I stifle a giggle at the image of Graham standing there flicking piss off his hair. It stung his eyes, he says, and was surprisingly hot.

He coughs. He's either coming down with something or his words are choking him.

"I know about Tom. The night you went to the cinema I saw you both outside. I shouted on you."

So it was Graham's voice after all that I heard.

"My mate didn't have enough cash, so we stopped to grab

some and I saw your face when he handed you a rose. The way it lit up. After that, I couldn't enjoy my night."

I stir the sauce. The ginger tickles my nose and I sneeze. Poor Graham, distracted from fucking around.

"I was furious. Kept thinking about you with him. What did he have that I didn't?"

Welcome to my world, fucker.

"So I left the club early and ran over here. But when you let me in, I could smell him. I knew he'd been here and that you'd slept with him. You were crying, Ronnie. Why would you cry over him?"

The chicken is sticking to the pan. Burning. I stir in the soya sauce. Okay, this is it. He's finishing things.

"I've spent the last couple of weeks working out my feelings. Asking myself why I was so jealous. Today I decided I was ready to talk, but when I saw Tom outside, I blew. Dragged him away from the door and told him to get to lost before I beat him up."

I grab a couple of plates from the cupboard and some knives and forks. The drawer could do with a good clean. The cupboard too.

"That's not like me. So my confession. The one you've dissected with a magnifying glass."

Here it comes. Don't throw the wok at him.

"It was never part of my plan, Ron. But the only answer that made sense is that I must love you."

What do I say to that? He stands. Switches the cooker off, takes my hand and leads me to the bedroom.

The smell of paint is fainter, but there's still a mess everywhere. I lift the plastic sheets from the bed and tell Graham I won't be long in the shower. But he shakes his head and pulls me into a kiss.

I giggle and tumble across the bed. "So you love me, huh?" I tease.

He slaps my arse, says, "Yep, I guess I do," and pulls me back to him. His lips caress the back of my neck but then he stops, points to the wall. "Ronnie, what does futfug mean?"

I laugh and unfurl from his arms and escape from the question. In the shower only one thought dominates. Twirls and swirls inside me.

This is it. I've won.

CHAPTER 34

Nikki – Mondello

I sit up, rip the nylon bedsheet off my body and sigh with relief. I've tossed and turned trying to kick it off for the last hour. A dining chair with stained green padding stands next to the bed. A fan sits on it whirring warm air. Its click-clacking is annoying, but it's not as bad as Gio's snoring. It's the worst I've heard and between the heat, the clacking and his snoring, I can't sleep.

My fingers pinch Gio's nose. He shakes his face left to right, but I hold on tight. His mouth splitter splutters then a grunt rattles from the back of his throat and forces his lips to part. I swear, when I was at a farm with Dad, we saw a fat pig rolling in mud that grunted less than Gio does.

He turns onto his side, muttering, wafting stale garlic around him. I cough and cover my face with my palm. Even sweat's Italian here.

In the darkness, the radio alarm's red numerals flash three a.m. Paola will be coming upstairs to knock on the door soon. We're walking up a mountain to visit the cave of Santa Rosalia. She's some kind of saint but I forget what for. They've hundreds here. People are always carrying crosses and statues, parading in the street under twinkling lights for one saint or another.

A night breeze creeps through the window and I crawl over the mattress towards it, blooming in its faint caress.

Paola loaned me her red halter-neck top to wear. I tried it on last night and I loved how my shoulders looked, even Gio whistled and approved. May as well get ready now. I don't want to be late. Gio grunts and I poke him with an elbow then slip into my flip-flops and head for the shower.

Flecks of turquoise and lemon streak the dawn sky and stain Palermo harbour a shimmering gold. We pause our climb of the mountain and soak in the palette that sprawls far below us. Mum has a painting above the fireplace at home. It's by somebody called Van Gogh and the sky is brushed the same. She bought it from a stall at the Sunday market, where everything was two for a tenner.

Trees shade the pathway and a cool morning breeze drifts around us. I hum our favourite song and clasp Gio's hand.

He draws me to him and kisses my brow. I smile. "It's paradise up here."

He shrugs. "It no more beautiful than you."

The bushes rustle and an emerald lizard flashes in the sunlight as it darts across a rock. I scream and stumble on the cobbled path, but Gio tightens his grip and saves me. A couple jostles past us, the woman pushing a blue buggy laden with bags. She throws me a dirty look. When she turns away, I stick my tongue out.

A rumble of engines. Gio tugs my hand and pulls me back against the yellow and orange wildflowers that pepper the trail. A thistle scratches my leg. Don't they only grow back home? I don't say anything in case Gio thinks I'm daft. A butterfly swirls onto my arm and flutters its blue wings before dashing on. A bus groans around the corner and drives up the middle of the road.

My head snaps to Gio. "A bus? Where's it going?"

"It go the Santuario di Santa Rosalia." He pecks bright orange pollen from his white T-shirt, rolls it between his fingers and flicks it away.

I throw my arms up into the air and pout. "You mean to say we could've got a bus instead of hiking up this mountain for two hours?"

He sticks out his bottom lip and I feel bad. "Aww, Gio. It's not that I'm not having fun, but it's so steep and everyone else has left us behind."

The bus grumbles by us, its wheels heavy, crumbling stone. Shirtless men, slimy with sweat, lean glaring from open windows. Their wolf whistles cling to the dust rising from the trail and blast into our faces. Gio dips his hand into his jeans pocket, pulls a knife, snaps the blade open and jerks his head towards them. It's like a scene from *The Godfather*.

I grab onto his arm. Hold him in place. But his anger rages and he shoves me back further into the wild bushes. I'm on the edge of the cliff. So high up. The sheer drop to the ground makes me scream. My head spins, my legs weaken and I close my eyes. Force my feet back to safety.

The bus is further up the dusty path. Gio is chasing it, shouting insults at the men, demanding they come out and face him. The men are laughing, pointing and carving the air with gestures. You don't need to speak Italian to know what they mean. But except for a glance or giggle, no one else pays them any attention. It's as if this is an ordinary occurrence. I run and catch up with him. This is ridiculous.

His face is scarlet and he's panting for breath. I grab his hand and pull him back. He must want to retreat because his body responds and he moves away. With another yell at the bus, he turns towards me and jabs a finger in my face.

"This why I no like you wear these clothes. These men think you easy fuck. It cause many problems for me."

My stomach tightens and anger burns my cheeks. My fault? I'm the reason grown men are fighting on a mountain like arse-holes? I made him take a knife and chase after a bus, like a maniac? My fault because I wanted to be pretty for once?

"Bastardos!" He runs his hand through his hair, closes the blade and puts it back in his jeans. "The men, they animals, Nikki." He twists his mouth and spits a bubble of saliva to the ground.

"I'm just wearing the same as any other woman here, Gio." My hands tug the red top I was so proud of this morning. "This is Paola's."

His hands rise and clasp each side of his head. "You got the blonde hair. My Papa, he say the skin you have, it too pale. The people, they know you no Italian here. The men sniff you out like the dogs and me have to defend the honour."

Beads of sweat drip from his chin and his T-shirt clings to his damp skin. He peels it off and wipes the cotton across his brow then loops it into the buckle of his belt. I bite the inside of my cheek. The staying home alone in the flat. Not being allowed to go out. The horrible shapeless tent dresses. The arguments about what to wear to the beach. It all makes sense now. He's been locking me up like Rapunzel, keeping me confined and away from outsiders. That's why he preferred me in the granny dresses with my face scrubbed bare. It's not that he thought I was beau-tiful like that. It was the opposite. He believed it made me invis-ible and drab. Someone no one would fancy.

Disenchantment threatens tears in my eyes. I blink them

back. The sun is higher and swirls of creamy butter melt into the turquoise sky. It won't be long now until it grows fat with heat and scorches the land. My hands fumble into my purse and I slip my sunglasses on. When Gio walks forward, arms outstretched to gather me in, I place my palms on his chest and shove him away.

He tilts his head and slowly grins. But I'm not falling for his charms. Not this time. I march up the mountain and he dawdles behind me the rest of the way. Now and again he sprinkles the air with *Bellas*, but I shake them off. For the first time it occurs to me he's really not so different from those stupid guys on the bus. All they see is blonde hair and a halter-top. Maybe that's all he can see too. In this place, the real me is gradually disappearing. All my flavour melting away. Is that what I want?

At the top of the mountain, we enter a small square, dotted with rickety stalls selling statuettes and trinkets. The air is different here. It's refreshing and scented with mulled wine. It's packed with people, but they talk in low whispers as if in reverence to a higher presence. Something grazes past my calf and I step back from a middle-aged man crawling along the ground. Gio pulls me close. "No to worry, Nikki. Some people come from bottom to top of mountain on the hands and knees."

"Why?"

He gives a nod to a stallholder and picks up a statue encased in clear plastic. It's a woman in a nun's brown habit, holding a skull and pickaxe. He twirls it around in his palms, then hands it to me. "This the Santa Rosalia. Long time ago in Palermo is very bad plague. Everybody die very horrible death. Nobody help us. But her save us all." He presses the statue to his lips, closing his eyes and kissing the plastic. "She live in this cave till she die. The people take her bones in parade and next day the plague it gone. People come here for the devotion to her. Some they come on the knees, like the man you see. To give the thanks."

My fingers trace a golden thread in the white marble base. My mum would love her. A collection of saints and crucifixes adorns her bedroom dressing table. She prays to them every night. She'd cherish an Italian addition.

"Gio, let's buy this." He drops his shoulders and turns out his pockets. There's only the blade and a strip of chewing gum.

"I no have the money on me, Nikki."

I sigh. He never has money. Everywhere we go, he pleads poverty. But he's out every day and night working. What's he doing with the money he makes? There are no casinos or bookies here, so he's not frittering it away gambling. Anyway, he said he'd never do that again. Not after last time. He'd not break that promise.

"We come next week. We buy then," he says.

But it's not good enough. I want it now, right at this moment. Otherwise, it will be tarnished with the memory of his cheap excuses. But wait, he's been mentioning a surprise for us. Something that's going to make us happy. That he just needs a little more time to make it happen. I bet it's our own restaurant. That's why he's skint – he's saving, trying to make up for the past.

A tug at my shorts. I look down, imagining another damp body, but my eyes meet the top of Francesca's brown curls. I gather her up into my arms and she hands me some crumpled money.

"Mama, she say buy the Santa Rosalia."

I look across the square past all the different people until I see Paola. She's standing at the steps of a cream church that's built into a wall, she smiles and waves over. She must have been watching me and Gio and seen the discussion. She knew we didn't have the money.

My lashes glisten with tears and I shake my head to show that I can't accept her kindness.

She shoves her hands onto her hips and nods her head up and down indicating I must.

Francesca giggles in my arms and Gio takes the money from my hand and slips it to the stallholder. He doesn't have the same conflict or pride.

I wrap the statue in the tissue paper that hangs from the stall and place it gently into my bag. I'll write and tell my mother later all about it.

Goosebumps spring onto my skin and I exhale a deep breath as we enter the cave. I hold out my hand and Gio clutches my palm to his chest. "Wow, just wow," I whisper.

In front of us stands a white marble statue, backlit in a blue haze. At her feet are hundreds of written notes and she's draped in strings of pearl and ruby necklaces. Gio explains they are all thank-you notes and offerings from people she's helped. The flickering light of more than a dozen candles bathe her glory. I'm not religious, but even I sense the serenity within these musky walls.

A mass is underway, the congregation pat their brows as drops of water splash from brass pipes in the ceiling. Gio leads me towards a glass display and my breath stills. Santa Rosalia reclines inside, gold and white marble sparkling under artificial light. She holds her own skull in her hand and a pickaxe for hacking her way through rocks in the cave. Such beauty. How Mum would love to be here with me.

There's a squeal of voices and a rush of bodies crowd into the cave beside us. It's a slap to the senses. Too boisterous for the presence of whatever rests in this place of worship. I turn to Gio and whisper, "What's going on?"

Far too loud, he replies, "Italians. We no like the rain."

Oh my God. Rain? I bounce on my feet and clap my hands. Finally, after months of harsh sunshine, Santa Rosalia has answered my prayers. I push and weave in and out of the bodies blocking the exit, them going one way, me the other. They smack their lips together and groan as if I'm stealing their parmesan. Gio follows me and shouts my name, asking me to come back, to slow down. I ignore him.

Stallholders cover their wares in sheets of thin blue plastic. Others pack their trinkets into wide wicker baskets as the rain, the glorious rain, pummels around them. I throw my head back, stick my tongue out to taste it and descend the stairs.

Within a few seconds, I'm drenched. Clean. Fresh. Soaked to the bone. Spreading my arms out wide, I circle around. Sacrifice myself to more.

Someone shouts, "You crazy! You die out here catch pneumonia or more."

When some more join in, I pause. An audience has gathered at the top of the church steps. Most of them scowl or stand with their arms crossed. Gio is in the middle with an eyebrow raised in concern. I laugh and shout up. "Come down, Gio, and join me. It's so cool. No more sticky pollen. No more sweat."

He shakes his head and someone pats him on the back as if giving him condolences for having a psycho girlfriend. Maybe I've gone too far. Embarrassed him in front of all these people. Worse than that. Made him look less than a man. Someone who can't control his woman. He won't like that.

But then footsteps flutter down the stone and Paola runs towards me. Mascara smudged under her eyes, hair wet and stringy. She's never looked so beautiful. We glance at each other and giggle. My heart fizzes and flutters with joy.

She clasps her hand at my waist and places mine on her shoulder. In the sweetest voice, she sings the first lines of Elvis Presley's "Return to Sender". And since my Mum's a huge fan, I know every word and join in. Then with a nod and a smile to each other, our feet splash through the puddles and we waltz around the square.

The rain drowns our misgivings and it's just me, her and fresh mountain air.

CHAPTER 35

Mrs Hawthorne – Edinburgh

"*T*ell me, Charles, why don't you watch television with me anymore?"

"Pardon?"

"I find things you'd enjoy all the time and you say yes but then never come and join me."

"That's quite untrue."

We're in the garden eating cheese omelettes for lunch. I usually add ham to mine, but I can't handle the guilt of eating meat anymore. It's not as if he ever says anything, but his eyes narrow and his lips move a fraction before snapping tight. The unspoken words flavour my meal with his distaste. This way is better, less stressful, and I sneak a burger when I'm out shopping with my sisters.

The garden's losing its summer blush and the cold nip in the air has snatched the light from its fading blossom. Even the willow is bare and neglected. Leaves litter the lawn in brown and fawn. Charles mutters at something in the newspaper, turns the page and I wrap my cardigan tighter around me. Jack scrambles up, pushes his nose in my lap and I dip a hand into my pocket for his treat. He runs off happily, munching away.

When my sisters and I were young, we danced in autumn, up and down hills in Princes Street Gardens. Dad chased us. Mum stood by, biting her nails and begging him to slow down before one of us fell. We'd laugh, run faster, kicking and crunching through the leaves.

I loved the crackles under our feet, the snap of the dried leaves, the giggles of our youth. Even if I could be bothered now, it wouldn't sound the same.

I cradle the cup of tea to warm my hands and try again.

"Charles, what are you doing every night in the summer-house?" The place I've never been allowed to decorate. The place that's always locked. He peers over his glasses, closes the newspaper and lays it down on the table. The smell of leftover egg catches my breath.

"Just listening to music or playing piano, that's all."

"But you're in there for ages."

"Sometimes I read."

I gather and stack the plates, place the dirty cutlery on top. The dredges of tea are sloshed into the lavender bush then I hook the cups on my fingers. "But we don't spend any time together, Charles."

He laughs. "You do say such silly things. Let me help you there. It's about to rain."

I sigh. Even laced with laughter his tone is dismissive. At first, he went in to practise piano once a week for an hour or so. It annoyed me because I'd love to have heard him play but he said he wasn't good enough for an audience. I attempted to persuade him otherwise on many occasions but always failed. Lately, he practises a lot.

I rinse the remnants of egg from the plates and pop them into the dishwasher. I won't switch it on yet. I'll wait until after dinner.

I walked into the summerhouse once, just before I moved in, to ask him what he wanted for lunch. He was startled as if he'd forgotten who I was. Now he keeps the door locked even when he's in there.

I finish wiping down the worktop and Charles hands me a glass of white wine.

"Shall we watch that new sci-fi film you mentioned last week?" he says.

It's a tad early for wine, but I take a sip anyway, nod my agreement and follow him through. I shouldn't have to push him to want to spend time with me. During the day it's fine. But in the evenings he disappears and, like that night after dinner at his friends, the strains of her funeral song drift from the garden to taunt me. For the last week, he hasn't come to bed. For some reason, we don't discuss it.

Jack jumps up onto the sofa and I let him curl around my feet. His fur is soft from his bath this morning. He nudges his nose into my pocket and I relent and give him another snack. Charles smiles, reaches for my hand, lifts it to his mouth and kisses it.

Something's missing from the bookcase. I can't quite place what it is. All our photographs and trinkets are there but the silver candlesticks are odd. They seem out of balance and are placed too close together. It's Clarissa's urn. They stood on either side of it but now there's an empty space. Charles must have moved it. But where to? He wouldn't have thrown it out, that's for sure.

To boost my confidence I take another sip of wine and whisper as if it's too harsh to say out loud. "What's happened to the urn?"

His thumb strokes my palm and he crosses his legs. I smile, encouraging him to speak, but inside my stomach flutters. Am I about to destroy the tranquillity of the love we share?

"You're quite right. I really must make sure I come to bed rather than falling asleep on the sofa downstairs."

"But what are you doing down here? I came down last night and you weren't anywhere to be seen. Then I saw a light shine in the garden from the summerhouse. You can't be playing piano at two in the morning?"

He drops my hand and stands. "I'll take Jack out for a walk. Then afterward we can settle down in peace to watch the film. I'll just run to the bathroom first. That's if you don't mind?" Jack clambers down from the sofa and runs around Charles's feet, tail wagging at the mention of a walk and Charles tickles him under his chin.

"Yes, of course, that's fine."

He leans over and pecks a kiss on my cheek and heads upstairs. My legs tense and I wait a minute then run to the hall. He always leaves his keys there. They jingle together as I fumble through them searching for the right one. Which one is it? The toilet flushes. I jump and they clatter to the floor. I pick them up and start again. His footsteps on the staircase tell me that he's coming back down. It must be the gold one. The others are the same as mine. I pull it from the ring and run back and settle on the sofa. The key pressed tight in my hand.

"I might go for a pint with Robert while I'm out," Charles says.

"Great, then I've time for a bath before you're back." I wave goodbye and close the door as he tugs Jack down the driveway. Am I really going to go through with this? It's wrong to invade his privacy. I would hate it if he did that to me, but I really have to find out what's going on here. To understand why he leaves me alone so much and evades my questions. But most of all, is Clarissa's urn in there? A future wife has a right to know.

I cross over the lawn and walk down past the willow tree, the bench and the forget-me-nots. I hesitate outside on the verandah. There's still time to change my mind, but then I'd never know. I turn the key in the lock. It clicks. My lips dry. I moisten them with a sweep of my tongue and open the door.

The room's dark. Charles explained the piano has to be protected from direct sunlight as it can affect the tuning. So the Venetian blind on the window is always closed. There's a faint smell of mildew and dead flowers. It hasn't seen fresh air in a while. I switch on the light and step back in shock.

There are photographs of Clarissa on every surface, including the walls. He must have rescued them from the skip. She hasn't vanished at all. She's present, here in this perverse mausoleum, and he spends his time in here beside her. Why? Can't he embrace the love in front of him, the one that's alive?

The photographs are going in the bin, even if I've to put them there myself. We'll discuss it when he comes back from the pub and if he can't agree, I'm leaving. I can't live with this madness anymore. But it won't come to that. Charles is kind. Maybe we happened too soon and he needed longer to let go. He must have found it so hard and then hid all this from me because he was ashamed of his actions. I'll help him. We'll put an end to this. But should I say I've seen it, or give him more time?

Where's the urn? It must be in here too. Maybe we could end this madness by scattering her ashes at sea. He did say they used to walk the dogs at the beach. It would be the perfect resting place.

I tilt my head to one side. There's something on the sofa. A piece of paper. An empty glass sits on the floor beside it. As if Charles has sat there many times with a whisky and read it. I chew the inside of my cheek. It couldn't be, could it? Is this the letter? The one that made Charles cry all those months ago? I walk over and pick it up. I scan the salutation. *Your forever wife, Clarissa.*

There's a tightness in my chest as I begin to read.

CHAPTER 36

Ronnie – Liverpool

"And then there's *Ludus*, meaning playful love, like when you have a one-night stand or a casual thing. And *Storge* is the kind of love you have for your mum or dad. And..."

"Will you shut the fuck up about Greeks and their stupid definitions of love, Graham?" I shove a piece of toast in my mouth and pull on my coat.

He laughs and picks up his briefcase. "I'm just saying that there are different kinds of love, that's all. That one word doesn't cover everything."

"No. You're trying to wriggle out of saying you loved me. I'm not dumb." It's been months and he's never said it again. Instead, all I get is this boring bullshit about what someone said about love two thousand years ago. What has that got to do with anything? I've obviously not won yet, because he's still a shifty bastard. *Ludus* and *Storge* and the rest of that crap is some kind of strategy. I just haven't worked out what, yet. But I'll succeed in the end.

"You all set for the big day, Ron? This is the promotion you always dreamed of."

Looking at his image in the glass, he adjusts his hair, checks from every angle. He loves that mirror more than me. Someday I might smash it. With a swing of my hip, I nudge him out of the way.

"You're obsessed with how you look." I check my own reflection. Hair is fine. I bare my teeth. Lipstick too.

Hands land on my shoulders. He twirls me around to face him. "You've got this. You're tenacious and you know your stuff inside out. They'll be lucky to have you. Go show them what you're made of."

This is what gets to me. One minute he's talking shit about Greeks. And the next he's my rock, the one person who truly has my back.

"But what about the presentation? I'm not sure it's clear."

He leans in and kisses me on the nose. There's something tender about being kissed there. More protective and sweet than sexual. It's like how a father might kiss his daughter. I'm not going there. Not today of all days.

"It's shit hot, Ron. We worked on it all night. You're gonna blow them away."

He's right. We sat all night together, writing and re-writing and refining, his sharp commentary helping me. Guiding me.

I shrug. He runs his hand through my hair and pulls my mouth to his. I push him away.

"What the fuck you doing, Graham? You're messing up my hair."

He throws his hands up and backs away, laughing. "Sorry, I got carried away. I'll save it for later." I raise my eyebrows. Graham can bring any situation back to sex. But at least it means he still likes me. Or am I just more easily available?

A taxi horn blasts from the street. There used to be a time when the driver would leave his car and knock gently on your door, but not anymore. The world's in too much of a hurry now for such manners. Lifting a hand to my mouth, I blow Graham a kiss and head out. Briefcase in hand, he follows. "Good luck!" he shouts and then sets off along the pavement for work.

The taxi driver asks where to and we drive off.

The call had come last Friday, asking me if I would be interested in taking over a large failing school. I was more than ready for a new challenge, so I'd agreed to be interviewed today. If I get the job, it will be a huge jump in salary and a boost to my confidence. Even as a headteacher I feel like an imposter in boardrooms cramped with men from the right schools with the right accents. But if they make me an offer and I relocate to a different city, what will it mean for Graham and me?

A group of adults stand at the school gates, puffing away on cigarettes. Weeds grow on either side of the neglected driveway and paint peels from the signage. The kids deserve much more than this. I pay the driver, ignoring the urge to jump back in and go somewhere else. But then, isn't this the only thing I'm good at? The one thing I excel in?

"It's rough here, better watch your bags, love." He winks.

"Just up my street then. It's much easier to polish a turd than people think, you know."

He laughs. "You'll need a big duster for this place."

I smile. These fuckers haven't met me yet. They're going to discover it's a life-changing experience.

Fried chicken sizzles from the kitchen, paprika drifting along the air to welcome me home. Graham's a fabulous cook, but every surface will be covered in gloop. Of course, he'll have a perfect dab of flour on his nose for me to kiss away. He does it every time. It was funny at first, but it's just one of his signature moves, to go along with the recipe. I slip out of my heels and stretch my feet. Bliss.

As I enter the living room, a tingle of apprehension crawls up the back of my neck. Candles burn from every direction and the table is decorated with a white tablecloth and rose petals. A silver bucket filled with champagne in crushed ice stands beside it. A card is propped against a wine glass, my name circled within a love heart.

It's unusual for him to go to so much effort. Normally we eat from trays while watching a film. Something is going on. He's either seeking forgiveness for something he's done or buttering me up for what's to come.

"Hey! How'd it go, baby?" His arms wrap around me and I rise on my toes and lick the flour from his nose as expected.

A sweep of my arm takes in the room with its decorations. "What's all this in aid of?"

His bottom lip droops out and he fakes a sob. "You're such a hard woman to please. Don't you like it?"

I like it, but what's the emotional cost of my enjoyment? Nothing comes without motive from Graham. It wouldn't surprise me if some random nude jumped out of a cupboard to join us in a threesome.

"Chill, Ronnie. I thought I'd show you how proud I am of you. I wanted you to know I'm here for you, no matter the outcome today. That's it, nothing else."

He walks back to the kitchen, shaking his head, and a pang of guilt twists my stomach. I'm being a bitch. He's doing a nice thing here, yet instead of thanking him, I'm investigating him like a criminal. Any other girlfriend would have been happy by this show of solidarity. But then, Graham isn't the typical boyfriend. And I've been stabbed in the heart too many times in the past to fall into the traps of grand gestures. I no longer mistake hearts and flowers for sincerity.

Graham returns with platters of fried chicken and herby rice which he places in the centre of the table with a smile. His moods never settle into a long-drawn sulk. Everything is always too easy and light to shake his world with any real depth. Nothing matters to him. The only thing of real substance is himself.

When the first bite of salty chicken crunches in my mouth and a drip of grease runs from my lips, a moan of pleasure escapes. "It's good, huh?" he says. I nod my agreement and as he offers me a napkin our hands touch for the briefest of moments. It's enough for our eyes to catch and for my guard to soften.

"They offered me the job and I accepted. It will mean moving away, but I knew that anyway."

This is it. This is the turning point. If I transfer somewhere else, what about us? I fill my mouth with a spoonful of rice and the words hang heavy in the air between us. It won't be long before the full implications land on his shoulders.

Graham lifts a napkin, cleans his hands and stands. With a smile, he lifts me from the chair and spins me around in the air. "I knew they'd see you like I do."

I laugh and tap his back. "Put me down, Graham. I'm not a little girl." I hate being spun around like a child. Something about it is so belittling and it makes me queasy.

He pours champagne and toasts my success. I'm relieved he's happy for me and is proud of what I've accomplished. But he hasn't said anything yet about what our future together will be like.

He grabs the card from the table and thrusts it into my hands. He's always believed in me since the first day we met. But if I don't find out where the promotion leaves us, I'll overthink it all night.

"Now don't go crazy, Ronnie, but ..." He's concentrating on his glass, spinning the champagne around inside. A wave of heat rushes to my head. If it's him or my career, then the career will always win. It's the only part of my life that's dependable and solid. There's just no competition.

"But you know how I've been going on about the Greeks and their definitions of the different types of love?"

What the fuck. Not this again. I nod and take a slug of champagne, wishing it was something stronger, like a double vodka.

"The Greeks have it all sussed. My religious upbringing was stifling. All the rules and door knocking. There was only one truth about love and to think otherwise was eternal damnation. But we don't have to fit into that mould. We can make our own rules."

His foot taps against the floor. Where's he going with this? I resist the urge to roll my eyes, as he rubs the back of his neck and exhales.

"I was scared to tell you I love you in case everything changed. In case it meant we were put in a cage and the lock on the door engaged. But that doesn't have to be us. We don't need to be trapped by love. We'll be scholars. Approach it from the broader sense, like the Greeks."

My hands stroke my necklace. My head tilts to the left. Let him finish. Don't interrupt.

"I mean we're in love, but we can still be us. Still be playful with others but realise it doesn't affect the many kinds of love we have for each other."

He takes a sip of his drink and places it down. From behind the cushion, he retrieves a Tiffany blue box and kneels in front of me. I press my fist to my mouth and step back. Tears rush to my eyes. What's he doing?

"Marry me, Ronnie. Let's live our own kind of love."

My mouth drops open. He laughs and reaches for my hand. I let him take it. Then my voice returns. "I haven't even met your parents."

"They won't be a part of this. Their religion would forbid it. It will just be us. We'll marry here in Liverpool, or in our new place after we get settled. I'll come with you. We'll get a house together. I can work from anywhere."

The proposal spins inside my head. I can't wait to undo the white ribbon to see what type of ring he chose. But is this what the Greek shit was all about? All that rubbish about how many different forms of love exist. Just an academic excuse to swing his dick. His declaration of love doesn't mean a thing.

When will he ever grow up from the teenage *sow your oats* crap? It's pathetic. Every man wants a woman to come home to and one to fuck down a dark alley. But at some point, they have to make a fucking choice. One or the other. They can't have burgers and steak every day, the greedy bastards.

I sigh. Maybe that's unfair. He's never had the freedom before. Not when all the rest of us did. And his true commitment is to me. Hasn't he just shown that with an engagement ring?

Yes, he wants to have sex with other people, but his emotions and his loyalty remain solely with me. The game could have ended with me moving away, us breaking up, but instead, I've won. Not just won his love but won a marriage proposal. And he'll never go behind my back. Not when he has a pardon. Graham will never leave me. He'll always be by my side and, one day, he'll get bored with all the sexual conquests.

It's true. We'll have our own kind of love. Love that's based on honesty.

"Ronnie?"

I jump into his arms. "Yes. Yes. I'll marry you."

I've not been for many years. Time softens the edges, but it's just a blister of emotions waiting to burst. A song. The way someone walks. The scent of a perfume. Even the glimpse of a colour she once wore. And the pain seeps out to drown me. I don't talk about her. I can't. The agony's too raw. But I have to go back. I need to face her. Tell her that her daughter is getting married.

CHAPTER 37

Nikki – Mondello

io stares silently out the window in the back seat of the car. Still angry about our visit to Santa Rosalia. The rain. Paola and me dancing. Men whistling from the bus and my red halter-neck top. He doesn't want to go to the beach.

I sit beside him, bare legs fused to the hot leather seat. I nudge closer to him, my skin stinging from its sudden release. He slides further away and continues to watch the countryside fly past. He's been like this for weeks. A big man sulking like a little boy.

Phillipo switches on the radio. "We need the musica," he says.

It blares into life, and I sing along to the English lyrics, excited for a day out, but Gio stretches between the seats and switches it off. Such a big pig. I slump back and cross my arms across my chest. He's always spoiling my fun. He'd best snap out of it before we get to the beach or there won't be much point.

Slender tree branches skim over the car and a few green leaves scatter into the sunroof and onto my lap. I caress them through my fingers, wishing things were better. Flashes of colour grab my attention and I look up. An orange grove just like the one when we first arrived. Where Gio leapt out of the car, climbed into the trees and brought me some to taste. I tap his arm. "Gio! The orange trees! Do you remember?"

He glances over, takes in the trees swollen with fruit and looks away. But not before the corner of a grin flashes on his face. "Don't you remember? It was so hot, and you opened the oranges and gave them to me, and it was such a relief to quench my thirst."

He turns, his grin wide.

"I was like the Tarzan," he says and beats his chest. I laugh and he joins in. It's what you have to do with little boys. Talk them around. Flatter their ego and make them feel tall.

Phillipo drops us off in town and we stroll along the Strada Statale. It's so different from Portobello. Huge pastel houses line the street, all of them with high metal gates. Rich people protecting themselves from everyone else. On the other side of the road, palm trees line the pavement. People stroll along, hand in hand like us, men in shorts and white T-shirts, women in bright strappy dresses. I smile as the breeze ruffles over my legs and arms. I'm just like them for once.

The sea lures me closer. I slip from Gio's hand, skip along the sandy pavement and run through the trees. Gio calls me back. "No, Nikki. This beach not for you and me. This the private."

I screw up my nose. The people here are having fun, screaming and laughing in shimmering water and I want to be a part of it.

"We go the public beach," Gio says and I wait until he catches me up then follow. We amble past a string of coffee shops, bars and bakeries that sweeten the air with sugary scents until Gio stops in front of a street vendor and I bump into the back of his legs. Stretching an arm above his shoulders to a rack full of sunglasses and inflatables, he grabs a pink hat from a hook, pays for it, then arranges it on top of my head.

"This keep you safe," he says and plants a kiss on my forehead which is now shaded under a wide floppy brim. I twirl around showing it off, a warmth in my belly that the sun didn't heat.

He turns and leads us off the path and down a couple of steps onto glittering sand. Beach towels in vibrant colours are spread together like the patchwork quilt my granny made back home. Weaving in and out of them, from one end of the beach to the other, a couple of guys selling ice-cold drinks chant. *Aranciata, Coca-Cola, Limonata*. My tongue wets my dry lips.

Bursts of laughter sprinkle around us as a group of teenagers leap into the sky to bat a bright yellow ball back over a high white net. The sea glistens behind them, the colour of turquoise, just like the photos I've seen in holiday brochures. Further out, where boats sail, bouncing on waves, it's a deeper blue, almost a navy. It shines and ripples in the sunshine, enticing me in. Welcoming me home.

Through clouds of suntan oil heavy with coconut and mango, we cross the sands and place our beach towels down next to each other. I jump up and down, excited.

Gio laughs and sits down, spreads cream onto his hairy legs, sunglasses hiding the glances he throws around at all the pretty ladies. I've no time for any of that nonsense and whip off my sandals. Toes curl in the heat of the sand and a bliss runs through me that only the sea can offer. I moisten my lips and the salt on my tongue tastes like freedom.

Pulling my sundress over my head and throwing my hat to the sand, I dash in my red bikini to the water. In Scotland, the sea is always cold even in summer. We whimper in, a piece of skin at a time. But here it's like a warm hug that cradles you up. I close my eyes, float on my back, arms and legs stretched out like a starfish, and let the water renew me. Replenish my soul.

My hand hits something and I squeal in fright, but it's only a shoal of tangerine fish swimming alongside me. Such a beautiful experience, it fills me with lightness. I might stay here forever. Be one with the waves. Even the chatter from the beach soothes my worries away. Makes me feel a part of something special.

A push. A pull. Something lunges from below the sea and capsizes me. Tips me over face down and pushes me deep into the water. I flap around, gulp a mouthful of sea and scream. What's happening? Am I going to drown?

Gio seizes me, lifts me high in the air and splashes me back down.

"Nikki! Here come the sharky. Watch out. It eat you all up." He laughs.

"Gio! You big idiot." I splash his face and he roars and splashes back and soon we're like toddlers in a paddling pool, drenching each other, our shrieks mingling with the bustle from the shore until we tire ourselves out. Jumping onto his back, I wrap my arms around his neck, legs around his belly and he clutches my ankles in his hands. Safe.

"Look, Gio." I point towards lemon paddle boats that sway on water further along from us. "Can we hire one, pretty please?"

"Let's go," he says and I wrap my arms tighter around him, feeling like a princess as he paddles us down.

Giggling, cheeks sore with laughter, I poke Gio in the side. We can't make the boat go forward no matter how hard we try. It's him, he's pedalling too fast, and even when I tell him to slow down, we just circle around like a couple of fools. Until, eventually, we get stuck in wet sand and no matter what we do we can't budge our way out. It's weird how others sail by us, perfectly fine. Maybe they balance each other out better than him and me. Throwing his hands in the air, Gio jumps overboard and swims up behind me.

"You do the cycle, Nikki. We beat this." Placing his palms on the back of the boat he pushes hard. I wriggle in excitement as we glide off, finally leaving the shallows of the beach.

"Wait me," he shouts.

And I giggle and throw a smile over my shoulder. "Hurry up then, slowcoach, and jump back in."

Apartments jostle against each other, all slightly different shades of orange. Balconies with shuttered windows, keeping the heat out, overflow with plants. Their flowers of lilac and cream trail down to the street and cheer it up. Chatting loudly, families with pasta and wine sit outside small cafés. A group of old women dressed head to toe in black sit at the edge of the pavement shelling crab.

As we idle along, the open doorway of a shadow-lined shop reveals shelves of figurines and crockery and bric-a-brac.

My feet dance in pleasure. Gio has money. I'm going to make the most of the moment. It's time to brighten up the flat and make it more like our home. Gio has already passed by, but I call him back and show him the shop. He groans, but I'm already making my way inside.

Two men with bushy moustaches, it must be a thing with Italian men, are leaning on the frame of the door. Gio bustles over so that he passes between them before I do and I sneak in behind. The men all exchange glances, but nothing is said. I can't be bothered with all the silly macho games. The shop is narrow, but its shelves stretch off forever with hidden treasure. It's a little piece of heaven and I clap my hands in excitement and delve in.

I'm rummaging among some pieces of fabric when Gio says, "Nikki. We here for hours and hours. It very long time. No?" He's talking rubbish. It hasn't even been half an hour. But he's getting fidgety, so I snatch up my choices, and he pays the shopkeepers who are now standing behind a big old-fashioned till.

We leave, and outside the sun hits me like a sledgehammer. But I'm holding a few of my new things tight, and I don't even mind when Gio mutters about having to carry the rest back on the bus in this heat. I can't wait to show Paola all my new stuff.

~

I keep changing my mind about where things should go, but it's such fun. Is the little white bookcase okay here or would it look better over by the window? The flat already feels less of a dump and I've only started doing it up. Imagine how pretty it will look in a few months. Deciding to leave the bookcase where it is, I stand back from it all and look around at my hard work. The painting of Mondello beach on the wall looks gorgeous. On the dining table, like sand under sunlight, spirals of shimmering gold sparkle from a large glass bowl. Perfect.

"Nikki! Enough of the decorating. You need get ready for christening," Gio shouts from the bedroom.

I scrunch up my nose. His nephew's christening. They're a big deal in Scotland but here in Sicily, the naming of a child is something else. It's sort of sacred. No member of the family would dare miss it. I can't be bothered to visit them all, especially the father with his gloomy dark stares. I'd rather bathe here in all the sparkles.

We walk along the street to the cream church. Crowds of people are already outside and I can tell instantly I'm dressed wrong. All the women are in bright colours, short skirts, flashing silk scarves. I'm dressed like a nun in a long black skirt and high collared white blouse. Gio had insisted, and I'd gone along with it to keep the peace. Everyone files into the church and I clasp Gio's hand and try to loiter at the back.

There's a hush. Phillipo holds a tiny bundle draped in white satin and lace, his wife by his side. Together, they step down the passageway between the pews. The priest is waiting at the font, watching them solemnly.

At the altar, the priest lifts the baby into his arms. For the first time, I get a clear look. Thick black hair. Red cherub lips. So tiny and innocent. Light from stained-glass windows falls on her like a blessing from God. The ceremony begins. I can't follow everything that's said, but I take in the solemn faces of those around me and let their emotions draw me in. My mum would love this so much.

The priest gives his final blessings and now the pious expressions give way to cheering and clapping. Everyone rises and clusters around the baby, kissing cheeks, hugging and slapping backs. Then we all spill out into the church courtyard.

Gio turns to me, wraps me up in his bear-like arms and kisses my neck. "We do this one day," he whispers. I nod, feeling fuzzy and warm inside. He takes my hand and we join the crowd as it meanders along the road to his father's house.

Tony's home is like a fairy tale. In the garden outside, strings of tiny pale lights glint among the tree branches and lemons and oranges tang the air. The tinkle of glass is everywhere. It's magical, and my eyes fill with tears. His dad stands under a frangipani tree greeting everyone, kissing all the men and women. Welcoming them all in. I drift to the side of the garden in case he ignores me again.

Gio has vanished and, without him beside me, I nibble at the skin around my fingers. All the conversation is in a language I don't fully understand. All the family members I've never met, but who are bonded by love. I shrink into the hedge.

There's a wooden bandstand at the end of the garden, the musicians playing songs I don't recognise. Even a bit of Frank Sinatra would be better than this. I tap my foot on the pathway, so it appears as if I'm joining in.

His face dead serious, Gio's dad appears and I'm a bit frightened by his presence. The last time he even refused my handshake. My feet still, my fingers twine together behind my back. But then he smiles and lifts his right hand. I'm not sure what he means but he nods encouragement and so I put my fingers in his.

He sweeps his arm around my waist and draws me into the centre of the garden, right in front of the band. Suddenly the music makes sense. It might be old folk tunes, but the beat is simple. My feet follow his, and soon we're waltzing in the moonlight under the twinkling stars. He draws me closer to him and in broken English, he whispers, "First, I no like you. But you good girl for the Gio. You keep him under what you call it, the thumb. He has the need of that."

Tilting my head back, I look up into his eyes and smile. It isn't the welcome I would have wanted. But it's something. He's happy someone is willing to say to Gio when enough is enough.

We swirl around and eventually, the song comes to an end and he lifts my hand to his mouth and plants a kiss there. The family breaks into applause. I've passed some kind of test. A girl, probably a cousin, pats my arm as I walk back to the comfort of the garden edges. There's a bounce in my step that wasn't there before.

"*Dovè Gio?*" I ask her.

She scowls and points across the fairy lights in the shrubbery to a wooden shed set aside from the main house.

"The men. They there. But you no go." She laughs.

But I'm dizzy with excitement. He missed the dance. He'd have been so proud. I run across the grass to the shed and grasp the door handle. I pause, heart fluttering with excitement. Gio is going to sweep me up into his arms when I tell him what's happened and all the men will cheer.

I burst my way inside. A small wooden table sits in the centre of the room. Half a dozen men are seated around it. There's a mountain of cash in the middle, and cards are strewn around its edges. An older man is drawing the money towards him, grinning widely. Gio has his head in his hands, moaning, his fingers scratching at his skin.

I look at the cards. There are no casinos here. No way to reach the horse racing tracks. No convenient bookies for a fool to throw away all his money. But, somehow, Gio has found a means. All those nights when he was supposed to be working extra shifts suddenly make sense. It wasn't work that called him. It was his disease. The mistress he couldn't reject. That's why we live in a pigsty with a cockroach infestation. That's why he never has any money. He hasn't changed. I tiptoe backward, pull the door closed behind me, and flee from the garden and Gio's lies.

CHAPTER 38

Mrs Hawthorne – Edinburgh

My Dearest Charles,

If you are reading this, I am long gone. No longer of this world but in another place where you cannot reach me. Yet I am sorry to have left you all alone.

I do hope that I battled death and didn't surrender to His call too easily. That you were proud of me in those last few days. But He was always going to win at some point. We both knew that. Thankfully, I went first, because to live without you would have been like living in my own personal hell. Forgive me for my selfishness, but you cannot imagine the torture your passing would have caused in every fibre of my being.

You know I loved you deeply. It was there in every touch, every word, and it sits within every memory. Look for it, Charles, if you must. It's easy to find in the photographs of our life together.

That girl, only seventeen, pirouetting on the stage, dizzy from all that glittered around her. But only ever needing the love of one man. The one that gave her the confidence to dance. You, my darling.

That glance only the camera spied. That touch of my hand on your

226

arm. *That smile you missed. Look, Charles. Look back, and you'll find it. Never doubt our love.*

Do keep playing piano. And if at times you feel it's too hard, or a song reminds you of our time together, think of me. And I'll be there right beside you, every time you need me. Play not for you, but for us, my love.

Yesterday when you served me soup (I am so sorry I couldn't eat it), you turned your face to the side. To hide how tears had blinded your eyes. It reminded me of our first kiss. Do you remember it? You were so shy. I'd liked you for such a long time but each time I gave you a hint, you missed it. Therefore, I asked you to be my boyfriend. Your hands flew to cover your face, but I could still see the blush underneath. I leaned in, parted your palms and kissed you. Right there in the school playground. And from that day onwards it was just us. We ruled the world, Charles, you and I.

But I am gone now and what I say next will distress you. I do so with pain in my heart for the little boy that blushed and will shrivel with hurt. Please remember, it doesn't tarnish our love or how much I adore you. But I can't take it to my grave. So, I present the facts.

I had an affair. It's no one you know, and I take his name with me. It lasted five years. You were so busy with work, and I was disappearing into the role of the Professor's wife. I used to be the star of the stage, the one adored by hundreds of fans every night, peonies thrown at my feet, my face on every poster, in every paper. But suddenly I was the understudy. Wilting within the endless graduations, the banquets with dry academics and the never-ending damp handshakes.

I know it's a cliché to say that it meant nothing. But it didn't, Charles. You had so much, all that adoration. What was wrong with me having some too? I don't expect you to forgive me. I know that's an impossible thing to ask. I only ask you to understand. I know you've room in your heart for that.

But if you can't, destroy this letter and throw all my possessions out into the cold. Burn our memories and curse me to the gods. However, if you do that, Charles, you deny the love between us. You cheapen it to the indiscretion of a silly affair. We were much more than that. We were the epitome of love.

If you ever sense someone behind you, if you ever feel a hand rest on your arm or hear a sigh of longing, of loss, it will be me, Charles. Watching for you. Waiting for you. For how could I ever truly leave my own dear boy? I'll be with you. Always and forever.

Remember us and, if you doubt us, look for the love. You'll find it.

Your everlasting wife,

Clarissa

The most beautiful girl in the world.

CHAPTER 39

Mrs Hawthorne – The Beach

*E*verlasting wife? A hot rage flies to my fingertips. I want to rip up the letter, do what Charles should have done in the first place. Instead of sitting there in his summerhouse reading it nightly. My fingers grip the paper tight. But it's a seashell I hold, not paper, and it's unyielding. It falls from my hands and splashes into the waves.

I pat the pockets of my cardigan, turn around, and search the sand at my feet. Ronnie and Nikki are further up the beach, their gaze hot against my face.

The Gatekeeper strolls down to greet me. I'm growing to hate his grin.

"They say that eavesdroppers always learn of things they wish they hadn't. Does that also hold true for those who read other people's letters?"

"How dare you? I've got a right to know how Charles feels."

"Right? What a curious sense of the difference between right and wrong you possess. Snooping and prying into poor old Charles and his petty little secrets."

For the first time, I understand Ronnie's anger. I want to slap him and watch that smile slide off his face.

Ronnie barges between us, shoving past him to stand beside me. "She's every fucking right. That bitch is trying to control Charles even though she's dead."

The Gatekeeper takes a step back, hands held high to the sky. "You, of all people, Ronnie. You? You seek to defend Mrs Hawthorne and her obsession with someone long gone?"

Nikki walks across the sand to stand alongside us. "That's not what Ronnie is saying. The past should bury the past. Charles needs to let go of Clarissa. Ronnie is right and so is Mrs Hawthorne."

The Gatekeeper laughs. "Is this our Bastille moment? Are you implying I'm abusing my position of power?"

Ronnie clenches her fists and storms up to him. She's fearless in a way I envy. "Fuck you and your Bastille Day. She just found out her man has been lying to her. And so has Nikki with that arsehole and his gambling. And me? Am I in some sort of better place?"

I've found her so hard to bear, with her foul mouth and her fouler morals, falling prey to Tom as a gambit for snaring someone else. But Graham has proposed to her. Yes, it would be an open marriage. Yes, that disgusts me. But I've read Clarissa's letter. I've plumbed the depths of a different kind of depravity. And yet I want to make things work with Charles. So are Ronnie and I really so different?

A cold wind springs up, scattering grains of sand across the beach. I shiver against the unexpected chill. "Ronnie," I say, "I'm glad for you. If this marriage with Graham leads you to your own kind of happiness, I wish you the best."

Her eyes narrow as she scans my face, looking for signs of false encouragement.

Nikki steps forward. She's biting her bottom lip. "But how can you say that? He just told her he'd be unfaithful. That he'd have sex with other people. How is that marriage?"

Ronnie flinches as if the unvarnished truth from the mouth of a child has punched her in the stomach. Compromise. Accommodation. Nuance. These are words that don't translate well into an eighteen-year-old's language. But Ronnie and I understand each other. I smile at her.

"So, what about his gambling, Nikki?" Ronnie says. It isn't a challenge. She's in earnest, her eyes imploring Nikki to follow her own star. "Me and Mrs Hawthorne have made our decisions. All you did was run away from the card game like a silly little girl."

I reach out and draw Nikki to me. "She's eighteen, Ronnie. Would we have acted any differently at her age? She lives in a world of black and white. We live in a world of greys. I have faith in her. I have faith in her dance in the rain."

Ronnie pauses, but a smile grows over her features and she joins us, seeking out Nikki's hand. "I've faith in you too, Nikki. But I've none in Giovanni. Be careful. Remember, none of us know how we died."

The sky darkens. The sun's dying embers reflect on the waves that crash into the shore, and the sand transforms to blood red.

The Gatekeeper coughs. "Faith is an overrated virtue, ladies. It has driven us to the brink, caused innumerable wars, and countless heartbreaks. I sometimes think the world would be better off it had never been invented. And it's so elusive. You say you've faith in each other. Do you really?"

I'm watching his face, squinting as the wind picks up, scattering grains of sand into our eyes. If his expression is revealing, I can't tell what it shows. But the Gatekeeper is crafty, so I continue to try.

"I propose to test this so-called faith. Let's find out where Nikki ran to once she left that christening party. And was Clarissa's letter anything more than an old keepsake? Did it warrant violating Charles's privacy?"

He's wrong. Clarissa tried to manipulate Charles from beyond the grave.

"And you, Ronnie, why don't you begin? Tell us the story of how that marriage proposal was the beginning of a blissful 'happy ever after' life."

Charles needs me. All this time I thought Clarissa was haunting me. But I was wrong. Charles was her target. I must go back. I should be next. But before I say anything, before I can state my case, the beach dissolves. And the Gatekeeper's scarlet eyes wink towards me.

CHAPTER 40

Ronnie – Edinburgh

The flowers cradled in my arms appear brash. Sunshine intensifies their natural colour to a brassy fiesta of artificial hues. I pause at a bin, remove the cream-coloured stems and discard the rest. My eyes narrow against the sunlight but my glasses remain tucked in my bag. Mum's lips pressed tight whenever I wore them. *You're not some Hollywood star. Take them off. Everyone will be looking at you and laughing behind your back.* She was very taken with what others might think. We always had to be perfect, beyond anyone's reproach. Our feet planted firmly on the ground with the stars shining down. But we must never reach for them. Never strive to be one. I've never been sure if she was protecting us from failure. Or keeping us in our place.

A haze shimmers above concrete headstones that rise from the ground in tones of white and black. The markers stretch wide and distant. Why isn't it raining? Heads should be bowed under dark umbrellas in this sombre location.

Wrought-iron gates add a solemn inflection. The stone angels that border the pathway evoke a certain reverence. But still, the sky should weep.

My chest tightens and I force myself to walk up the winding path that's punctuated with benches adorned with gold plaques. *Willow, a wonderful daughter who was taken too soon. Uncle Bob, who loved to sit and watch.* It would be nice to sit with Willow or Bob. Perhaps they'd whisper who they once were and tell tales of a wonderful life. But if I rest I might outstay my welcome. So I persist.

Turning the corner, I bend forward, clutch my stomach and pause. I'm getting too close. I've not been here since the funeral many years ago. She's buried next to Gran.

A burst of laughter. My head swivels. A group of teenagers loiter on a bench. Girls sprawl along it, their arms wrapped around knees bent to their chests. Boys sit above them perched like pigeons on the backrest. Legs dangling in shorts. Cigarettes hang from their mouths, and they pass around cans of lager. A girl grins at me and throws an empty packet of crisps to the ground.

My lips clench together but they're unable to suppress the rage on my tongue. I storm towards them. "Have some decorum. Pick up your rubbish. Your lager cans and butt ends. And get the fuck out of here."

The tallest boy shuffles towards me, hands deep in his pockets, a sneer sliced on his face. His mates rise to join him, squealing and hooting, excited by the sudden charge in their day. A girl with stringy brown hair fans herself, grabs a boy's shoulders and leaps onto his back. They hurl words like hyenas circling prey.

"Hey, you not got anything more to say, Mrs?"

"Yeah, she's lost her voice now, eh?"

I tilt my head back and laugh. Their so-called intimidation is infantile at best. I've faced down better in school playgrounds.

Just for a moment, I switch on my headteacher role. "Grow up. You have five minutes, then it's the police. Starting now." They flinch and I walk through them. They fall away easily, as is often the case. It only takes one. Then the rest back down. Just kids, bored and finding their place in the world. Doing all the wrong things at the wrong time, trying to fit in. Although I shouldn't have lost my temper and wished them to grow up too soon. Not when this burial ground awaits.

Fresh roses lie on her grave. It isn't surprising. They visit every Sunday to replenish and pay their respects. Another ritual I'm not part of. Not their fault. It was me that forced them away. Me who cut them off. The hum of a mower and the scent of freshly cut grass snap into the air. I wrinkle my nose at the intrusion and also the pollen. Everyday people, going about their jobs, keeping the grounds maintained as if this is just an ordinary day. My eyes squeeze tight, and I rock back and forth on my heels, afraid to take the first step onto spongy ground.

When I was nineteen, I stood in her bedroom while she was fixing her hair for a night out with her mates. Every Saturday, they'd go down to the local pub for dancing and drinks. She worked two jobs to afford that one treat.

"I'm pregnant," I said.

The hairbrush paused in her hand, and she swallowed hard. "And do you want it?" her reflection spoke back. It was as if she couldn't place herself fully in the conversation. As if she was trying to make it less real. I shrugged. "Don't worry. Whatever you want, we'll sort this together," she said.

Why did I ruin her evening? I could have waited until morning, but I was selfish. I wanted her to take my pain and make it her own. Within a week it was gone. Never spoken about again. There had been no recriminations. No *bad girls* thrown at me. But I felt like shit for letting her down.

The baby would be twenty-one now. Had Mum ever thought about it, mourned the absent love from her arms? Like me.

I slip down to my knees in front of her headstone and trace her name. *Joyce*. The dust coats my fingertips chalky white. I wipe them clean across the grass. She'd never left this little village. Never felt the Mediterranean sun on her pale shoulders or dipped her blood-red painted toes into a warm sea. Always too busy making ends meet.

The cancer devoured her piece by piece, like chewing maggots descending on rotten meat. My proud mother. The ferocious warrior who never had a chance. Even her closest friends couldn't bear to watch her being consumed alive. Visits tapered off.

"She can fight this," said a doctor as if it would be her fault if she died. It took all my strength not to spit in his eye. You don't die because you didn't try hard enough to stay alive.

In my twenties, I caught her once, gazing at her face in the bedroom mirror. Her eyes were glazed, and I hoped the drugs would prevent her from witnessing the horror we could see. I asked her what she was doing. "I've dwelt too much on my beauty. Cared too much about how I looked. God's punishing me for being vain."

Fuck you, God.

I collapse on top of her, bring my knees up to my chest and curl into a ball. Grass soft against my damp cheek. My fingers scratch through the grass and roots and find the soil. I dig my nails in deeper. Pull out clumps of earth. If I could just touch her once more. If I could draw her to me and breathe in her perfume. One last time. That's all I ask.

But it's pointless. What's left of her here? I roll onto my back and sobs shake my body. Would she have cared so much about beauty if my dad had stayed? Or if other men didn't value women the same way? Measure their worth by how they'd appear on their arms or look under their weight while they fucked them in bed?

My hands clench and my fists pummel the earth. But you

could have tried harder to make Dad stay, Mum. Why didn't you laugh at his jokes rather than roll your eyes and wander off? You could have faked a liking for football. Joined in with his passion. Would a couple of hours have been too much to pay? You were too strong, Mum. You made him feel weak in comparison. Did you not know that each chip of disapproval pushed him away?

I heard you crying when he was gone. Saw you pretend to enjoy the nights on the town. When all you wanted was to be back in his arms. You are smart, Mum. Why couldn't you understand that a woman has to be what a man wants? That you must keep your true self hidden and focus on the prize. If you'd tried harder to keep him, life would have been so different. You wouldn't have been so sad and lonely. And I would have had my dad.

I stroke the earth, gathering the dirt and the grass back to where it belongs. Mum would dislike an untidy grave.

I hate how everyone comments on how beautiful you were as if that's all that defined you. You were a thousand tiny little things. A smile of encouragement at the swing park when I was too shy to ask another girl to play with me. A song rising from the kitchen on a freezing winter's day. A burst of laughter that lightened dull Sundays. Such a brilliant artist. We should have framed your prizes. Now I don't know where they are. When something knocked me hard to the floor, you taught me how to get back up. But most of all you were my home.

My fingers play with the dirt gathered under my nails. But I've got news, Mum. You'll be so excited. He only asked me a few days ago, but I rushed up here to tell you. I'm getting married. His name's Graham, and he's so smart and kind. He's a school inspector, so he has a really good job. You'd love him. And don't worry. He won't ever leave me. Not like Dad left you. He doesn't fall in love easily. He didn't even want a relationship at first, but he's fallen for me because I fought hard. We're buying a house together and soon maybe children. I wish you could meet him. I wish you could be there at the wedding. Dress me in your veil. I still have it, Mum. I kept it safely wrapped up in the box for when it was my turn.

My hands spread against the grass, and I push myself upright. But that's the future and you're trapped in my past. My palms rub against my thighs to shake off the dirt.

I wish you were here. Your arms wrapped around me. Do you remember when we were young? You'd carry me from the bath and wrap me up in a warm towel. I'd giggle and tuck my head into the crook of your arm. You'd tell me I was too big to be carried at seven, but you still would for years to come. On the carpet in front of a blazing coal fire, you'd dress me in pink cotton and tell me a story as you brushed my long hair.

I wish I could travel back in time, sneak into that scene and whisper to that little girl, *Cling onto this moment. You haven't got long. Turn around and study your mummy's face. Examine every detail. You won't remember it when she's gone.*

I lay my cream stems next to the vase. Without water, they won't last long. I shrug. Everything dies.

My lips touch the gravestone. I can't do it alone, Mum. I miss you too much. Come back to me. Come back. I beg you. If you ever loved me. Come back.

A shiver runs through me. Eyes dart to the sky. The haze that shimmered above us has lost its shine. It's dull now. A misty fog.

CHAPTER 41

Nikki – Mondello

*H*ead bowed, Gio stares at the floor as if searching for something to save him. His hands comb through his hair and with a long sigh, he lets them flop and hang loosely. He can't look at me. He knows I'm right. That we can't go on like this. Living like beggars. He's still my Gio, still the guy that makes my heart soar, but things need to change. I can't live like this anymore. "You've got a problem, Gio."

He shakes his head in silence and slumps down into a chair at the kitchen table. Sunlight streams from the window to bathe his despair. He hunches over and burrows his head in his arms.

Stroking my throat and swallowing my disgust, I place my palms flat down on the table, opposite him. He needs to stop feeling so bloody sorry for himself. Admit what he's done and find a way for us to move forwards. I believed in his dreams. He painted such pretty colours of the way we'd live our lives here. Our own little pizzeria, a beach house, all under the glorious

Italian sun. Well, the sun is still here but it only highlights the dirt of our lives. The dreams glossed over with fresh coats of his lies.

"Gio, how could you do it again?"

His head lifts in slow motion. His eyes red-veined are heavy with tears and his hand swipes snot from under his nose. "I no bad person. I do it for you, Nikki. No for me."

Stumbling back, my hands clutch the edge of the table. He did it for me? Me? He never accepts blame. Never acknowledges what heartache he's caused. And he wants me to feel sorry for him. But I don't. My hands clench into fists. I want to hit him, scratch him, rattle the pity out of him. Wake him up to what he is. I detest this side of him. I slam my fist against the table.

"You didn't do it for me. You did it because you wanted to. Because you can't stop yourself. Because you're an addict."

His nostrils flare and he thrusts the table away. It hits me in the stomach and I bend over winded and shocked from the blow. Stomping around the room, his hands clamp into his hair and, like a wild man, he tears at it while muttering in Italian.

"Look at the state of you!" I shout. And it's true. I've never really noticed before, but there are days, even weeks, when he lets himself go. His hair is greasy and his unwashed body reeks of old garlic. He walks towards me, T-shirt stained with splashes of spaghetti sauce and grey joggers baggy at the knee. Who knows when he last changed them? Yet, last week at the christening he was the same gorgeous man I first met. My eyes roll. Of course, it's a pattern. He's like this when he's trapped in gambling. So deep in the hole of losing that he doesn't care about anything else but how to escape. And the only way to do that is another bet.

"Nikki, I don't do it again. It was the bastardo, Phillipo. He do the bluff pretend he have bad cards. Make a fool out of me. I would won if he tell the truth."

I blink. "You'll never change. You disgust me."

Gio growls, grabs my golden bowl, the one we bought in

Mondello, and throws it against the wall. I gasp as it shatters into pieces.

"It this place, Nikki. It too much hot." The dining table is hurled into the air. It slams against the ceiling, splinters, breaks, and crashes back to the floor. It spreads out on the tiles like an unfinished jigsaw.

I back against the wall, my mouth open in disbelief. It's not him? It's this place? The place he lured me to with his promises of "happy ever after" and a fairy-tale ending. He was gambling just the same at home, but on different things. It isn't the different country that's at fault. It's him.

"All the people they say, 'Come, Gio. Drink the beer. Play the cards.'" He picks up a chair and throws it along the floor. It skitters across the tiles and lands at my feet. "I not got the problem like you say. It this place. It not good for me."

Maybe it's time for me to wake up to the reality of what my life has become. The wall has another fresh hole in it from Gio's bashing. The night we came back from the mountain trip, I'd asked him about money and he'd punched a hole then, too. The shitty dining table lies in bits on the floor. We've nowhere to eat now. The second-hand tied-up fridge that I refuse to eat out of. The brown-stained sofa that was only temporary but has never been replaced. It's a dump. All the little things I bought in Mondello just emphasise it. I lean against the wall and slide down to the floor. Bring my knees to my chest and wrap my arms around them.

Gio shuffles across the tiles towards me. His face slack and mouth open. If any more crap comes from his lips I might scream the place down. His hand rests on my knee and I flick it away with a scowl.

"Nikki, it got the hold of me. I don't let it do it again."

"What do you mean, again?"

He smiles. "I know what do next time. I know not make same mistake. I take it slow. Put the small money on and I walk away."

My lips part and a scream tears up my throat. "Next time? Next time? You don't get it, do you? Even after all this. You're scum, Gio. You'll never change."

He kicks out at the remnants of the table, then rushes into the bedroom. Has he gone for more things to break? I follow him as far as the doorway, ready to tell him that this time I don't care. He's kneeling at the bed, groping underneath the mattress. He grunts in triumph and I back away. I know what he has hidden under there.

He bursts back into the living room, waving his knife. He's lost his reason. He grips the material of his T-shirt, gathers the cotton into his fist and slices with the blade. The shirt rips open to show his bare chest. "You take knife and you stab my heart!" Sweat is dripping from his face and his eyes are glazed like a madman.

"Enough," I whisper, and climb to my feet. He moves in closer and leans a hand against the wall just above me, the knife in his clenched fist. His face is so close to me now that when he yells, bubbles of foamy spittle hit my cheeks. I use my arm to wipe it off and wish my mum could walk in. Save me like she's done so many times before. But I was a child then, and this is no skint knee from a fall in the park. A kiss and a plaster won't help me now. I have to leave. Get out. Let him calm down.

"Nikki, I bad man. I no want hurt you. I sorry." He throws the knife to the floor, leans down, kisses my nose, and brushes the hair from my eyes.

Where are we now? My head is dizzy. I can't keep up with all the different mood changes. What version of Gio is this? And then I get it. This is "come here little girl, come and be good and let me make everything better". It would be so easy to comply and give in and let him wrap me in his arms and forget everything.

"We start again. We go live with my father and my brother. He'll give me job. I take it this time and we save the money. We have good life, my Bella Nikki."

His brother will give him a job? Hasn't he been working with his brother since we got here? "If you've not been working, Gio, where've you been going every day?"

He shrugs. "I was try be professional card player. But I do the job, okay. Nothing to worry about now."

I duck under his arms and push him against the wall. All this time, when I was alone in the flat, waiting for him to squeeze some time in for me. He wasn't even working. And everyone must have known about it, except me. It wasn't just his jealousy that was keeping me isolated. He was keeping me away from the truth. "Gio, you're a liar, and I hate you."

With a guttural roar he picks up my statue from the shelf on the wall. Santa Rosalia. The gift for my mum. "No, Gio. No."

But it's too late. He smashes it to the floor, falls to his knees and sobs. "Sorry, Nikki. I sorry. I buy you new."

"No, you won't." And I walk away.

In the bedroom, I collect my suitcase from under the bed. Check my passport is there and pull out an old box of sanitary towels. Mum had put money in it for any emergencies. She wanted reassurance that I'd always have a way home. I told her I'd be fine, but she'd insisted. She made me promise never to tell Gio about it. *The men in your life don't need to know everything, Nikki. Always keep something back for yourself. Something that only belongs to you.*

I throw off my flip-flops. I won't need them where I'm going. I change into my trainers. I'll never have a home with Gio. Never have nice things. Life will always be like this. No matter how hard I try to make things pretty, he'll destroy everything. I'm just an accessory, a Barbie doll. Someone to make him feel tall. His true love is gambling and I won't be second best to anyone or anything. Not anymore. I'm going home and I'll make something of myself. Be somebody. Maybe start college. I'll never rely on a man again.

But one day, after all this pain, if I do find myself fancying someone, he'll love me beyond anything or anyone else. He'll never leave me or make me feel second best like Gio has, or abandon me like Dad.

I walk back to the living room and he's lying on the floor. Clumps of his hair lie beside him. He looks up with his gorgeous brown eyes, and he says, "My Bella Nikki?"

I laugh. Spit in his face. "Fuck you and all your fucking Bella Bella shite."

A growl rumbles from deep within him. He springs to his feet and picks up the knife. A glint of steel flashes in the sunshine. "You stay. I the good man. You see, Nikki. You see." He's smiling, almost pleading. Fear trickles down my spine. I edge backward, closer to the front door. Closer to freedom.

Gio stumbles forward as if he's drunk. But the point of the blade does not waver. "You no leave me. I no allow." I can't take my eyes from the glinting metal. One more step back on trembling legs. Our eyes meet and I'm caught by the madness that shines there. Blindly, I fumble behind me, search for the door handle, but my fingers only trail over the door's wooden surface.

Tears blur my vision. "Gio, it's me. Nikki. Your Bella Nikki. Remember me? I promise we'll be okay. Put down the silly knife. Let's go and get some pizza. We haven't eaten and I'm hungry. Then we can cuddle up in bed and sleep. I bet you're tired, Gio. Like me." Trying to keep his attention on my face, my hand searches, seeking out the handle and my escape. The warm metal of the doorknob slides into my palm, and I twist and pull. The door opens and I turn to flee. But he springs forward and slams his hand on the door above my head. It thuds shut. And I scream.

I turn back to him, just as the knife slices towards my throat.

"I nothing left to lose," he whispers.

CHAPTER 42

Mrs Hawthorne – Edinburgh

$\mathcal{C}$larissa's letter tumbles from my fingers. It flutters on the breeze, but it's her laughter coaxing it along. My arms hang loosely at my side, and I stare at a mark on the wall. Jack must have scratched the paintwork with his paws. It will need to be repaired. I'll ask Charles if he's any leftover paint when he's back.

Charles. He lied. It was all a monstrous lie. There was no perfect marriage. There was no perfect wife. Clarissa Ballerina was a fraud.

How could someone do that to a person they loved? Someone they cared for? Why, on your deathbed, would you confess to an affair? What did she have to gain? It must have crushed Charles to read it. I pull out a cigarette and light it. Watch the end burn.

My feet tap against the wooden floor again and again. Think. What did she have to gain? Ash gathers on the cigarette. I flick it and survey the room.

Photographs of her surround me. Images taunting from the past. Charles and her at some fancy wedding. Hiking in green anoraks, dogs running beside them. A formal affair, him in a dinner suit, her in a red velvet gown. She smiles with friends around a table, Charles by her side, all of them wearing silly paper hats. A beach where she's sunning herself, Charles relaxing at her feet. Now they're cuddled up in knitted scarfs, snow pure behind them.

I throw my cigarette onto the floor and slap my forehead. Of course. I turn in a circle, her gaze falling on me from every direction. This is it. This is what she gained. A shrine to her stardom. The summerhouse her theatre, with Charles her audience. Clarissa, the star. She was back where she wanted to be. Centre stage. Sparkling in the limelight.

She'd have suspected Charles was too kind to throw away the mementos of their life. But she had to be sure. Had to be certain. She wouldn't be hidden in a shoebox at the top of a wardrobe. Gathering dust. Forgotten. And so she stuck in a blade of guilt and twisted it. Made his love bleed. Yes, she'd had an affair, or so she said. But whose fault was that? She accused Charles.

In her deathbed confession, she got what she wanted. A guarantee that he'd save every image. Broken by her betrayal of trust, but blaming himself, they were vital to Charles. In scanning each picture, he was searching for signs that she'd loved him. Wasn't that exactly what she'd instructed him to do? *Look, Charles… look for the love.* Unravelling in a twisted maze of obsession and haunted by his fruitless search for the truth, Charles had become ensnared by the past.

But she hadn't counted on me.

As the saying goes: The show's not over till the fat lady sings. And it's time for the main attraction. Time for you to exit the stage, Clarissa Ballerina.

"Alexa. Play CeeLo Green, 'Forget You.'"

I drag a chair over to the wall, stand on it, grab the oil

painting and throw it to the floor. "Fuck you." My arm runs along a low bookshelf. Another ten pictures gone. "Fuck you too." There are another six on an office desk. They slam to the floor as well. The windowsill has five, each in silver frames. I get closer. These are younger versions of them. A few show them in school uniforms. So sweet. I raise them above my head and hurl them aside. Any more? The piano, of course.

How lovely. Charles is gorgeous here. Clarissa standing beside him in Chanel and pearls. Is that a smile she wears? I hold it closer. Charles is looking at her, but her eyes are elsewhere. Who is the man at the edge of the frame? Is he the one she's smiling for? I flinch. What the hell am I doing? I fling the photo across the room. "You nearly had me there, Clarissa Ballerina. I was going as crazy as Charles for a second."

Music. Now, where's that bloody song? The funeral song. The one that taunts me most nights. An old-fashioned hi-fi sits in the corner and on top rests a stack of CDs. Greedily, I file through them but it's not there. I scratch my hands in my hair. He's not the type to ask Alexa to play it. Charles is too traditional for that. It must be somewhere. I press the eject button and there it is, waiting to be played. To hell with this. "Alexa. Play Pink 'So What'."

Seizing the hi-fi with both hands, I swivel it back and forth until it topples and falls. The CDs and albums arranged carefully inside spill out, clattering to the floor. A bundle piles at my feet. I kick them across the floor. I bet they spent ages making these choices, ensuring each artist set the right tone. No Bay City Rollers or David Essex. Only serious contenders like Bob Dylan or Nina Simone. Fuck their sanctimonious taste. "Alexa. Play Abba 'Waterloo'."

Should I? Little porcelain dolls. About twenty of them lined up behind glass doors of a miniature mahogany cabinet. Dancers striking delicate poses in tulle of all colours. Why not? But I need a hammer. There's one under the sink. I rush to the house and grab it along with a brush and a roll of black rubbish bags. Racing back, the autumn leaves crunch under my feet. Funny how the sound makes me lighter. Alive once more.

I lift the hammer high and the glass in the cabinet smashes. The dolls stare. I grab them and rip the tulle from their bodies. Pound them into smithereens.

Dancing around the room, I sweep up the spoils of my battle into bin bags. The photos, the porcelain, the musical anthems. All the final fragments of the life Clarissa left behind. I scramble about making sure there isn't a trace left of her and stand back to admire my artistic endeavour.

I scream and raise my foot. A shard of glass has pierced through my shoe. I hobble across the grass to the kitchen and dampen a tea towel under warm water. My teeth clench as my fingers prise the glass out. Blood trickles along the sole and I press the towel firmly against the flow.

What time is it? Charles won't be much longer. He'll be furious when he sees the carnage I've raged.

But wait. Charles read the letter the day I got back from lunch with my sisters. He was sobbing down the phone. That was before we officially got engaged. Before I moved in. So, all this time he's been complicit. Hiding her letter. Hiding all the photographs. Hiding the truth of his marriage. The bastard.

Spittle builds up at the side of my mouth. I smear it off with the back of my hand. He's made a complete fool of me. I slip my other shoe off and limp back towards the summerhouse. Fingertips circle my temples. An edgy feeling overpowering me as though I need to flee from this place.

How could he have lied so long and made me feel so inferior to the façade of his marriage? I rummage in the bin looking for their wedding photo. There must be one. I need to see it.

She's stunning in her bouffant veil, dark tendrils of hair framing high cheekbones. Bridesmaids in long chiffon dresses stand beside them, pearls in their hair. His arm is around her waist and in her hands are pale pink peonies. They weren't just her favourite flowers. It was her wedding bouquet and he still buys them for me. A droplet of blood splatters the photo. My hand has been cut on all the broken glass. I smear it across their faces and rip them apart.

The hammer rises above my head, and I smash it down on their history. Frames splinter, glass cracks into a thousand broken pieces. I've gone mad. But the noise soothes my scars. All the broken promises across a lifetime of years. Smash. All the happy ever after lies. Smash. All the *call you in the mornings*. Smash. For every man that called me special. Smash. Every time I started to let myself believe. Smash. And for every time I tried. Smash.

"Stop. Stop right this very minute!" Charles shouts.

He stands in the doorway, face pale and body trembling. Jack is cradled in his arms. It's as if time has returned to our first meeting. He's the image of how he looked in the park. But this time it's not grief that scares him. It's me.

"Put the hammer down and get out of my summerhouse."

I'm long past being told what to do by a man. I lift my arm above my head ready to strike again but then I pause and blink. Underneath Jack's fur lies a bunch of peonies. Charles must have bought them when he was out. Rage reddens my skin. The hammer slides from my hand and thuds to the floor and I leap towards him, screaming and scratching.

He steps backward and turns to protect Jack. But not before I've plucked the stems from his arms. I shred their petals into tiny pieces and scatter them like confetti onto the shards of their life.

I turn and ask him. "Why, Charles? Why?"

He puts Jack down, out into the garden, and closes the door behind him. His hands rake through his hair, and he opens the venetian blind and stares out of the window. He won't look at me. Barefooted, bleeding, face wet with tears.

I'm breathless. My head spins and I collapse onto the piano

stool with my head sunk in my hands. "Why did you let me think your marriage was perfect?"

He turns towards me, but all the warmth of my Charles has vanished. "My marriage was perfect. If there was an affair – and I'm undecided on that – then it was my fault."

"Your fault? Your fault she betrayed you?"

"I was working too many hours. I forgot who she was."

"But why did you lie to me? I never felt good enough to walk in her shoes. I asked you so many times to open up about your feelings."

"I let her become my shadow while I followed my own stardom in academia. She should never have felt invisible. She was the star. I let her down badly. I drove her to whatever she did."

He walks past me, glass crackling under his shoes and pulls open what I assume is a back door. I stand, not quite believing he's going to walk out and leave me. But it's a large storage space. Newspaper cuttings and theatre brochures paper the inside. The colours are faded, their edges aged a soft lemon. But there she is, dazzling in a pirouette. In another, in pink tulle, she's caught mid-leap. A large photograph framed in gold sits on a shelf in the centre. She's in black velvet, mesh and feathers. Odile in *Swan Lake*. A glass vase of wilting flowers stands to the side. He must have been planning on replacing them with the ones I ripped up.

I was wrong. The summerhouse isn't a shrine. It's this cupboard, hidden and private. And there next to the photograph of her starring role is the peacock urn. And before I can think, I jump over and snatch it.

"Return that to me now." His voice is low and void of emotion.

No normal person would behave the way Charles has. No one else would build a shrine to someone who hurt them so much. Who would mourn that kind of love? But wait. Have I not done that all my life? Chased men who didn't love me enough. Made excuses for their bad behaviour. Searched for the smallest of signals in their conversations. Examined every word and action for signs of love. All he wanted was proof too. Have I not done the same with every man, even with Charles? Accepted less than I deserved. I wouldn't listen to friends or take any advice, but maybe I can still save Charles. Still save us.

"Charles, I'm sorry. Don't you see she didn't really love you? She cheated and had an affair. Who knows how many? But I love you. I see how wonderful you are. I can bring the light back into your world. You don't have to search any longer. Love stands right here."

"I don't want your notion of love. Not after your behaviour today. I would choose Clarissa a thousand times in any lifetime over you."

I smash the urn to the floor. Her ashes spill out in a thick clump. I spread them with my feet. Fragments of bones scratch the bare skin of my soles. They're not as smooth as I thought. "What do you think of your whore now, Charles?"

A scream cuts the air. It's not mine. Grabbing my hair, pulling it at the roots, he throws me to the floor. He looms over me, his eyes brimming with tears. Are they for her or me? He picks up the hammer and kneels beside me. I screw up my eyes and the first blow knocks my head to the side. Blood streams across the floor and the arid ashes slake their thirst. Perhaps love, for me, was always going to end this way.

CHAPTER 43

Ronnie – Liverpool

I'm so fucking ready to marry Graham. Worked so hard to snare him.

From church windows, a stream of light will shine on the crisp white tulle of my dress. It will crackle and shimmer a rainbow of colours. And with the reddest of roses clutched in my hands, I'll float up the aisle.

Music will soften the air and then, as if spun from golden threads, the most delicate cherubs will appear. They'll circle around us and scatter specks of golden glitter. At the altar, he'll turn and whistle his appreciation and we'll tenderly clasp hands. Eyes only on each other. I'll hold on tight. In case the bastard tries to do a runner.

I laugh. Maybe the cherubs are a touch too far. All of it is, since we're marrying in a registry office, and not the fairy tale version of my youth. Still, it's the thought that counts, right? And the money we saved bought us a Maldives honeymoon.

One last look in the dressing room mirror and I remove Mum's bridal veil, fold its delicate lace back into lemon tissue paper, and close the satin box. I'll still wear it, but I'll buy a tea-length sweetheart gown and embrace a fifties theme.

Graham isn't inviting any of his family, but a few of his new friends are coming. I don't like them. They're cheaters, liars and dirty rats. But I'll rid his life of them after the wedding. He'll settle down into married life much better that way.

As for my guests, I'm not sure. Friendship has always been a transitory transaction for me. One made out of necessity or comfort at a given time or place. It's not that I'm selfish or not giving of myself. I've had some great friendships. But they're fleeting. They last as long as I remain in one place. I haven't the inclination to compete from afar with all the new people that replace me. My time had to be focused on my career and finding "the one".

I could invite relatives from back home, but there'd be so many questions and hushed tones. Graham is right. We're better doing this on our own.

Music booms from my bathroom. It's weird how, in just a few weeks, we will be moving in together. But then I suppose we've been living in and out of each other's homes for a while, so we'll barely notice the difference. At least the new bedrooms won't ever linger with other women's perfume.

"Graham, I'm going downstairs for a drink. Do you want me to bring you up a glass of wine?"

"I'm good. Enjoying your strawberry bubble bath and catching up with a work paper before I go and meet James. You're still okay about me going out tonight, aren't you?"

My hand pauses on the stair banister and my fingers scratch at a speck of dust. James, one of his rat pack. I laugh to make my response appear more carefree than it is. "Sure. At least I won't have to listen to that awful music you're playing. But we've got some houses to look at near the new school in the morning. So, don't make it a late one."

"Ah, you're getting old, Ronnie. You'll be wanting slippers and hot chocolate next."

"Yeah. Yeah. Whatever. You'll still fancy me. Remember, I've seen where you've been, and they weren't five-star locations like me." His chuckles follow me into the kitchen where I open the fridge.

No wine, except for a drizzle in the bottom of a bottle of white. Typical. We must have drunk more than I thought last night. Sighing, I grab my purse and house keys, shout "Back soon," though he probably won't hear it, and open the front door to a wall of summer heat.

James stands there, fist dangling in the air. "Oh, Ronnie. I was about to knock."

It's bad enough that Graham goes out on the pull with this bastard, but now I've to welcome him at my home? Forcing a smile, I tell him, "Graham's not ready. He's in the bath. And wasn't he meeting you down the pub?"

The rat grins like he's spied some cheese, and scurries past me into the hall. "Yeah, but well we haven't properly met, and I thought why not pop around earlier and meet the woman my man is about to marry." His eyes graze up and down the length of my bare legs and I wish I'd worn trousers. "It's not a problem, is it?"

He's probably disease-ridden. I'll need to disinfect the house with bleach after he's gone. "Nah, it's fine. Graham won't be long and it'll be good to get to know you better."

He wanders through to the kitchen, unsteady on his feet. He's obviously had a few drinks before arriving here. Dutch courage. But for what? The fridge door opens, and he stands peering in. "Do you have any wine, or maybe a beer?"

The cheek of it. "Sorry, no. I was just on my way out for some. We finished it off last night."

"I bet you had sexy times all pissed up, huh? Women are much looser that way. More adventurous."

My teeth tug at the corner of my bottom lip. What is he really here for? It's not to get to know me, that's for sure. I should call Graham and tell him to hurry up, but I've never really spent time with one of the rat boys before. Graham never lets them in the house. They always pick him up outside or he meets them elsewhere. What's behind James's smile?

Opening a drawer, he takes out scissors and a drinking straw. He knows where everything is, so he's been here before. When? He shakes a small plastic packet filled with white powder and winks. "Want a line? Or does the great headteacher refrain from such things?"

What the fuck is he doing? Before I can stop myself, I reach over and grab it. Like he's a school kid with contraband in the playground. "You can't bring that into this house." A thought slashes through my mind. Does Graham take cocaine as well? Is that why he's always full of energy even after a night out?

For a minute, maybe more, James and I stare at each other, then he edges over. And I realise it's not just beer that's glazed his eyes. It's this drug too. He's high. "Look. Let me go and get Graham and tell him you're here, and you can both sort this out together, okay?"

He runs his fingers slowly up my arm. "I don't think so, Miss Ronnie. Graham's told me all about the stuff you two get up to. You're a very dirty girl, aren't you? Why don't you give me the coke back and we can have a little party of our own."

Flames of rage burn inside me. He's far worse than I ever thought. I turn, but he clutches my arm. "Oh, come on now. Graham has his fuck-toys and you don't give a damn. What about a little bit of fun for us, eh? Come on. Let's have a party. Maybe Graham will join in."

I push his filthy hands away and take a deep breath. "Graham is nothing like you. You'd think as a friend you'd not be hitting on his fiancée."

James grabs my wrist and unfurls my hand, takes back the coke and laughs. "Oh. Fiancée. Yeah. That'll last too. You dumb bitches are all the same. You're a passing fling. Nothing more. This has all happened before. You're not special or that. But you think you are." He licks a finger, dips into the packet and rubs the powder along his gums. "He told me this is our last night together. He needs to kick it all on the head for a while. But that's not gonna happen. He'll come back to me in the end. He needs a good wingman."

"Grow the fuck up. You're pathetic. Get out." Grabbing his arm, I pull him out of the kitchen and into the hall. He stumbles, falls onto the wall, then rights himself. My hands shape into fists at my side. It's hard to keep them there. I want to punch him so much. But that's what he wants. He's trying to split us up. Stop the marriage, so he can have Graham all to himself. "Last time. Get the fuck out of my house."

He sneers. "Come on. Give us a kiss and a feel. I'll let you into a secret about Graham if you do."

I should shout upstairs for Graham and let him deal with this, but anger's raging inside me. I grab him again and push him out the door. "There's nothing you can tell me about Graham that I don't already know. I get it. It's all about the cult. It fucked him up. But you, you've no excuses, except that you're a clown."

His head tilts back, and he laughs. "Oh, he told you the cult thing. Yeah. You're not so clever, Miss Headteacher. He uses that line on them all."

I press a fist to my mouth and bite down. "You're lying. Get out before I tell him what you've done."

"I wouldn't do that," he sneers. "You think you're so above everyone, with your airs and graces. But you're not. You're a dumb fuck. Graham's been playing you for months. There was never a cult, sweetie. Ask him." And with that, he leaves, pulling the door closed with a bang.

I rub my forehead. Is he right? My head spins. I sit down on the bottom step of the staircase, letting the house keys spin around my finger, and remember that first chat. He'd grown up in a cult-like religion, not allowed to mix with other children. Engaged to be married since he was fifteen. He spent his life knocking on doors and handing out leaflets. But then his family disowned him. Shunned him. Except he hadn't grown up like that at all. None of that happened. James didn't ask, *What cult?* He already knew it was all made up.

It crashes into me. I was so obsessed with being the partner he needed that I accepted his reasons with no hesitation. Made my own excuses for his sexual behaviour. Jumping on the feeble explanation of his lost youth to defend him. But Graham hadn't been part of a cult. It was lies. I'd accepted because it let me excuse the way he treats women. A lie. A lie. Everything about him. Everything about us. A lie.

My cheeks burn. How could I have let this happen? Was I so intent on not being my mother that I'd become a worse version? Tears sting my eyes. I stand, turn around and scale the stairs. It's time to confront him.

Each step closer to his treacherous body rips me further apart from my happily ever after. The wedding. The marriage. Destroyed. My hands clench and my nails dig into the flesh of my palms. I grip tighter, welcoming the pain. At the top of the staircase, strawberries swirl in the air, but they don't mask the stench of his putrid lies.

A gurgle of mouthwash, and a spit in the porcelain basin. Two quick spurts of deodorant – familiar sounds – and the bathroom door opens. He steps out, a blue towel around his waist, a knot tied at one hip. A grin spreads his mouth open.

"Hey, honey. You gave me a fright there. Was there someone at the door? I thought I heard something."

His skin, still damp from the bath, glows with not one imperfection to blemish it. His green eyes are as vivid as the night I met him. They twinkle still. How does such beauty conceal an ugly soul? Why didn't I look deeper? Have I been blinded by the surface it's encased in?

His eyes dart to my hand clutching the keys against the banister railing. He blinks and shakes his head, and his eyes catch mine. "What's wrong?"

"I can't stand liars."

He fidgets with the knot at his hip. Ties it tighter. "Liars? Who's been lying to you, baby?"

A laugh bursts from me. Even now, when he knows something is up, he'll keep up the *honey, sugar, baby*. Words to soften and make me feel cared for. He moves closer, heading for the bedroom. I turn and stand in his way. I'm so very tired of men hiding.

"Ronnie, what's got into you?"

"You were never in a cult. It was all an excuse to fuck around. Am I right?"

"You're insane."

I edge closer. How many women has he hurt with his lies? How many trusted him to be who he said he was? When you fuck someone who is lying about their identity, it's rape. I jab the house keys repeatedly into his chest.

"Am I right? Am I right?"

A vein twitches in his neck. I jab him again. His skin tears. Scratches of blood appear.

"Get off me! You're getting needy again. Insecure."

"James has been here. He's a sleazebag. Maybe even worse than you. But he's told me all about you and the things you say and do."

"You should have left things alone," Graham whispers. "But you could never do that, could you, Ronnie? Always had to know what I was up to. Always sniffing around, watching. Why didn't you tell me James had arrived?"

My hand swipes under his towel. Fingers clench around his balls, squeeze tight. He whimpers and pushes me to the floor. My head bangs against the staircase and pain blinds me.

"Sorry. Sorry. But you're a fucking bitch at times." He stands over me, feet planted on either side of my body. Despite myself, a sliver of fear makes me shiver. He shakes his head. "I'm not going to hurt you. I'm not that kind of person."

"No. You're a liar. Aren't you?"

He nods. "I always tell women the cult thing and throw in a fake marriage. It's amazing what women will put up with to fix a man. They all want to be the special one. The one that changes them. The one that heals them. Maybe it's a mothering thing." He lifts me to my feet and kisses my forehead. "At first, I thought you were like the rest. Just a fling. But then I started to like you. How could I confess it was all a lie, after so long? And we've been having fun, haven't we? You can't deny that. So it wasn't all bad. The wedding was a problem, of course. But I thought after the ceremony, you'd forgive me. You always do."

His dick is pressing against my stomach. Protruding rock hard from his body. He's turned on by this. "After the honeymoon, I would've confessed about the cult thing. Then we would've carried on living our own definition of love. You would've got used to it by then. And we could've met each other's families with the slate wiped clean."

He moistens his lips. "But you've ruined all that now." He kisses my chin, then his tongue licks slowly up my face. Saliva coats my skin. I keep still. Let him. He stands back and I smile up at him. "It's better it's all out in the open anyway. I love you, honey," he says.

I grip his arms, swing my shoulders back, then lunge forward and smash my skull into his nose. A sharp *crack* stings the air. Blood spurts and dribbles onto his chest. I step back. He wails, and fumbles his fingers to his face, blindly searching for the damage.

"Fuck you, bastard," I whisper, pain flaring between my eyes. My vision blurs and I step back, my feet shuffling underneath me, toes curling over the edge of the top stair. My hand wraps around the banister, fingernails clawing the wood for traction. But it's no use. My damp hand slides off.

His mouth jerks open and he stretches his arms out to catch me, but I fall, screaming as I plummet through the air. "Ronnie!" he shouts. "Ronnie. Oh my God!"

My head slams against the landing at the bottom of the staircase.

And everything fades.

CHAPTER 44

Ronnie – The Beach

Graham's voice is faint, far away. Something about God? A crack. Scream. Blood bubbles around me and seeps into the sand. A face. Graham's? No. Nikki's.

She takes my hand and pulls me to my feet. Kisses me on the cheek. "I can't believe this. I'm so sorry, Ronnie. Did he push you?" The waves lap around my ankles. My mind spins, searching for the answer. Did he push me, or did I fall?

The Gatekeeper sits on a rock that's shaded green with seaweed. He's cradling Mrs Hawthorne in his arms. The hammer. Never expected Charles to have such hatred. She must have been so afraid in those last few moments. When he loomed over her, how did she feel? I clutch my stomach and vomit into the sea.

Nikki's hands drag slowly down her face. "I can't do this. I can't. It's too much."

She's just eighteen. She doesn't deserve this. Just a baby. I take her hands in mine and kiss her forehead. "Go sit on the rocks and rest. Everything's going to be okay."

Dry grains of sand spun silver by moonlight stretch out around us. The campfire, cocktail bar, everything else has vanished except for the beach. What does that mean?

"Oh, Mrs Hawthorne. I'm so, so sorry," Nikki sobs, kneeling beside her. Her head shakes as if she can't believe the old woman's fate. "How could someone do that to you?"

Mrs Hawthorne smiles. "It's okay, Nikki. I don't feel pain here. I just feel sad. I thought it would have ended so differently."

"I wish it too. You deserved more from Charles after giving him your heart and trust."

"As did you, dear Nikki. I found it so difficult to see what Gio did to you. If only you had left straight after the christening. But then men, they have a way of making a woman insecure in her thoughts."

Life has frayed our edges but in death, we have become friends. Comforting each other and sharing our disappointments and joy. Perhaps we found our reflections in each other's stories along the way? Perhaps we were never so different after all.

The Gatekeeper leans down and strokes Nikki's hair. The knife. And so young. But why is he touching her in such an intimate way?

I cup some water into my hands and rinse my mouth clean. The salt deepens the bitterness of what's happened to us all. Our only crime, if any, was love.

"Come, Ronnie," the Gatekeeper says. His voice is lighter, the harshness smoothed away. It could be a trick of the breeze.

I brace my shoulders and walk towards them. "I can't believe what's happened to you, Mrs Hawthorne. Charles is such a mild-mannered man. I would never have seen it coming."

The Gatekeeper giggles. "Surely by now, after sharing so much, we're on first-name terms?" Why would he laugh at such a time? He's still an evil old bastard despite his signs of affection. He smiles at me before looking down at her.

"Veronika, don't you remember a time when they called you *Ronnie*? And before that, when you were just *Nikki*?"

What's he on about? Even now, he's playing more tricks. Haven't we been through enough?

Her blue eyes grow brighter. It's as if a fog has been lifted from her gaze. She turns her head towards me, then to Nikki. My heart races and my palms lift to my cover my mouth. What does this mean? Why do we all have similar names?

I sink to my knees and the coarse sand grates against my palms. Everything's too bright, too loud. Each grain of sand scratches my skin. The moonlight gleaming on the water, too dazzling to bear. The salt scent of the waves stings my nostrils. Nikki's breathing is like a roaring in my ears. The glitter in the Gatekeeper's eyes is pin-sharp as if I'm watching him through a giant magnifying glass.

"And talking of names, Ronnie. After all your adventures with Graham. All those ups and downs. All that closeness." The Gate-keeper gives a short laugh at the idea. "Why don't you tell us his surname?"

I would blurt it out, spit it in his face, just to blast his grin into oblivion. Except. The name won't come to me. I pinch my skin. Think. Think.

"Can it be, Ronnie, after so much effort to snare him, you don't even know his last name? Try harder."

"Fuck you, you old sadist!" I scream. But the catch in my voice betrays the courage of my words. Because the memories are flooding back. Graham at the podium, flustered by my teasing, fiddling nervously with the name card in front of him. I can't read it clearly. The writing's blurred. That old school inspector in his tweed suit. It was a business meeting. Of course, he'd use formal introductions, not just first names. But what was Graham's? And that bar. I shoved him away and he bowed in defeat. And then he said, "I'm Graham." No last name. The airport in Paris. His name is covered by his hands. Why hadn't I seen that before? Questioned my memories?

"My thoughts," the Gatekeeper says, "have turned lately to Poe's story, *The Masque of the Red Death*. One day in the future, Ronnie, you'll understand its fascination for me. In the story, people hide from a terrible plague by attending a great costumed ball. Like all such events, the most telling moment is, of course, when the masks are removed at the end of the evening."

I leap to my feet. Fear running down my spine. "No. No. Leave everything as it is. This doesn't have to end. Not this way. Take us back to the beginning. Back to the waves. Please, I beg you. Back to the waves. We were happy there, just drifting."

The Gatekeeper dips forward slightly. "The waves are of no further use to us. I feel, for our own tale, the time has now arrived for us to reveal our true selves."

My vision alters as if an invisible camera has spun its lens, and everything springs into sharp focus. I turn to Nikki and Mrs Hawthorne. I see them as they are for the first time. The moonlight should be casting them into shade. Instead, every detail leaps out at me. I devour every plane and contour of their faces. Nikki utters a soft cry. The same thing is happening to her. Our masks have been stripped away.

We're different ages, but time can't hide the similarities of our features. Now that we see each other, really see each other, we understand.

We're one and the same person. We're all Veronika.

I get up and walk over to where Nikki is kneeling. Her face is so familiar to me. The mirror has shown me its reflection a thousand times. It's my face when I was eighteen. I reach out and my fingertips trace the line of her sharp jaw and brush over her full lips. Her tears are gone, but mine have just begun.

All those wasted years of yearning and being rejected, of seeking out that one man who would create joy. Who would love me. And it all ended with a selfish gambler incapable of caring for anyone but himself. I cup her cheeks in my hands. She doesn't say anything, but her trusting eyes find mine. Was I ever so young, so innocent, so vulnerable? I kiss her and beg, "Nikki, I don't know what this is. Or what it all means. But if you get the chance, don't turn into me. Don't make the same mistakes I made. You're worth so much more."

"Will I really be a headteacher just like you, Ronnie?"

I kiss her lips. My lips. I'm kissing me. "I have no idea. I was. And you are me. So maybe."

She giggles. "Well I'm not going to the sex parties, that's for sure. But it will be cool to be a headteacher."

Mrs Hawthorne stands beside me, stroking Nikki's hair. She's hypnotised by the texture and sheen of it and is winding it through her palms. "It feels so vibrant, so new," she says. Then she turns to me, and her fingers trace my face. "Oh, Ronnie, you're so beautiful. *I* was so beautiful. Why did I never see that?" She wipes the tears from my cheeks.

I see myself in her too. The years have etched lines deep into her skin, but she's me. "You married him?" I whisper.

"Graham Hawthorne? Perhaps I did, perhaps I didn't. It's not decided yet, is it? Was he the worse mistake of our life? Who knows, dear? There are always bad choices to make."

I nod. "Charles." I gather her into my arms and all three of us huddle together and cry.

What does it all mean? If this is all me, what happened to us? We've come to the end of our story, but nothing is clear. Are we ghosts of our past failures wandering around unable to let go of what we thought we'd found? Our hearts so starved of love that even in death we still seek it out. How fucking depressing.

Nikki bites on her bottom lip. I did that a lot when I was young. It means she's worried about what she might say but can't hold it in.

I stroke her arm and smile. "What is it, Nikki?"

She shakes her head. "It's okay. It doesn't matter." She buries her face in my chest. I tilt her face upwards. Was I always so scared to speak my mind? Afraid to offend someone?

"Spit it out, Nikki Wikki," I say.

The words are alien on my tongue. Words I've never uttered before. But I'd heard them all the time. It's what my sisters used to call me when I was young. Nikki Wikki, Judie Fruity and Mary Fairy. Three little girls clasping hands dancing in the garden. At the beach making sandcastles. In the snow on sledges sliding down hills covered in ice. When Gio came to the door to ask me to go to Sicily, Mary was eating her dinner with me, and Judy was out with her friends. When Mrs Hawthorne had her sisters around for dinner, they weren't just hers; they were mine. How had I not recognised them from the stories? Felt their love?

The Gatekeeper coughs. "It wouldn't have done for you to know everything all at once, Ronnie. You had to witness it all from someone else's eyes."

His frame wavers in the pearly light and the moonbeams are drawn to it, lighting him up. Coruscating. We turn our eyes away from the glare and when we look back, he's gone. In his place is a woman. Her blonde hair is perfectly styled. Her red lipstick gleams. A carefully drawn beauty spot rests on her cheek. Estée Lauder floats on the air.

"Mum?" Nikki says.

It can't be true. A bliss so fierce runs through me that its sudden pain leaves me breathless. How can it be? How did I not notice the way he spoke to me? The tease in his laughter? The glint in his eye that was so familiar? All the years without her and she's been here beside me, all this time. My body hungers for her touch. But can I? What if she disappears? What if it's the Gatekeeper up to his old tricks? It's too much to bear. I force my head away from her. I'd rather walk into the waves.

"Veronika?"

Warmth creeps into my veins. I remember the voice so

clearly. Sitting in front of the fire listening to fairy tales as she brushed my hair. Reciting multiplication tables as we strolled hand in hand to primary school. The kiss of her lips whispering *Good night, my princess.*

I race towards her and wrap her in my love-starved arms. We weep for all the missed years, for all the seconds she wasn't there. At long last, I'm back home, a child once more.

I collapse at her feet, cradle her hands and gaze up. She's as beautiful now as she was before the disease destroyed her and there's so much I have to say. So much stuff she's missed. All the tiny inconsequential scraps of everyday life we'd have shared. The gossip from a neighbour, the shade of a new lipstick.

Nikki and Mrs Hawthorne weep beside me and Mum cuddles us in. All of us safe now, where love lives.

But for how long?

CHAPTER 45

Ronnie – The Beach

"*M*um, what's this place? Why are we all here?" I ask, nestled at her feet. Nikki's arms wrap around Mum's legs. Mrs Hawthorne and I hold her hands. All three of us are scared to break contact with her skin in case she disappears.

The Gatekeeper's harsh tones have disappeared, replaced by my mother's soft Scottish accent. "Ronnie, you should remember. After all, I've given you all back your memories. A clever girl like you really should have worked it out."

The graveyard. The weird haze and my words begging her to come back to me. Is that all it took? Is that the secret to all this?

"Are we in Heaven?" Nikki asks.

Mum grins down at her. "There are some things I'm not allowed to tell you," she replies. "But I'll tell you this much. It was me who brought you here. I wanted you to see yourself through different eyes. To know your life from a different perspective. Women are very good at giving each other advice, but they seldom listen to it where love or romance is involved. Now you've seen for yourself what you are, and what you used to be, and what'll happen to you if you continue this way."

I screw my face up and trickle sand through my hand. She gives me her signature lopsided smile. "Ronnie, I want you to understand. Three times, I gave you the chance to tell me what love meant. And what happened? Three times you told the same dreary story about how you would find love from a man, and then your life would be perfect. Is that it? Is that all your life amounts to? Being someone else so a man will love you?"

I sigh. It was always like this. Under Mum's gaze, every tiny misdeed was magnified and blown up. "But when Dad left you, you were so unhappy. Your life was ruined."

She throws her head back, and her laughter sparkles in the night sky.

"You dafty! Is that what you think? That I spent my days pining for that old misery guts? Your dad didn't leave me. I kicked him out. If he was here right now, I'd tell him to get lost. Nothing would have changed him. Believe me. I tried. He's always been a waster."

Nikki's lips draw back into a shocked grimace and the child in her punches the sand. "You kicked him out? That's not true. I was there at the bottom of the stairs watching. Sorry, but Dad left you."

Mum lets go of my hand and ruffles Nikki's hair. It's as if something's flown into my body and snatched my breath away. My fingers search until her hand is back in mine.

"You saw wrong then, Nikki. Why do you think he didn't keep in contact after that? I'll tell you why. It was punishment for me kicking him out. He was furious and spiteful. And he knew the best way to hurt me was through hurting my daughters."

"But you were heartbroken. I heard you crying!" Nikki says.

"Aye. I cried. That's true. But not one of those tears was for your dad. They were for you and your sisters. All the pain you suffered at losing him. Or for worrying about how the rent would be paid, or how tired I was after cleaning folks' floors to put food in your mouths and clothes on your backs. For the shame of what the neighbours would say and the horror of the words *broken family*. Oh, back in the day, he was charming and handsome, but it didn't last long. He became a drunk, and vicious with it. I couldn't have that and after too many chances, it was time for him to go."

"But Nikki's right. He did leave you. I... sorry, we, watched you both in the mirror from the bottom of the stairs," I say.

"No, Ronnie. Jesus, this is hard. It was bad enough when there was only one of you. What you saw was me telling him to get out. I'm not the sort to wither away just because some man turns out to be an arsehole. Is that what you told yourself? That without a man, you'd be a wee old maid?" Mum shakes her finger at me. "It's a big beautiful world out there, Ronnie. It's time you went and got some of it for yourself."

My mouth hangs open. Of all the revelations since I arrived back here, this is the one that sinks deepest into my soul. Dad didn't leave us at all. Mum kicked him out. I've spent my whole life trying to prove myself for all the wrong reasons.

Mrs Hawthorne says, "I understand you didn't want us to recognise each other, Mum. But I don't understand why you masked yourself too."

"Come on!" Mum replies. "If you'd known it was me, you'd have told me a right load of rubbish instead of the truth. Have you forgotten all those lies you told me when you were trying to get out of trouble at school?"

I laugh. I can hardly deny it. Oh, my good God, she's seen all the sex scenes. The clubs. The orgies. A blush paints me scarlet.

"And you can keep those sniggers to yourself, Ronnie Stevens," my mother says. "You've got a long way to go yet."

"How do you mean, Mum?"

She stands and organises us into a line. Youngest to oldest.

Just like she did with me and my sisters, inspecting us before we set off for school. We stand tall, push our shoulders back and hold hands.

"Ronnie, I want you to learn from these stories. About life. About love. About yourself. You have to remember it's never too late to change the future."

Nikki looks at her from under her eyelashes. "What about me and Mrs Hawthorne, Mum?"

She smiles. "Nikki, you're going back to your own wee life. You'll be fine and I'll tell you a secret. Yes, you do become a headteacher." Mum moves down the line. "And you, Veronika. Don't you fret. All that stuff with Charles was just one possible future. That doesn't have to be you. If Ronnie sets herself straight, realises she deserves more, your life will be different. Happier."

Mrs Hawthorne tugs my hand. "You'd better get a fucking grip, Ronnie. Because I'm not going through all that shit again."

Through her refined accent, the swearing sounds awkward but there's enough of me left in there to make me laugh. "I got so posh, didn't I? How did that happen?"

"Living down south for too long and well, to be honest, some of it's put on."

We all giggle and Mum goes back down the line, hugging and kissing us. Saying goodbye. When she gets to me, tears roll down my cheek but I keep my head high.

"I'll miss you, Mum," I sob.

The moonbeams flare, the shimmer surrounds us. They draw Nikki and Mrs Hawthorne closer to me. And closer. And then the light dancing across their bodies merges with mine. I close my eyes, and when I open them, I'm alone. But I'm not empty anymore.

"You mind what I told you, Ronnie," my mother says. "Love yourself the way I love you."

The beach whirls. I'm caught up in the air. The fog engulfs me and pulls me elsewhere. This time I embrace it. I have things to sort out.

"Ronnie? Oh, thank God you're alive. I've been so worried."

My eyes squint against the light. There's a tube coming out of my arm and a machine beeping. Nurses stand around me, frowning with concern. Someone clasps my hand. Is it Mum? But the face comes into focus and it's not.

"Hello, Graham." I smile.

CHAPTER 46

Ronnie – Liverpool

*T*he medicinal scent of antiseptic rises to a ceiling of white fibre tiles. I turn my head on the hospital pillow and my mouth tightens in pain. A clear plastic jug, half-filled with water and ice, lies on a grey plastic cabinet. Beside it stands a metal pole. A brown box hangs from it, its front covered in tiny computer screens and dials.

"Welcome back to the land of the living," someone says. A nurse smiles down at me. Her auburn hair pulled into a tight ponytail underneath a white cap. Then it comes back to me. The nurses' grave faces. The IV. And Graham's *Thank God*.

My fingers trace my hand but find nothing. I sigh in relief that it's gone. "Where is he?" I ask, my voice hoarse.

"Mr Hawthorne? Well, you woke up momentarily, then fell back asleep. He said he couldn't stay, had some sort of important thing to do, but that he'd drop by later on."

Something to do, or someone. Blonde or a brunette? He

wouldn't care. He likely just *dropped by* the first time to make sure I was still alive. That it hadn't become a police incident.

"You gave us a bit of a scare when you first got here, you know. Blood everywhere. But it turned out it was just a scalp wound. They always look worse than they are."

"Where am I?"

She crosses over to the jug and fills a paper cup with water and places it in my hand. I gulp down greedily. It softens the burn in my throat.

"Liverpool Royal Hospital. And it's no wonder you're thirsty. You've been asleep for most of the day."

"What's wrong with me?"

She laughs. "Amazingly, nothing except for the gash on the back of your head. I hear you took quite the tumble down a flight of stairs. You're lucky nothing was broken."

She looks at the readout on the computer equipment, nods in satisfaction, and mutters to herself. Turns. "We can do away with this now," and unclips a white peg from my fingertip.

Placing my palms down on the mattress, I push myself up to sit. But pain stabs my side and shoves me down. Memories filter in. Graham shouting. Plummeting through the air. Grasping for the banister. The floor rushing towards me. I blink back tears.

"You'll need to be careful for a couple of days. There's nothing broken, but your ribs are a bit bruised." She hands me a mirror. "That other bruise on your forehead is going to take a lot of covering up. I'm not sure how you managed to bang the front of your face and the back of your head at the same time. You must have somersaulted down those stairs."

I blush, too embarrassed to explain that the bruise is a consequence of butting Graham in the face. "When can I go home?"

"Doctor says one more night for observation because of the knock on your head. But I'm sure you'll be out of here tomorrow, first thing."

I don't argue. Attempting to get out sooner would make me a

fool. She bustles around the bed, scribbling on forms, collecting notes and adjusting my pillows just so.

"I'll check in on you in a little while," she says and closes the door softly behind her.

My thoughts drift to a dream from last night. About stuff I'd buried deep in my mind for years. It must have been the medication, or maybe it was a reaction to my near-death experience. However, I'd survived one of those before.

Gio was a gambler who'd swept me off my feet when I was young and naive. He tried to kill me once, but at the last minute snapped back to reality and threw his weapon to the floor. He'd begged for forgiveness. He said he'd get help and, like a fool, I'd agreed. Two weeks later, he lost his wages at a racecourse and I was back at Mum's door. Telling her everything. Letting her mend my broken heart.

When the sadness lifted, I visited my Gran's and sat in the living room with a bacon roll. I didn't eat eggs anymore. Grandad reminded me with a cuddle, "Love is a choice, wee Nikki. Remember people must bring you sunshine or you make it for yourself."

He was right. So I'd made my first choice there and then. "I'm not Nikki anymore, Grandad. From now on, my name's Ronnie and I'm going to university. I'm going to be somebody."

He'd patted my arm. "That's right, Ronnie. With a name like Veronika you've plenty of choices, so you can be whoever you want."

I turn onto my side thinking back to when Gio had disappeared in Blackpool stinking of aftershave, and I'd called Suzie for support. Where was she now? My God, the fun we'd had together. The boozy nights out, the drunken nights in. The long phone calls talking crap. And Paola's warm smile as she drew me into the safety of her family. How had I allowed Gio to steal all that away from me? And what about Tara? We'd been best friends. I grin at the memory of us in that bar. Tara, with her bouncy blonde hair, yelling at a pack of snobby guys and sending them fleeing, dicks between their legs.

I clamp my hands over my eyes. How could I have talked her into a threesome with Graham? Disgust clings to many parts of my past. Our relationship had changed forever. Or had it? We'd been Thelma and Louise, rip-roaring through the night-time clubs and bars. Was there a way back to that friendship, torn apart by Graham and his sleazy desires?

And my sisters. The car rides to the seaside, jumping up and down in the back seats and anxiously waiting for the first glimpse of the sea. Shopping trips to Princes Street looking for just the right dress for a Saturday night out and a cheeseburger in the Wimpy when all was lost. Mum saying it's impossible to not find something to wear in a road full of shops and us giggling and trying the catalogue. Quarrelling and squabbling together, but always making up in the end, as bonded as only sisters are. How had I drifted away from such love? Mum's right. It's a big beautiful world, with beautiful people in it. It's time I got myself back into it. The thought is freeing. But it came from a dream, didn't it?

A knock on the door. The nurse peeks in around the edge. She smiles. "Someone to see you."

Graham slides past her into the room. "Ronnie, you're looking better already."

"I'll leave you two to it. Just press your bell if you need any assistance, Ronnie." Graham throws her a wink, and she walks off down the corridor with a skip in her step.

A thick white plaster is taped across his nose. I suppress a giggle. His nose bends to the left into a weird shape. His handsomeness is marred, spoiled forever. I should be guilty. But I'm not.

He sits on the edge of my bed and flashes me a grin. "We got ourselves into a bit of a mess with things." He smooths out the green hospital blanket and tucks me in. "But we can get things back on an even keel. I'll always love you."

Is he worried I'm going to call the police on him? He's not worth the effort. And anyway, I'm still not sure if I fell or he pushed me.

"And my proposal still stands, Ron. We'll get married and live life our own way. Who cares what anyone else thinks?" He jerks his thumb over his shoulder. "That nurse, for one. A bit of a looker, eh?"

I ring the bell by my bedside. I need an audience for this. The nurse puts her head around the door again, eyebrows raised. Then I finally reply to Graham. "You're a cheating, fucking bastard. I wouldn't marry you if my life depended on it. You're not worthy of me. You don't get to have me. So take your slimy proposal, shove it right up your stinking arse, and find some stupid bimbo who'll fall for your lies. Though with that nose and your tiny dick, good luck finding one who'll be interested. Now fuck off."

The nurse's eyes are wide open. And so is her mouth.

Graham stands, clapping his hands. "What a performance, Ronnie. You nearly had me convinced for a minute there. It's okay. I get it. You're jealous of the attention I'm giving the nurses while you're in such a state. But there will always be plenty for you too. Don't worry. Now just get yourself better and I'll see you around." A wink and he struts out.

I scrunch up my nose in disgust. What a sleazebag. Thank God we didn't move in together yet. I'll apologise to the nurse later. But I knew he was going to hit on her. I just hope my little performance saved her from that.

I slump back against the pillows, feeling lighter than I have in years. It's as if I've been set free. Even the air is clearer. My pain duller. That was one change. More are going to come. And as to whose ideas they are, does it matter? The nurse told me I'd been sleeping all night and day. So maybe I did just dream about Mum and Nikki and Mrs Hawthorne. Who cares? Whether it was Mum who told me, or I told myself, it's time to change my life.

"Mrs Hawthorne? If you're out there in some parallel universe. I hope you saw what I've done. I changed our future."

God, for some reason I need a ciggy. I swing my legs over the bed and ease my way across the room to the Formica built-in wardrobe. Fumble in my handbag for the pack of cigarettes I always hide there just in case. I'll need to sneak outside when the nurse is busy elsewhere.

Something gritty is in the lining. I pinch it up and hold it out to the light. Grains of sand roll between my thumb and fingertips then cascade onto the floor.

CHAPTER 47

Ronnie – Edinburgh

*T*he traffic outside my flat window sounds louder than it used to, and I've only been away for a day. I exhale slowly and allow the noise to wash over me. Relieved at least to be home. Pain still nags at my ribs and I've had to plaster concealer over my bruises but I've more important concerns to fret about. There's something I must do.

Of course, I could just hide here and drown my anxieties in a glass of Cabernet. And leave the past to ferment in the scent of sour grapes. But what would that achieve?

The train ticket's burning a hole in my purse. But then it occurs to me. There's more than one errand to run. And why not order them in a way that suits me best? I ring for a taxi and gather my things.

As I exit the station, all the old familiar buildings, with a nod to the past, welcome me home. The pub we first got drunk in, under layers of foundation and eyeshadow to look older than our years. Across the road, Blockbusters, where we spent hours on a Friday night choosing perfect videos to watch. The bus stop where we'd sit eating chips, hoping for boys to stroll by.

A taxi drives past. I wave my hand and after a few seconds, jump in. He asks all the usual questions. Where you from, lass? What brings you back? Then he drops me off at the end of the street. Typical. He couldn't be bothered to find the street number.

Is this such a good idea after all? I could turn back. Run away. Gritting my teeth, I grind down the insecurities and consult the yellowing fragment of paper which shows an old address of a past life. It's been so long. Time passes, people change. Do these few words written in fading ink identify an address where someone still thinks of me? Cares? But my mother's words echo. There's still time to make a change. I straighten my back and march down the road.

It's a nondescript door. The paint's faded. Children's bicycles sprawl across a tiny unkempt lawn. A faded nylon tent gives evidence of secret hideaways, where children escape the rules of adulthood. This is a home where family life supersedes the priorities of neighbourhood niceties. It's now or never. I take a deep breath and ring the bell.

When Suzie answers, my eyes narrow, trying to place her. I've carried her image in my mind for such a long time. A grinning teenager with mischief sparking her eyes. But she's aged, like me. Here and there, the odd wisp of grey in her long dark hair. Laughter lines creasing the corners of her eyes. She glares at me as if I'm a debt collector. "Yes? What do you want?"

How do I respond? I step back from the animosity. But then her eyebrows rise, and her hands reach up to her mouth. "Nikki. Oh my God. Is it really you? I haven't heard from you in twenty years." She bursts forwards, stepping across the threshold, and hugs me tight in her arms. I sink into them. And all the years of separation dissolve into that one moment of recognition.

In her living room, coffee cups and plates and half-eaten fairy cakes are strewn around us. A beef stew bubbling in the oven warms the air. Her son, a skinny twelve-year-old, is wolfing down leftovers while looking over at me red-faced now and again. I laugh. "Just you keep going, Malcolm. It'll save your mum from having to clear up."

Suzie and I spend the whole afternoon giggling and reminiscing. About our school days and how she was always the one who was late, sitting outside the headmaster's door, like a child on the naughty step. About drinking cider at the park and the crushes we had on Donny Osmond lookalikes who grew into middle-aged men with pot bellies. It served them right. About her two kids, Malcolm, and Ellie, who's only three and is sitting on my knee playing with my hair. About my career, and how I'd driven my way to school headship. Suzie grinned and asked if I used the naughty step too and I told her, nah, the staff and kids were too scared of me to misbehave, and we both laughed.

"What about that Italian guy you were seeing then? Your mum said you went to Italy?"

I screw my nose up and roll my eyes. "Just another waster, Suzie. You were right when you told me he wasn't good enough."

She smiles. "A lot of people told you about guys that weren't good enough, Ronnie. I could never work out why you thought you had to change to get someone to love you. Why you were so obsessed with boys. You didn't have to pretend to be someone else, you know."

I nod. "Well, all that's in the past. I'm never going to pretend to like cricket, Radio Four, or a nice brisk walk in the park ever again."

We raise our coffee cups to the air and cheer.

"Give me a minute," Suzie says and walks out to the hall.

I lift Ellie's fingers and whisper, "This little piggy." She squeals and squirms on my knee, just the way I did when my mum told it to me. Fragments of conversation drift through the open doorway. Suzie's phoning all the old gang. I wonder what they'll say.

"Yes, yes. She's exactly the same. As funny as ever… She calls herself Ronnie now but she's still… A school head… I know, she's been away too long… on Friday? I'll ask her… yes, I'll tell her… okay, bye."

She comes bouncing back into the living room. "Marie says to tell you lots of love, and we'll all meet Friday evening. Jen and Gill can make it too."

I grin. Why not? "That's great. Let's do it!" I slide Ellie off my knee and get up.

"But now I've got to get going. I've one more person I have to catch up with. See you Friday." We hug and she escorts me to the door, waving as I make my way down the garden path. I'll flag down a taxi later but for now, I want to just walk and feel the sunshine. I need all the nourishment I can get before my next visit.

The block of flats is run-down. One of the stairwell windows is broken, and empty crisp packets flutter at my feet. The communal door hangs loosely from its hinges, worn out, uncared for. As I climb the steps the smells of old cooking oil and something worse invade my nose. I shiver, remembering my flat in Mondello.

On the third floor, the stairwell windowpanes are grimy and block out the light, making the flat numbers hard to read. When I ring the bell, nothing happens so I rap on the door and after a moment it creaks open.

He's withered, shrunken. His once broad shoulders are stooped, and the sleeves of an old grey cardigan are rolled up over scrawny arms. The arms that once twirled me in the air.

"Hello, Dad," I say.

He grunts and shuffles back inside. I follow. Living room walls are stained nicotine yellow and a heavy coat of grease sticks to the air. Dad sits on a brown sturdy chair, the kind they have in old folks' homes. Isobel, his new wife, nervously darts from the kitchen to give me a hug and a kiss on the cheek. I flinch and wipe my face clean. She throws a sideways glance at Dad and returns to her sanctuary among the pots and pans.

"You look well for yourself, Nikki," he says.

He doesn't even know my name. That's how long he's kept his distance from me.

"I go by *Ronnie* now, Dad."

He clicks a Zippo alight. Mrs Hawthorne flicked that same lighter on and off until the gas ran out, after he died. Destroyed by her loss and regret.

"Ronnie, eh? Well, you'll always be my wee Nikki."

The sheer hypocrisy. My fingers clench the fabric of my jacket. But I keep the obscenities inside. He's not getting off that easily.

"Do you want a cup of tea?" He flicks ash from his cigarette into an ashtray full of butt-ends.

"No. And I don't want to sit down and talk about the weather either. I want answers."

"What do you mean," he mumbles. I stare at him, and he draws his tatty cardigan around himself. His gaze is everywhere except where it should be. Directly on me.

"The day you left. The day Mum threw you out. Do you understand what that did to me?"

"It was all so long ago, Nikki. Just let things be." He lights another cigarette even though it's just been seconds since the last one.

"It's Ronnie!" I shout, despite my best efforts not to. "Ronnie!"

"All right, all right. Ronnie, then."

"Do you remember that day? I know you do. And do you

remember leaving me in the street when you drove away? I know you remember that too because I saw you watching me in your rear-view mirror."

He hunches up in his chair and looks to the front door. Pots rattle in the kitchen as though Isobel is trying to drown out our argument.

"It was for the best, hen."

"The best? I was standing there, tears falling like rain down my cheeks, my arms out to you, begging you to come back. Do you know how long I stood there, waiting, hoping?"

"I couldn't come back, could I?"

"Why not? You knew I loved you. I was your little princess. You told me you'd always protect me. But when it suited you, you fucked off without a backward thought."

The images are in front of me as I talk. Building sandcastles at the beach. Following him to the water's edge and watching him collect water for the moat. Him pushing me on the swings, singing songs as we giggle. Snuggling into him as I tell him about my exploits at school, his eyes filling with pride. Sunday morning stories cuddled together in bed. Him running behind me cheering, when my stabilisers came off my pink bike. All those moments. All that love. Where was it meant to go when he left?

"Why not, Dad?"

He straightens his back, his voice harshening. "You bloody well know why. Your mother always had a thing about the drink." He fakes a whiny voice. "You'll never amount to anything if you keep boozing." He snorts. "As if it was her business. She was always above herself. Too high and mighty. I was never good enough for her." He shifts in his seat, memories of old outrage folding his arms.

"But what about me? If you wouldn't change for her, couldn't you change for me?"

"The leopard never changes its spots, Nikki."

Laughter bursts out of me. This is his excuse for being such a waster. Some stupid old cliché. I can't even be bothered to correct him on my name.

"You're just like the rest of them, Dad. All those men I let into my life. I spent years telling myself I was the problem. But it wasn't me. It was you. It was them."

"You don't know what you're talking about."

I sit down on the chair across from him. Photos of us as children are scattered around the room. On the back wall, there's one of him and his grandchildren cuddling in. My sister's boys. Over the years they'd forgiven him. But I hadn't. I'd never spoken to him again until now.

"Yes, Dad. Yes, I do know what I'm talking about. It's taken me a long time to realise, but now I know only too well. We women live in a world where we're surrounded by men like you. Selfish, emotionally detached, unable to be honest even with yourselves. And what happens? Fuck all, that's what happens. Nobody says a word. Woman after woman gets their self-esteem destroyed. Nobody talks about the injustice. Fuck's sake, we don't even admit it to ourselves. We're ashamed. Think it's all our fault. We let our voices be silenced by the fear of being seen to be needy or weak. Or a crazy bitch. We water ourselves down."

He leans forward in his seat, scowling. "There's no need for that tone. You're just like your mother. I don't know why you can't be like your sisters. They still come around now and again."

I laugh at the effrontery. "Do you know what happened that day you drove away?"

He looks down at his slippered feet. Silenced.

"I'll tell you. You, with your big strong arms that hauled coal all day long. You took my sense of self-worth into those powerful fingers and you crushed, and you crushed, and you crushed until there was nothing left."

He sniffs and dabs his eyes.

"I thought no one could love me and if they did, they'd leave me one day, just like you did. If my own father couldn't stay, how could anyone else?"

I stand and wander through to the kitchen for a glass of water but I'm really giving him time to think. Isobel hands me a glass. Behind her, a large pinboard is attached to the wall. I move closer. Newspaper cuttings. Magazine articles. Ofsted reports. It's an homage to me and my career. Almost a shrine to who I am.

It would be so easy to see this as love, to run and cuddle at his feet. Be his little girl again. But I'm done with taking fragments of emotion from men and searching for their meanings. It isn't enough. If someone loves you, it's their role to show you. But then I remember the pain Mrs Hawthorne felt when he died. Am I brave enough to try? I drown my feelings with a gulp of water and walk back in.

"Dad, we're not going to end like this. I want you back in my life. We've so many years ahead of us to enjoy. We all make mistakes. But I'm not your little princess anymore. And I'm not Nikki. You come back to me on my terms, not yours. Do you understand?"

His bottom lip trembles. "I'm sorry, Ronnie. I'm really sorry. I was a coward and weak. But I always loved you."

"No you didn't, Dad. That's not love."

Isobel is in the hallway standing by the door, wringing the edges of her apron. She gives me a nervous smile. "You told him, dear. You told him right off."

My footsteps light against concrete stone, I stride into the future. Mum's voice curls in a soft Estee Lauder mist around me.

Remember, Ronnie, love yourself, the way I love you.

I smile and whisper back, "Don't worry, I won't water myself down for anyone, anymore."

EPILOGUE

Ronnie – Twenty-five years later

*A*voiding a patch of hard sticky gum, I settle onto a park bench. My hand grazes against the ragged edges of carvings in the wood. My fingers trace along their ridges. Whoever MK and LG were, I hope their love spun an eternity.

Mary calls me over to where my family gathers on the grass. She's pushing Dad in his wheelchair towards them. And like a toddler in a buggy, he's tapping his shoes against the footrest, hurrying her along. A cigarette dangles like a weapon from his grinning lips. This was her idea. A celebration to mark his 90th birthday.

Under the shade of a sweet chestnut tree, my sister, Judy, is fussing with a gingham bag, setting out plates and plastic forks on a tartan rug. She smiles and pats a space beside her and I ease myself down.

Dotted around us, clusters of families sit with picnic baskets and coloured blankets. From a smoky barbeque, the smell of sausages and burgers tang the air. A couple of boys kick around a football and Judy points them towards the play park at the top of the hill. They scamper off, passing the ball between them. Déjà vu shivers up my spine.

My brother-in-law pops the cork on a bottle of fizz, and soon we're all laughing and talking over one another. Until my dad recounts one of his tall stories about how he once fought a dragon in Wales. And although we all shake our heads, we're entranced by his storytelling.

My eyes squint against the sun into the distance. A man walks along the path into the park. He pauses, as though the heat has wearied him, and slumps down onto the bench I just left. He adjusts his tie and plumps up a red silk handkerchief in his jacket pocket. A little white dog curls at his feet.

My handbag lies beside me on the grass. It's attracted the attention of some of the park's bees. Hopefully, a gentle kick with my foot will make them settle elsewhere. But instead, this angers them, and they buzz closer to me. Much more of them than I first thought. Screaming, I draw back.

The burst of noise draws the dog's attention, and he jolts up, barks, and bounds over. His owner jumps to his feet and runs behind him. "Jack! You silly dog. Come back at once," he shouts. But the dog ignores him and the man can't catch up.

I flinch as it scrambles up onto my knees. His tail is wagging in circles as he peers into my face. In the warm molten brown of his eyes is my startled reflection. He gives another bark then snuffles around me and his nose burrows into my cardigan pocket. Almost as though he expects to find something there. Like a biscuit or treat for a good little doggie.

Our laughter sprinkles his antics, and my niece runs over and wraps her arms around his white fluffy neck. Panting, his owner arrives. He fumbles for the dog's collar and tugs him away. "How do you do? I'm Charles, and this rapscallion is Jack," he says, holding him back. "I'm dreadfully sorry about his complete lack of decorum. I've no idea what got into him. He's usually a rather timid little chap." Charles's eyes, cornflower blue, fix on me and he scratches his chin. "I hope you don't mind me saying. But you seem familiar. Perhaps we've met?"

His gaze draws me in as though I have fallen through a mirror and am looking out from the other side. Charles. Jack. The picnics. Even the bees buzzing around my handbag. I've seen all this before. A stray cloud covers the light of the sun, casting darkness across the ground, stretching all the way to the bench where Charles once sat. My eyes follow the edges of the shadow and, in the sudden gloom that surrounds the bench, a shimmering shape sits. A woman smoking a cigarette. Observing all the fun of the summer's day, but not a part of it. I know who she is. I know her pain. She was me. But then she looks over and smiles.

A burst of wind whisks the cloud away. The gloom evaporates and as the vision fades, the warm laughter of my sisters draws me back.

I haven't answered Charles, and he takes it as a rebuke. "I must be mistaken. Come along, you naughty dog. I'm so sorry for the intrusion. Please do enjoy your day." He cradles him up into his arms like a baby and strolls away. Jack peers over Charles's shoulder and his barks give way to plaintive whimpers. Just before they exit the park gate, a final sad yelp floats towards me.

Tears glaze my eyes. In a future that could have been mine, a lonely man met an unhappy woman sitting on a park bench. They made each other happy for a while until it ended badly. But I could change it this time. Make it end well. It wouldn't take much to fix it.

Another bottle of fizz pops and Judy lights up dad's birthday cake. As she carries it over to him, Mary and I follow behind. We stand before him just as we did as children so many years before. His eyes glistening with tears, he blows out the candles and whispers "Thank you, girls." His glance settles on me. "For everything." I bend forward, take his wrinkled hand, not unlike mine, and bring it to my lips. The pain of his passing will come soon, but not today.

Judy slices up cake, wraps it up in lemon serviettes and passes it around. Dad picks at a dollop of strawberry jam and licks a finger coated in fondant. "Even the cake's melting in this heat. We should've gone to Yellowcraigs like we did when you were wee. Had a paddle in the sea." He grins.

"Can we? Can we please?" my niece squeals..

I steady myself with a palm on the grass. Salt brushes my lips and seasons my senses. An urge to find Charles and fold him into my arms overwhelms me.

But then a wave of other memories flood into me. A young girl lost and alone in a foreign land until she met Paola, who taught her to dance on a mountaintop and gave her the strength to break free. Tara, with her halo of fierce curls, who stood up to anyone who watered her down. The friends from school and how they folded me back into their lives. The warmth of my sisters and all the memories that shape us. *And me?* And you, little Francesca, who swept the cockroaches away.

I'm not the same woman I was before. Love already surrounds me.

THE END

ACKNOWLEDGEMENTS

Thank you to my wonderful agent Clare Coombes for dragging The Storytellers out of the slush pile and loving it so much. I'm so grateful for your kindness and support.

Thank you to my publisher Bloodhound Books, especially Betsy and Fred for being so supportive. The lovely Tara who found the time to squash my anxieties at any time, day or night. Morgen and Shirley, thank you for making my book sharper. Abbie who adored my story from the start and Hannah for her support in marketing.

To all the people who helped me along the way, thank you for your time and support. There are so many of you that I would be too worried to list everyone in case I missed someone out. However special mentions to, Stephenie for the confidence. Laure for her wisdom and insight. Lynn, my rock, and with me from the start, always believing in me and my book. Mairi, my partner in crime. Thank goodness we take turns at being anxious. Julie who gave me wonderful feedback and Belinda who made me laugh when she got the twist. Rachel for letting me hear her theories as she read along. Tracy and Paul for giving me the courage to think it was good enough. Emma for all the amazing support since. I am so grateful for all your kindness.

To my sisters, Gillian and Amanda, and daughter Francesca, thanks for reading each chapter as I wrote them. Gillian, for always saying *love it* and fretting over the hammer. Amanda for her criticism and for being so excited. My daughter, Francesca, for being The Storytellers' biggest fan and for truly getting the book. Your belief made me stronger. And Paola, my younger daughter, for all the dating stories that made me flinch in horror.

To all the shitty arses out there treating women so badly, thanks for giving me so many ideas for my imaginary characters. But grow the fuck up.

Thank you to everyone in the Debut2022 group for their support and insight. Strap in Patricia, there are so many brilliant reads coming this year.

To my husband, Andy, thank you for being there every time I needed you. I would never have done this without your encouragement and love. I know I'm one of the lucky ones.

To Dad, The Storyteller. I wish you were able to show it off down at the bookies. Mum, you'd go mad at the bad language. I miss you both so very much and, just like Ronnie, wish I could talk with you one last time.

Finally, but most importantly, thank you to all the readers and bloggers who take a chance on a debut and read this book. It means the world to me. If you enjoy it, please do leave a review on Amazon, Goodreads, etc., as reviews are so important - especially when you're just starting out. Also, I love hearing from readers - you'll find me on social media if you fancy getting in touch. It would make my day (but only if you liked it please).

BOOK CLUB QUESTIONS

1. If you somehow ended up in a place like The Beach, how do you think you would handle it? How would you view your younger self? What might you tell them?
2. Ronnie pursues Graham because he's a challenge. She thinks that making him fall in love with her will prove her self-worth. Can you understand why she thought that way? Have you ever done something similar or seen that pattern in a friend?
3. Nikki, Ronnie and Mrs Hawthorne all seek to accommodate their partners. They are, in different ways, willing to change for love. But are compromises like that always bad, or are they a necessary feature of relationships?
4. Why do you think Clarissa confessed about her affair? Would you confess something on your deathbed? Could there ever be a reason to do so?
5. After discovering who she is, Nikki asks Ronnie a question, but she doesn't complete it. What do you think her question was?
6. On the beach, Ronnie saw the pain Mrs Hawthorne felt

when their father died. Was Ronnie right to give him a second chance when she returned to her life?

7. In the epilogue, do you think Ronnie should have given Charles another chance? Could it have worked out for them this time?

8. Did the episodes on the beach really happen? Or was it all just a hospital-bed dream? Did her mother reach out from beyond the grave to save her and, if she did, why at that particular point in her life?